Praise fo[...]
and h[...]

"Jaci Burton's stories are full of heat and heart."
——#1 *New York Times* bestselling author Maya Banks

"A wild ride." ——#1 *New York Times* bestselling author Lora Leigh

"Jaci Burton delivers."
——*New York Times* bestselling author Cherry Adair

"One to pick up and savor." ——*Publishers Weekly*

"Jaci Burton's books are always sexy, romantic, and charming! A hot hero, a lovable heroine, and an adorable dog—prepare to fall in love with Jaci Burton's amazing new small-town romance series."
——*New York Times* bestselling author Jill Shalvis

"A heartwarming second-chance-at-love contemporary romance enhanced by engaging characters and Jaci Burton's signature dry wit."
——*USA Today*

"Captures everything I love about a small-town romance."
——Fresh Fiction

"Delivered on everything I was hoping for and more."
——Under the Covers Book Blog

"A sweet, hot, small-town romance." ——Dear Author

"Fun and sexy." ——Fiction Vixen

DESIGNS ON YOU

TITLES BY JACI BURTON

BOOTS AND BOUQUETS SERIES

The Matchmaker's
   Mistletoe Mission
   (an eNovella)
The Best Man Plan
The Engagement Arrangement
The Accidental Newlywed Game
The Backup Bride Proposal

BROTHERHOOD BY FIRE SERIES

Hot to the Touch
Ignite on Contact
All Consuming

HOPE SERIES

Hope Smolders
   (an eNovella)
Hope Flames
Hope Ignites
Hope Burns
Love After All
Make Me Stay
Don't Let Go
Love Me Again
One Perfect Kiss

PLAY-BY-PLAY SERIES

The Perfect Play
Changing the Game
Taking a Shot
Playing to Win
Thrown by a Curve
One Sweet Ride
Holiday Games
   (an eNovella)
Melting the Ice
Straddling the Line
Holiday on Ice
   (an eNovella)
Quarterback Draw
All Wound Up
Hot Holiday Nights
   (an eNovella)
Unexpected Rush
Rules of Contact
The Final Score
Shot on Gold

WILD RIDERS SERIES

Riding Wild
Riding Temptation
Riding on Instinct

Riding the Night
Riding to Sunset
    (an eNovella)
Riding the Edge
    (an eNovella)

STAND-ALONE NOVELS

Wild, Wicked, & Wanton
Bound, Branded, & Brazen
Housebroke
Designs on You

ANTHOLOGIES

Unlaced
    (with Jasmine Haynes, Joey
    W. Hill, and Denise Rossetti)
Exclusive
    (with Eden Bradley and Lisa
    Renee Jones)
Laced with Desire
    (with Jasmine Haynes, Joey
    W. Hill, and Denise Rossetti)
Nauti and Wild
    (with Lora Leigh)

Nautier and Wilder
    (with Lora Leigh)
Hot Summer Nights
    (with Carly Phillips, Erin
    McCarthy, and Jessica Clare)
Mistletoe Games
    (Holiday Games, Holiday on Ice,
    and Hot Holiday Nights in one
    volume)

ENOVELLAS

The Ties That Bind
No Strings Attached
Wild Nights

DESIGNS ON YOU

JACI BURTON

BERKLEY ROMANCE · NEW YORK

BERKLEY ROMANCE
Published by Berkley
An imprint of Penguin Random House LLC
penguinrandomhouse.com

Copyright © 2024 by Jaci Burton, Inc.

Book design by Elke Sigal

Library of Congress Cataloging-in-Publication Data

Names: Burton, Jaci, author.
Title: Designs on you / Jaci Burton.
Description: First edition. | New York: Berkley Romance, 2024.
Identifiers: LCCN 2024014168 (print) | LCCN 2024014169 (ebook) |
ISBN 9780593439616 (trade paperback) | ISBN 9780593439623 (ebook)
Subjects: LCGFT: Romance fiction. | Novels.
Classification: LCC PS3602.U776 D47 2024 (print) |
LCC PS3602.U776 (ebook) | DDC 813/.6—dc23/eng/20240329
LC record available at https://lccn.loc.gov/2024014168
LC ebook record available at https://lccn.loc.gov/2024014169

First Edition: December 2024

Printed in the United States of America
1st Printing

Having siblings is the best.
Always there to lend an ear or a helping hand,
as well as being a vital link to your childhood.

Ange and Gary, you are so missed.
Love you forever.
I'll see you again someday.

DESIGNS
ON YOU

〰〰〰〰〰〰〰〰〰〰〰〰〰〰〰〰〰〰〰〰

CHAPTER ONE

Natalie Parker grabbed the housewarming gift from the back of her SUV, along with the enormous houseplant, juggling both as she made her way to her sister's new house. As she barely made it to the front door without dropping both, she was utterly grateful she'd decided to get a sitter for her two kids. At seven, Cammie was inquisitive and already thought she was an adult, wanting in on every conversation. And four-year-old Christopher was constantly in motion and oh so exhausting.

She adored her children. She also needed a night off, and her sister's housewarming party was exactly what she needed. A glass or two of wine, conversation of the adult variety, and she'd be happy to settle back into mommy mode again tomorrow.

Pressing the doorbell with her elbow, the only free appendage she had, she waited, listening to the sounds of barking and music and laughter and—oh, for God's sake, someone answer the freakin' door already before she dropped everything.

The door opened, and her sister, Hazel, beamed a smile at her. "Oh, Nat. I'm so glad you came. Let me help you with these. This plant is gorgeous. Is it for me?"

"It is," she said as she followed Hazel inside, past a few people Natalie didn't recognize. "You have that big window that faces south. The plant will go nicely there."

Hazel laid the plant down on the floor in the eating area just outside the massive kitchen, and Natalie placed the gift on the island. "The plant is beautiful here. Thank you, Nat."

"You're welcome. Happy housewarming."

"Thanks. We're excited to finally be moved in. Thank you for helping with the décor."

"Well, it could use some additional touches, but for now, it's livable."

Hazel laughed. "I'm sure you'll continue to make suggestions."

"Now that I'm back working again, I always have new ideas."

"Good ones, too. Are Mom and Paul coming? I asked her, and all I got was a maybe."

She shook her head. "Paul has a client dinner, and Mom told me she has a headache and she's going to bed early." She followed up that statement with a shrug. "Sorry."

"It's fine. It's Mom and she's weird."

Natalie laughed at how matter-of-fact Hazel was about their mother's quirkiness. "You are so right about that."

While Hazel opened a bottle of wine, Natalie took a moment to look over the place. After months of house hunting and a lot of arguments, Hazel and her boyfriend, Linc, had finally settled on this twenty-eight-hundred-square-foot, two-story beauty. And the five acres was perfect for what they needed. Lots of trees and plenty of backyard space for all of Hazel's dogs.

"It turned out beautiful, Hazel."

"Thanks to you. And Linc, of course. It was worth living in a reno zone the past eight months. Good thing we set up a kitchen so we could at least eat amidst the mess."

Nat wrinkled her nose. "I can't even imagine, especially with all those dogs you have. You haven't added more yet, have you?"

"Not yet. But now that the house is finished and the backyard is almost done, I'm ready to start fostering again. I know all the pups will be so excited."

"Right. Like you need more than five dogs."

Hazel laughed. "I won't be keeping the ones I foster."

"Uh-huh. That's what you said about the five you have."

Hazel shrugged. "Those are different. Gordon and Mitzi are seniors with health issues and Penny belongs to Linc. Lilith is hard to warm up to people and Freddie is . . . well, he's just ours."

"Right. What will you say about the next cuddly creature you're supposed to find a home for? Decide that one is a keeper, too?"

Her lips curved. "I guess you'll just have to trust that I've got this."

Trust. Yeah, not one of the things she had in surplus right now. Not after what she'd been through with her ex. But then again, this wasn't her life, so Hazel could do whatever she wanted. "Hey, if it makes you happy, you can have ten dogs."

Hazel handed her a glass of wine. "You seem tense. Are things not going well?"

"Actually, things are fine. I've got the house to myself, and Sean is finally over having fits about the divorce, and the kids have adjusted, so it's all just great." She took a couple of long swallows of the wine, exactly what she needed.

JACI BURTON

"Then let's join the party." Hazel took her hand and dragged her outside. The weather was perfect—a little humid, like Orlando always was. But it was still spring, and the oppressive summer heat hadn't yet hit, plus Natalie wore a sundress and sandals, so she felt fine. Since her divorce, she'd changed a lot—including her wardrobe. Gone were the smart, crisp slacks and buttoned-up blouses and painful shoes that Sean always preferred, because, after all, one must always be dressed for the country club. To him, appearances were everything.

Ugh. Now she wore sundresses and shorts and capris, and she even let her hair grow out and wound it up in a bun on occasion. Anything and everything that was the opposite of her ex's expectations of her. She'd never felt more free. More herself. More like her old self, the person she'd been before her ex had tried to mold her into who he'd wanted her to be.

But that part of her life was over.

There was a crowd outside. She recognized a few of Hazel's friends, including Sandy, who ran the foster animal organization. She also saw some of Linc's friends that he'd made since he officially moved in.

Her lip curled in a sneer as Hazel led her over to the group. Linc's brother Eugene Kennedy was here, too. He was telling some story, or, knowing him, probably a joke since he seemed to find everything funny. A couple of younger women were hanging on his every word as if he were some kind of . . . prophet or rock star or something.

Whatever. Sure, he was pretty and all. Ridiculously tall, with lean muscle, glorious black hair, and piercing blue eyes. Any woman would be instantly attracted.

Any woman but her, of course. She was older than he was, and she didn't do that instalust thing. Plus, he liked to joke around and act like a kid, and she had way too many responsibilities to fall for that nonsense.

"Is everyone having a good time?" Hazel asked as they stepped outside. "For those who don't already know her, I want to introduce you to my sister, Natalie."

Eugene's head jerked up at the mention of her name. Their gazes met, and his lips curved into a sexy smile that shot right to all her feminine parts. Damn her betraying body, anyway. Why was he holding eye contact with her? And why didn't she just look away?

Finally focusing her attention elsewhere, she greeted the people she didn't know, and Linc hugged her. "Glad you could make it," he said. "Where are the kids?"

"Babysitter. I needed a free night."

"Yeah, you did," Hazel said.

Linc put his arm around Hazel. "Babe. I want you to meet some people."

"Sure." Hazel looked over at her. "You'll be okay?"

Natalie nodded. "I'm fine. Go."

Hazel wandered off, and she did as well, heading toward the kitchen, where there were several charcuteries set up. She grabbed a plate and some fruit, nuts, and cheese and took a seat in the eating area, watching the people wander in and out of the house.

"Hiding?"

She could have sworn she was sitting in a dark corner where no one could see her. Leave it to Eugene to find her. "Shouldn't you be out there picking up women?"

He pulled up a chair next to her, stretching out his long legs. "Pretty sure you're a woman."

"So that's your pickup line?"

He let out a low chuckle. "I wasn't trying to pick you up. Unless you'd like me to, in which case I'll give it my best shot."

She took a swallow of wine. "Don't bother. I'm not interested in boys."

"So you like women, then?"

"That's not at all what I meant and you know it."

"Oh. Okay."

"I like men just fine." She gave him the once-over. "Not . . . boys."

Not at all insulted, he picked an almond off her plate and popped it into his mouth. "Don't knock me until you've tried me."

Rolling her eyes, she got up. "You're ridiculous."

As she started to walk away, he said, "You're only saying that because you want me."

Every single time. Ever since Eugene moved here, there'd been this . . . back-and-forth thing between them. It had been instantaneous, like a constant buzzing around her. Antagonistic, electric, infuriating.

Exciting.

She hated it.

*E*ugene circled the house, thrilled for Linc and Hazel to be finally settled. He knew living in another renovation zone had been a hassle for them this past year, but they hadn't once complained about it. And while he'd stayed in California to finish up a project before officially moving out here to start his new job, he'd been back and forth a lot, getting to know Hazel better. And all five of the dogs, of course.

He'd never figured his brother for the settling down type. Linc had previously lived a vagabond lifestyle of renovating a house, then moving to another state to do the next one. Eugene had barely been able to keep up with what city Linc had been living in.

Not that he'd really cared. He had his own world and that had kept him happy. But seeing his brother in love? Yeah, that had been a shocker. After meeting Hazel, he could see the reason why. She was perfect for Linc, had turned the freewheeling workaholic into someone who seemed more caring, more settled. And definitely in love.

Eugene took a long swallow of his beer and walked outside, finding Linc sitting at a table with Hazel next to him, all five of the dogs either on their laps or lying on the ground next to them.

Yeah, pretty good life for his brother.

Eugene wasn't anywhere near ready for a life like that.

His gaze tracked to where Natalie sat chatting with some older guy who could be her grandpa. He shook his head. Leave it to her to play it safe. He'd have to fix that.

He'd learned plenty about her from listening to Hazel and Linc talk. Natalie had been through it with her shitty ex-husband, who not only treated her like she worked for him, but then fought her every step of the way in the divorce. But instead of breaking her, it only made her more determined to never let a man control her life again.

A woman like that was just the kind of woman Eugene found attractive. He had to admit he found her fascinating as hell. And beautiful, with her dark hair and piercing green eyes, not to mention her incredible body. Plus she had the smart mouth to go with the already perfect package. What more could a guy want?

They'd tussled since they first met, and he'd been happy as hell that she'd thrown his teasing comments right back at him. He could tell he got under her skin, but he hadn't even given her his best stuff yet.

That was yet to come.

CHAPTER TWO

Natalie pulled out wallpaper samples, standing at the big table in the interior design shop where she worked. She stared down at the plethora of samples and let out a satisfied sigh.

She worked. She had a job. She was free, independent, able to make her own decisions now. She did work for someone, but Delilah was an absolute delight, her design company was perfect for Natalie, and even more importantly, she trusted Natalie and gave her the freedom to do whatever she wanted for her clients.

Sean had never wanted her to work, preferring she stay home to take care of the house and kids. As someone who'd been so excited to get her degree and plan her career, she had no idea what had happened to her, how she had lost herself so fully. Because she was full of zest and desire, and she could have capably handled a marriage, kids, and a career. So how could she have let Sean sideline her life like that? How had she so completely given up control?

Shaking off thoughts of the past, she loaded up the wallpaper samples along with a few other awesome plans for her client, then headed out on the road, grateful to crack the window and feel the spring breeze flowing in her face.

Her phone buzzed, and she waited until she pulled up in front of the client's house to look at it, seeing that she had missed a call from Hazel. She sent her a quick text to let her know she was meeting with a client and she'd call her back once she was finished.

It took about an hour to go over the samples with her client. They were renovating the living room and kitchen, and right now everything was a dusty mess, but Natalie didn't concern herself with the construction aspect. Her job was to show the homeowners the fun, pretty things, like wallpaper and paint colors and hardware and countertops. Marianne was open and enthusiastic about updating her twenty-year-old home and loved all of Natalie's ideas. She threw in a few requests of her own, and Natalie made notes. They wrapped up, and she headed out, telling her phone to call Hazel while she drove.

"I'm so sorry to bother you while you're working," Hazel said.

"It's no bother. What's up?"

"Are you and the kids free for dinner tonight?"

"Cammie and Christopher are with Sean tonight, but I'm available."

"Oh great. Can you come over? I'm trying out a new seafood pasta recipe."

Her mouth watered at the thought, especially since her sister was a phenomenal cook. "Count me in. Thanks for the invite."

"You're welcome. See you about seven."

"See you then."

She clicked off and sent herself a voice note to add tonight's dinner to her calendar. Then she made voice notes about her visit with Marianne.

So far, today was going exceptionally well. Even better, now she wouldn't have to find something for dinner tonight.

*E*ugene left his office and drove to the house—one of the many he'd looked at since moving here. He had yet to find one that would suit his needs. And the small executive rental the company put him in was nice enough, but not for what he needed since he often worked at home. He had to get out of there.

He pulled up in front of a two-story white house with black shutters, the landscaping utterly perfect. It was private, and he liked his privacy. The Realtor met him at the front door.

"Hey, Mark," Eugene said. "Love the outside of the place."

"You'll like the inside even more. It has everything you need."

Mark had shown him enough spaces that he'd learned that Eugene didn't need him to talk up a place. He wanted to walk around and get a feel.

Living room had arched ceilings, but a slider leading to the backyard. He would change that to accordion sliding glass doors to let in more light and give him a better view of . . . He opened the door and stepped outside.

Oh yeah. Killer backyard. Pool, lush green landscaping, and a pool house in the back. Plenty of space for parties. Big covered patio. Needed an outside kitchen, though.

He walked back inside and went to the kitchen, which was closed off to the living room. That would have to change, along with the décor, which was about twenty years old. The kitchen was dark, the dining area small, so opening it up would help all of that. And every room needed updated lighting.

There were four bedrooms, so he wandered through all of those. Mostly cosmetic things like changing carpet to tile or hardwoods, but the rooms were all big, and that helped. And there was a bonus room that was set up as a media room, which would be perfect for his office. With a few modifications, of course.

Once he finished, he turned to Mark. "I like this one."

Mark looked surprised. "Seriously?"

"Yeah. Why?"

"Because you haven't liked anything I've shown you for the past month."

Eugene laughed. "Hey, I have certain needs, and I don't want to have to raze a house to make it livable. This one needs some adjustments, but I think I can make it work. But I want my brother to come look at it since he does renovations."

Mark nodded. "Sure. Just let me know."

"Will do."

When he got out to his car, he called Linc. It took him a few rings to answer.

"I'm in the middle of installing a bathtub. What do you want?"

Eugene laughed. "I might have found a house."

"Yeah?—No, don't put that there. Hang on.—Hey, Eugene, come for dinner tonight and tell me about it."

"Sure."

"I'll text you the time. I gotta go."

He hung up and Eugene grinned.

The day was looking up.

CHAPTER THREE

After meeting Sean to drop off the kids—which was never without scathing looks or some kind of whispered quip about how much this was hurting his children—Natalie shook it off and drove over to Hazel and Linc's house.

"I have wine, sangria, and beer," Hazel said as she let her in, the dogs happily greeting Natalie with whimpers and wagging tails.

"Hi, pups," Natalie said, so used to them now that she bent down and gave them all some pats and ear rubs. "Sangria sounds great."

Natalie—and the dogs—followed Hazel into the kitchen. Hazel pulled the bottle out of the fridge and opened it, pouring two glasses.

"Where's Linc?" she asked.

"In the shower," Hazel said, sliding a glass over to her. "His work day was long today. He should be down shortly."

"You're both working so hard lately. Him on renovating houses and you with your job at the restaurant."

Hazel led her to the table and they both sat. "I know, but we love it. We're working toward our future, Nat. And working hard is how we do it."

"Except that Linc already has money."

"Right," Hazel said, taking a sip of her drink. "His money. And I need to feel like I'm on at least somewhat equal footing. He respects that, so we're taking things slowly."

"I suppose I can understand that. After living off of Sean's income for so long, it's nice to be earning my own for a change. Even though he pays child support and temporary alimony, I can appreciate not having to ask for money from a man."

Hazel nodded. "Exactly. And the only reason you didn't have a career before was because he demanded you be the stay-at-home mom."

Natalie swirled the liquid around in her glass. "I could have argued. I didn't."

"But you're free now."

She let out a soft laugh. "Better late than never, I guess?"

"First, it's not late. And, second, give yourself some credit, Nat. A lot of women would have stayed in that type of relationship until it swallowed them up. Until they were left with nothing. You didn't. And you fought for what you and the kids deserved."

Leave it to her sister to build her up. "Thanks. But I've still got a ways to go."

"One step at a time, sis."

"Yeah." She took a longer swallow of her drink this time. "Anyway, how was your day?"

"It was good. Yours?"

"Pretty excellent, actually." She told Hazel about her client appointment and how that went.

"You're doing so well with your job, Nat. Your boss must be so pleased."

"She is. Which motivates me to keep doing what I'm doing."

"Hey, everyone. Linc told me to let myself in."

Natalie blinked, then looked over at Hazel, who didn't meet her gaze. Instead, she got up to give Eugene a hug. "I'm so glad you could make it. What can I get you to drink?"

"A beer would be great, thanks."

Eugene came over and pulled out a chair next to Natalie. "Hey, Natalie."

"Eugene. I didn't know you'd be joining us."

"Well, I'm nothing if not an excellent surprise."

Hazel snorted a laugh in the kitchen. Natalie rolled her eyes and heaved a sigh. "Yes, that's you all right."

Linc came into the kitchen. "Hey, y'all."

"Hi, Linc," Natalie said. "Long day?"

"Very. But good day. Wrapping up the house I've been renovating. We'll be staging next week and putting it on the market."

Hazel came in and handed beers to Linc and to Eugene. "That's awesome, babe."

"Yeah . . . babe." Eugene smirked and took a swallow of his beer. "Perfect timing, too, because I think I found a house."

"Really?" Hazel asked. "When?"

"Toured the house today. I think it might be the one."

"That's great," Linc said. "Where is it?"

Linc gave them the address and Natalie coughed.

"That's like a block over from where Nat lives," Hazel said. "How cool is that?"

"Just so cool." Natalie tried to smile, but she was certain it came out like a grimace. That was all she needed was Eugene dropping by to . . . well, she didn't actually know why he would want to come to her house. It was probably all in her imagination because the two of them had nothing—

"Yeah?" He looked over at Natalie, his expression revealing nothing. "So, we'll be neighbors. I can come over and borrow sugar. Or something."

She resisted rolling her eyes. "Uh-huh."

He gave her a lopsided grin, then turned his attention over to Linc. "Anyway, it needs some renovations. And serious design work."

"The reno I can do," Linc said, then motioned with his head over to Natalie. "Nat's who you need for help with the design stuff."

Oh no. She absolutely would not, could not, get involved with Eugene in that way. Or any way.

"Oh, Nat, how much fun would that be?" Hazel asked.

"Uh . . ." Not one who was ever at a loss for words, Natalie found herself unable to answer Hazel's question. Because the idea of working with Eugene did not seem fun at all.

"Can you both come by the house and take a look at it? I wouldn't want to put an offer on it until you look at it, Linc. And it definitely needs to be modernized, design-wise. I'd really like your opinion, Natalie."

She couldn't very well say no to that since it was her job.

Linc nodded. "Tell me your schedule and we'll make it happen."

Linc and Eugene settled on tomorrow morning.

"I have a client meeting then," Natalie said. "I can do late afternoon."

"I'm meeting with the real estate agent then, so that won't work for me," Linc said.

"That's okay," Eugene said. "I'll free up my day and make both happen."

"Awesome." Hazel got up. "Let me get the shrimp ready and then we can eat."

"I'm excited for you, bruh," Linc said. "Buying a house is a big step. I know you've looked around a lot."

"Yeah. I'm relieved to have found one that'll work for me." He looked over at Linc, then at Natalie. "Thanks to both of you for agreeing to help me out."

Natalie hadn't agreed to anything yet, but she couldn't help but note the sincerity in his voice. "It's my job, so I'm happy to see if I can assist you."

Again, that smile of his. Enigmatic. Sexy as hell.

Was she reading signals wrong? That was entirely possible. She'd been out of the game a long time. For all she knew, he was simply being friendly, and she didn't have a clue.

She'd look at his house, and if it was something that required her expertise, she'd do her job.

But that was all she'd do.

CHAPTER FOUR

Since Eugene had made a cash offer, the closing had come about fast, which had been one of his requirements to buy the house. Fortunately, the couple who owned the house had already moved out, so the entire transaction had been conducted in a matter of a few weeks.

Now, as he walked through the house, he couldn't believe he owned it.

He'd never minded condo living. Back in California it had suited his purposes. He'd often worked late nights and weekends at the office where he had state-of-the-art equipment. This was a different situation.

Not that the facility here didn't have its own awesome setup for their designers. They did. He had an office, a full staff, and all the state-of-the-art design gadgetry he could ever wish for. But this time he wanted separation, some space to create on his own without the constant buzz of people coming and going. Having his home office—one that was soundproof so he could play the explosions and noises at the appropriate decibel level the audience would need—was key.

He'd have to live in his rental house until Linc finished renovations, but his brother had walked through it with him before he signed the papers and told him the place was in good shape and would only need the cosmetic changes. Though he suggested they do a few upgrades to the air-conditioning and electrical, which Eugene had agreed was a good idea.

Linc had told him if he did it himself, it would take a few months, otherwise he could hire a crew to cut down on the timeline, but it would cost Eugene more money. Eugene didn't care about the money. He was ready to move in, so Linc told him they'd be ready to start as soon as Eugene got the keys.

Now all he had to do was get Natalie on board. She'd had to bail on the design walk-through before he bought the house, but Linc assured him she was the best. And seeing her design touches on Linc and Hazel's house showed him she knew her stuff.

Speaking of Natalie, he heard a soft knock on the door, and he smiled as he took a quick glance at his watch. She was definitely prompt.

"It's open," he yelled, and she turned the knob and walked in.

"You should lock your doors," she said.

"Why? You planning to burgle? Because there's nothing in here."

She laid a couple of bags at his feet. "No. Just something to consider for the future."

"Not a safe neighborhood?"

"Honey, no place is safe anymore. But as far as neighborhoods, this is one of the better ones. We all watch out for each other."

"Good to know." He liked that she called him "honey." Also, she held his gaze for a beat, and he sure didn't mind staring into her beautiful green eyes. There was something liquidy and mesmerizing about them, as if she held secrets of the universe or something.

Dude. You've created way too many fantasy games.

His mind was not wrong about that.

"Anyway, this is my house. Care for a tour?"

"Actually, I'd like to look around on my own, if you don't mind."

He shoved his hands in his jeans pockets. "Sure. Go ahead."

He followed a few steps behind while she wandered, her iPad in hand. She pivoted, taking a full two minutes to stare at the living room before moving to the kitchen. She looked around, made a sound of disgust and headed outside.

"You know, I thought out here we could—"

She raised a palm to stop him. "Not now. Why don't you wait out here while I finish my tour?"

"Uh . . . sure."

She wandered inside, so he pulled up one of the lawn chairs he'd bought at the discount store and checked his work emails. The team was already up and running, so all he had to do at the moment was approve their design notes. He'd sent preliminary schemes and drawings to them last week regarding the game setup. Normally he dealt in the virtual world, and while to some extent that would still be true, this was his first foray into bringing the virtual into reality.

Overwhelming? Hell yeah. But he couldn't imagine anything

more exciting. Creating games was one thing. A ride? It was like a dream come true.

Natalie came down the stairs. "Okay, here's what I think. I don't know what you and Linc have discussed renovations-wise, but I have a few ideas if you'd like to hear them."

He granted her a half smile, very interested in what she had to say. Would her ideas be the same as his or would they be complete bullshit? "I'm all ears."

"The kitchen is a gut job. But it's a good size. Plenty big enough to put in an island for added seating and prep space, providing that appeals to you. Also, it's closed off from the rest of the house." She pointed to the wall that he'd absolutely hated the first time he walked through. "We should lose this wall, open things up."

He followed her into the living room where she stood by the sliding door. "You have a stunning backyard. It's an entertainer's paradise. Get rid of the slider and put in an accordion sliding door that will bring in so much more light."

She walked him outside. "I'd change nothing out here. It's glorious. But, if you want to truly entertain, maybe you'd want to add an outside kitchen. It keeps the heat out of the indoor kitchen during the hot summer months and makes it easier for entertaining purposes."

She paused, waiting, he supposed, to see if he disagreed with anything she'd suggested so far.

He didn't.

"Go on."

"The laminate flooring has seen better days." She gave him

the once-over before continuing. "I think wood floors, or even wood-look tiles would be perfect for this house. Though if you go with wood, I'd suggest tile in the kitchen and all the bathrooms."

"Uh-huh."

She made her way up the stairs, and he followed, trying not to focus his attention on the way her ass swayed as she walked. Hard when she was two steps above him and her sweet behind was directly in his line of sight.

She wandered into one of the guest bedrooms. "All your bedrooms are fine. I'd update the flooring and they need some paint. And light. God, this whole house needs some light, Eugene. It's dark as a cave in here. I can suggest lighting that'll improve every room if you tell me what your plans are for the rooms."

They made their way into his favorite room. "Okay, this one. Huge. Obviously a bonus space. What are your plans for it, or do you have any?"

"Media room," he said, coming fully into the room. "I'll be working in here, so I'll need it fully soundproofed. Dark. I'll take care of ordering the appropriate sound system and digital needs along with furniture."

She shrugged. "Fine."

The last room was the primary bedroom. It was sizable, which was one of the things he liked most.

"King-size bed," she said. "These three windows will provide a lot of natural light. Dresser, two nightstands, good lighting, maybe a reading chair or two."

She turned to face him. "Thoughts?"

"I have lots of thoughts about my bedroom."

She cleared her throat. "And what would those . . . thoughts be?"

Her cheeks popped two pink spots, her eyes turning to pools of emerald green. The intimacy of the room seemed to instantly surround him, engulfing Eugene in the kind of heat he only felt when he was naked and rolling around with a woman. Yet here he was, fully clothed and standing in an empty bedroom. Just Natalie and him.

He'd thrown out the teaser, hoping she'd toss back a sarcastic remark. That she'd responded with an unexpected heat nearly brought him to his knees.

"You know, I like all your ideas for the bedroom. Big bed. Chairs. Nightstands. Lights. It's all good."

She blew out a breath and took a step back. "Perfect. Now the bath." She took several quick steps into the en suite, obviously not able to get away from him fast enough.

He smiled and followed her.

"Good-sized en suite," she said. "Plenty of room for an oversize shower." She finally turned to look at him. "I'd add a soaker tub. Vanity over here. Lots of bright and also ambient lighting. Some woman will appreciate it someday."

"Yeah, well, I'm not looking for *some* woman."

Again she opened her mouth to say something, then closed it and nodded. "Anyway, as far as design, I have some samples downstairs if you'd like to look through them."

"Sure."

Once they were on the main floor again, she opened the bags

she'd brought in and laid samples on the kitchen counter. Some were loud and colorful, which made him want to gag. Others were simple and more to his liking. He wondered which ones she'd suggest.

When she stepped toward the set he liked best, he sighed in relief.

"Black and white for the kitchen with black on the bottom and white on the top," she said. "A marbled white quartz for your counters. Black hardware. It's sleek, modern, somewhat masculine without being overly so. We'll add pendant lights above the island. I'm thinking something industrial."

"Yeah, I like that."

Then she set out flooring options, so many it made his head spin.

"If you go with wood flooring, you'll want to choose kitchen tile that blends both with your wood floors and with the kitchen cabinets and counter."

Natalie offered several options for wood and tile. All were good ones. But he found himself gravitating toward the wood-look tile.

"These look like wood. I'd bet they'd clean up easier, too."

She nodded. "They would."

"And then we could lay these all the way into the kitchen, making the whole area feel larger."

"Yes." She smiled, and damn, that lit up her face. He'd like to see a lot more of that smile.

"Okay, let's do that," he said, running his fingers over one of the smooth, cool tiles. "This one."

"Excellent choice. Now on to the bathrooms."

He couldn't hold his groan in. "This is going to take an eternity."

She laughed. "We're almost done." She pulled out more selections.

"Couldn't you just choose for me?"

"And what if you hate what I put in the primary bath? Or one of the other bathrooms?"

"Based on the samples you brought, I doubt I'd hate anything."

"This will go fast." She shuffled some of the selections around so there were fewer options. "This for your primary. These for your secondary bathrooms."

He looked them over and liked them all immediately. "Done."

"We still have to choose lighting and paint, but I'd say we've got a good start."

"Great. Let's go have lunch."

"I have to make notes of your selections. And don't you have to work?"

"I can work tonight. And I'm hungry. You can make notes while I'm driving."

"I have my car."

"I'll drive you back here after we eat. Which hopefully we can do soon."

She cocked her head to the side. "You're cranky when you're hungry."

"I am not. But can we go now?"

Her lips curved. "Yes. Let's go."

Finally. He pulled his keys out and led her to the door, already tasting the juicy hamburger he was planning to eat.

*D*uring lunch, Natalie glanced over on occasion to watch Eugene devour a hamburger, fries, and a side salad like he hadn't eaten in a week. And he did it while talking a mile a minute about anything and everything, which was fine with her because while she half listened to him going on about something baseball, she made notes about his selections.

"How's your chicken salad?" he asked.

She didn't look up from her notes. "It's fine, thanks."

"You're very good at your job."

This time she did look up. "You think so?"

He shoved a fry in his mouth, chewed, and swallowed, then nodded. "Yeah. You know what looks right and what fits, and you aren't afraid to state your opinion. I like people who have strong opinions."

"Really."

"Well, yeah. How are you going to know what someone is thinking or how they feel unless they tell you?"

She couldn't help but laugh. "You don't know my ex-husband."

He took a swallow of his iced tea and studied her. "Obviously he didn't want you to share your opinion on things."

"On anything. He just wanted to dictate and have me obey."

Eugene made a disgusted face. "He does know this is the twenty-first century, right?"

"I guess you could say he's more of an old-school kind of guy."

"How so?"

"I stayed home, kept the house clean, cooked meals, raised the kids. I wasn't supposed to have an opinion on anything because he made all the decisions. Where we went on vacation. What we did on the weekends. How money was spent. I only wish I had known that before I married him."

Instead of giving her that sad, sympathetic look she'd gotten from so many of her friends and family, he just shrugged. "But you're not married to him anymore. You're free. Independent. So now you can do—and say—whatever the hell you want, right?"

He understood. "Yes, I can."

"Good for you."

She popped a chip into the salsa and slid it into her mouth. She chewed thoughtfully, watching as Eugene polished off the last of his fries. She slid the chips and salsa to the center of the table, and he grinned, grabbing a chip and loading salsa on top of it.

"We probably need something stronger than iced tea," he said, motioning for the server. "Margaritas?"

She shouldn't. She had work to do. Then again, it was Friday, and Sean had the kids for the weekend, which meant she could do her orders and paperwork tomorrow. "It is close to the end of the day."

Their server came over. "Two margaritas, please. Oh, and more chips and salsa."

"Tell me about your new job," she said.

"I design games. Or that's what I did before. Do you play games?"

"Not really."

"Too bad. They can be fun. Strategic. Challenging. We should play together sometime."

We should play together sometime. A sudden rush of heat permeated her body. He'd been discussing games, of course. Her dirty mind had imagined other types of play entirely.

"I'm not much into games."

Their server brought their drinks along with fresh chips and salsa. Eugene took a sip of his margarita, then asked, "You play games with your kids, don't you?"

She shrugged and took a swallow of what turned out to be a very delicious margarita. "Christopher's idea of games is throwing his ball outside or playing some Spider-Man game on his tablet. Cammie is more into paint by numbers and some dollhouse game. I think they're both a little young to play the kinds of video games you're talking about."

He nodded. "Not really. There are tons of interactive games that can be played as a family."

"I'm not sure."

"Hey, this is what I do. You have to trust me. If you want some quality time with your kids, and something they'll enjoy, believe me. I can find video games they'll enjoy."

"Okay, this is where I admit that I'm not good with all the button-pushing and stuff."

He laughed. "That's all right. I can help. Invite me over some night and I'll bring several games. And I'll help push your buttons."

Did he do that on purpose or was it some innocent comment that she read as a double entendre?

No doubt it was her imagination. What with the divorce and

all the arguing she and Sean had done prior to the divorce, sex had been nonexistent for more than a year. To be honest, well before that, too. It wasn't a surprise that it was prominent on her mind, especially in the company of a very hot guy.

A very hot younger guy, Natalie. He's not for you.

Yeah, whatever. She could still enjoy looking at him.

"Sure. How about next Saturday? I have the kids next weekend and nothing on the agenda Saturday night."

He pulled out his phone and typed something in. "You're on my calendar."

"Are you sure you don't mind spending a Saturday night with my kids? They can be a lot."

His lips curved. "I like kids. I'll bring games. We'll have fun."

That's what a lot of people who didn't have kids said. They were so clueless. "Okay. I'll make dinner."

"Even better. It's a date."

He popped a chip in his mouth like what he'd just said meant nothing. Which, to him, it probably had. And, actually, it wasn't a date at all since her kids would be there.

It was going to be fun. Just fun. With her kids.

And she'd learn how to play video games.

So much fun.

CHAPTER FIVE

*E*ugene had spent the week in meetings and planning and writing code. He'd buried himself in his office, working on the calendar, meeting with his teams so they had the appropriate direction they needed, and planning out the next six months so everyone would know what they were supposed to be working on. So far, it was all going well.

He'd assembled a team of the best in the business, which had been one of his requirements. Fortunately, a lot of the best in the business had jumped right on board the project, which made his job a hell of a lot easier. And doing what he did was fun, too. He didn't have to wander around, managing people. From art to production to code, everyone was more than competent at their jobs.

But he had to admit he was happy when they finished off the week. His brain was tired and he needed a break. He took his team out Friday night for dinner and drinks, where they all talked about anything and everything but work. They discussed movies and games and their families, giving Eugene a chance to get to know all of them on a more personal level.

He needed to know his people, not just wave and smile as they passed each other in the hall. Getting to know his team members had always been a priority.

After a very long dinner, he'd gone home, played a few games, then gone to bed, immediately passing out.

Saturday morning he got up and went to the gym for an intense workout, followed by a stop at the local coffee shop for a drink and a muffin. He sat in the shop and ate while scrolling through his phone, answering some emails.

He'd had his favorite locations for coffee and breakfast in San Francisco. Since he'd moved here, he'd tried a few spots, but this one seemed to be good. It was busy but not noisy, which meant he could kick back and conduct business while he enjoyed his muffin and coffee. Plus he'd always liked people watching, and this place provided plenty of that.

After he finished up, he headed to the grocery store to get some essential food items for next week. Fortunately, he didn't have to clean since that service was one of the benefits of his executive rental, which he appreciated. But he did have to do laundry, a necessary evil.

When he finished folding the last load, his phone buzzed, and he picked it up to see a call from Natalie.

"Hey," he said.

"Hi. I thought you should know the kids go to bed about nine. I know you wanted to play games and all, so I thought we'd do dinner around five, if that's not too early for you."

"It's not too early. Can I bring something?"

"No, I've got it all taken care of."

"Okay. Text me your address."

"All right. I should warn you that the kids are very excited about tonight."

He grinned at her warning, as if excited kids would be a problem for him. "Me, too. See you, Natalie."

"Right. See you soon."

He clicked off, laid his phone down on the desk, and wandered into the other room where he had his temporary office. He should have asked Natalie if they had any kind of gaming system. Judging from his prior conversation with her, he'd guess no. He grabbed a box and started piling in his favorite system, along with about five games he thought kids Camryn's and Christopher's ages would enjoy.

He loaded those up in his car and headed out, stopping at the liquor store to pick up a bottle of wine. She might not want to drink it tonight, considering the kids and all, but she could always have it another night, and his mother had taught him that when you were invited to someone's house, you had to bring something.

Natalie lived about twenty minutes from his rental place. She had a really nice house—a craftsman in striking gray and blue colors, with a nice wide porch and white columns.

He made his way to the porch and rang the bell. He heard a voice through the doorbell camera.

"I'm unlocking the door. Just come in."

It was Natalie's voice, with kids yelling in the background. He grinned and turned the knob. The door opened to a large foyer. The place was wide and open, with sight lines all the way to the bifold doors leading out to the backyard.

Two beautiful children with Natalie's dark hair came running up to him. The girl was older, and the boy had a cheeky grin as wide as the ocean.

"Mommy said your name is Eugene," the girl said. "I'm Camryn but everyone calls me Cammie. I'm seven years old, but I'll be eight in three months. I'm in second grade. This is my brother, Christopher. He's four but he'll be five next month. How old are you? Are you going on a date with my mommy?"

"Cammie. That's quite enough of an inquisition."

Natalie walked in, looking amazing with her hair falling in silken waves. She wore dark capris and a colorful sleeveless top, baring shoulders he wanted to—

Well, he wouldn't think about her skin while her kids were present.

"I wasn't . . . in . . . questioning him," Cammie said. "I was getting to know him."

"That she was. Nice to meet you, Cammie. I'm not in any grade because I graduated. I am thirty years old, and no, tonight I am not going on a date with your mommy. But I am going to hang out with all of you if that's okay."

Cammie nodded. "It's okay."

He lifted his gaze to Natalie and gave her a smile. She looked decidedly uncomfortable. He meant to change that.

But for now, he crouched down to look at Christopher. "And what about you?"

"Momma said you brought games."

"I did."

"What kinda games?"

"Fun ones, of course. Do you like *Mario Kart*?"

Christopher frowned. "I dunno."

He grinned. "You'll like it. Trust me."

"Games later," Natalie said. "Dinner first. And can we let our guest move inside the front door, please? Cammie, Christopher, go wash your hands. Dinner is almost ready."

"Okay," Cammie said, heading upstairs, Christopher trailing behind her.

Eugene followed Natalie down the hall and into a nice, spacious kitchen. He'd expected all white, not the dark wood cabinets and white counters, complemented perfectly by the décor. Definitely a modern farmhouse vibe.

"What would you like to drink?" she asked. "We have wine, beer, tea, or soft drinks. And water, of course."

"I'll have an iced tea." He didn't want to drink alcohol around the kids. Besides, he wanted to be clearheaded when he worked with them on games.

While she fixed him a drink, he took a look around the open area. It was perfectly styled, and yet didn't feel like he had to watch everywhere he stepped or sat. It felt comfortable, like you could take your shoes off and relax.

"I can tell an interior designer lives here."

She stiffened as she handed him the tea. "You think it's stuffy."

"No, I think it's perfectly designed for a family. It's thoughtful. Oversize island with appropriate stools for both adults and kids. I'll bet the kids love sitting there."

Visibly relaxing, she smiled at him. "They do. They help me whenever I bake. It's a huge mess, but we always have so much fun."

He could envision her standing at the island, laughing with her kids while they made cookies together. "That sounds awesome."

"It really is."

"The huge sofa is made for cuddling up with your kids, too. I imagine you do that on movie nights."

She tilted her head to observe him. "Actually we read there together every night before bed. But, yes, there are plenty of movie and popcorn nights."

He nodded. "My family always did Friday night movie nights when we were kids. With pizza, of course."

"Of course."

The sounds of pounding footsteps let him know the kids were coming back. "Mommy, look," Cammie said, holding her palms out for inspection. "Clean hands."

"Me, too," Christopher said, mimicking his sister.

"That's a very good job. Let's set the table so we can eat."

He also liked that Natalie let the kids help set the table, something he'd been taught to do at an early age. It had always made him feel important, like his mom trusted him not to break the dishes or stab himself with a fork.

And if the fork was on the wrong side of the plate, no one cared. Apparently Natalie didn't, either. Eugene sure as hell didn't. Getting kids involved was the important thing. Appropriate table settings could come at a later time.

"I hope you like salad and casserole," Natalie said, placing something that smelled really amazing in the center of the dining room table.

After she brought over the salad and some freshly sliced bread,

Natalie scooped the food onto the kids' plates. Then Eugene cut a slice and offered it up to Natalie before putting some on his own plate. He filled up the salad bowls and grabbed two pieces of bread, helping Christopher butter his.

"It's lazana," Christopher said.

It took Eugene a few thoughtful seconds to realize he'd said "lasagna."

Cammie nodded. "Filled with cheesy goodness."

"You made lasagna?" Eugene asked after Natalie sat.

"Yes. Why? You don't like lasagna?"

"I love lasagna. Thank you again for inviting me to dinner."

She gave him a curious look, as if she couldn't believe he was grateful to be invited over for a meal. "You're welcome. Dig in, everyone."

After that, there was eating and talking and laughing. Cammie told him about all her friends and her gymnastics class, and Christopher's topics varied from his favorite soccer ball to something about a big bug he saw out in the backyard. Eugene promised they'd go out after dinner to see if they could find it.

Natalie engaged the kids with questions about what they'd done earlier today. Apparently she'd taken them to a nature preserve, so the kids talked about their favorite parts.

"I liked the butterfly garden the best," Cammie said. "Did you know that there are over seven hundred and fifty types of butterflies in the United States? And that they start out as caterpillars, then spin themselves into a cocoon?"

Eugene was impressed. "I did not know that. How many butterflies do you think you saw today?"

"I don't know. Maybe all of them. And I saw cocoons, too."

"Whoa. What did you think of the cocoons?"

"I loved them. They're like little cuddly nap spots where the butterflies get ready to show off how pretty they are."

He grinned. Eugene could tell from Cammie's wide eyes and look of excitement that she'd enjoyed the butterflies a lot.

Natalie gave him a warm smile and that made him feel good, though he had no idea why. He was just having a good time. Plus, there was no denying he'd enjoyed the food.

So far it was a great night.

Next up would be game time, and then the night would really be fun.

After Natalie did the dishes—which, surprisingly, Eugene helped with—they all gathered in the living room to play games. She had planned to beg off and watch while she caught up on some work, but Eugene insisted this was a family event, and Cammie and Christopher insisted as well, so she joined in.

He'd brought everything, including the game console. The kids were so excited as they filed through all the games. It was clear he understood their ages. They started out with a hedgehog game, which both the kids enjoyed. It kept their interest, both of them laughing as they maneuvered the characters through jumps and obstacles. Natalie had to admit she found herself immersed in the colorful world along with her kids.

They played several more games, including a dance game that left them all breathless and laughing. She could have done this all night. So could the kids, but she could tell they were wearing down.

"Okay," Natalie said. "It's time to get ready for bed."

"Aww." Christopher looked disappointed.

"Hey, buddy," Eugene said. "We'll play games again. And if it's okay with your mom, I'll leave the game console here, and you and your sister can play anytime you want."

Natalie looked at him. "Oh. You don't have to do that."

He laughed. "Trust me. I have a lot of these things. And I only loaded appropriate games for their ages on this one. I can show you how to navigate the system."

"Okay. Give me a few minutes to get them ready for bed?"

"Sure."

"Thanks, Eugene," Cammie said, slinging her arm around his neck. "You'll come over again, won't you?"

Christopher climbed on the couch and sat next to him. "Yeah, you'll come over and play with us?"

An unexpected rush of warmth fused through him as their small bodies pressed against him. "You couldn't keep me away."

He looked up at Natalie, who was giving him warm looks, too. Well, hell.

"Okay, you two, let's go," Natalie said.

"G'night, Eugene," Christopher said.

"Bye, Eugene," Cammie said.

"Goodnight kids. See you soon."

He leaned back and took a sip of his iced tea, totally thrown by these feelings.

He liked kids. Always had. He designed games for all ages,

from kids to adults. He didn't have children of his own or even nieces and nephews. Not yet, anyway. But he understood kids and what they liked. He'd done research studies and could design the hell out of a game that was age appropriate. And now he was designing a ride for kids of all ages.

He pulled out his phone and scrolled through his emails. Some of his staff had obviously been working today, because there were reports and questions about code and design that he'd answer later. But nothing urgent, so that was good.

He got up and went through the back door, wandering outside of the caged pool area to investigate the oversize backyard.

There was plenty of lawn area for the kids to play, lots of trees that provided privacy and shade, and even more space to the side to build out a guest house, pool house, or even a playhouse for the kids, if that's what Natalie wanted to do.

"I'm sorry," Natalie said, coming up to stand beside him. "The kids wanted two stories tonight."

He turned to face her and smiled. "Hey, they come first. Besides, it gave me time to check out your awesome backyard."

"Oh, thanks. It is nice, isn't it?"

"Yeah, it is. Do you like it?"

She let out a short laugh. "You know, no one ever asked me that. Sean chose the house. The location. It came with a membership to the country club. Status symbol, of course. Important for his business. I thought the house was nice, the pool awesome for the kids, and lots of space for them to play."

"But you didn't get input."

"No." She wandered around the yard, her thoughts obviously

somewhere else before she turned to him and smiled. "But it's fine. The kids love it here, and the schools are outstanding."

"That's good." She looked so wistful, and he figured her heart was still hurting over the divorce. All he wanted to do in that moment was pull her into his arms and let her know everything was going to be all right. "You miss him?"

She frowned. "Miss—oh, my ex? No. I miss the life I thought we were going to have, way before we got married. But do I miss him, the person? No. He wasn't who I thought he was going to be, husband-wise. I wanted a partner. He wanted something else entirely."

"Wanna talk about it?"

She shook her head. "Not tonight. But thanks for the offer."

He followed her inside, sat with her, and showed her how to work the game console. Even played a game together from start to finish so he could make sure she had a handle on the buttons.

"Oh, that's pretty easy."

"Yeah, it is."

She laid the console on the sofa. "The kids had fun. I appreciate you showing them these games. We'll have fun doing this together."

"I know you will."

Their gazes met, and something electric passed between them. They had chemistry. An energy he felt even without touching her. He wanted to explore that.

"Go out with me."

He wasn't sure how to read the surprise on her face. Hopefully it was a good thing.

"Excuse me?"

"A date. Dinner, or something."

She shook her head. "No. Thanks, but no."

That was pretty definite. He stood. "Okay. Thanks for dinner, Natalie."

She looked pissed as she walked him to the door. "Sure."

"I'll see you later."

She nodded and held the door open while he walked out.

He half turned and gave her a smile and a wave as he walked down the steps toward his truck. She gave him a short wave, then closed the door.

Frowning, he stopped at his truck, leaning against it, sending her a text.

Why did you say no?

It took her a minute to answer. Are you texting and driving?

He grinned and answered: No. I'm standing in your driveway.

A minute later she opened the door and came outside, walking fast. She stopped inches in front of him. "I said no."

"I got that. I respect it. But there's this chemistry between us, and you can't deny it."

"I—" She paused, looking at him, and there it was again. An invisible string of heat flowing between them. One step and she'd be in his arms, his mouth on hers. It vibrated between them.

"You feel it, don't you?" he asked.

She breathed in, then out. "You're younger than me."

He rolled his eyes. "Like that matters. It's a few years at most, Natalie."

"You walked out after I said no."

"What was I supposed to do?"

She threw her hands up. "I don't know. Ask me again."

Okay, he was starting to understand. She wanted to be pursued. Maybe her ex hadn't done that. Maybe the dude had the expectation that she'd fall all over herself to be with him. Eugene had no such illusions.

"I don't know if you realize this, but you are beautiful. Intelligent, sexy as fuck, and, Natalie? You're a damn catch. Any guy would be lucky to be with you. Would you please go out with me?"

She blew out a breath. "Yes."

"Great. You let me know your schedule, and we'll make plans that work for you."

"Okay."

He reached out, his fingers touching hers, and . . .

Zap.

His lips curved. There it was. And from the way her eyes went wide, her breathing quickening, she felt it, too.

He curled his fingers around hers, leaned in, and . . .

"Mommy?" Cammie stood on the sidewalk looking half asleep. "I need water."

Natalie jerked her hand away, and he took a full step back.

"Coming, baby." She gave him a regretful look. "I've gotta go."

"No problem. We'll talk later."

She headed to her daughter, putting her arm around Cammie, who turned and waved goodbye to him before Natalie closed the door.

Eugene smiled as he climbed into his truck.

Yeah, that was a much better ending to the night.

CHAPTER SIX

*T*he artwork and pillows that Natalie had ordered for Hazel and Linc's house had finally arrived, so Natalie called Hazel to check her schedule. She was off work from the restaurant today, and Hazel asked if Natalie wanted to have lunch with her. They arranged a time, and Natalie loaded the pieces into her SUV and drove over.

This would give Natalie some time to go over some design options for the backyard. Hazel had a decent enough setup for the dogs to frolic and for entertainment purposes, but with all that land, they could do so much more. Linc had told her to draw something up for them and present options to Hazel, so she had.

She appreciated that Linc hadn't taken over any part of the design process for their new home, allowing Hazel to make the lion's share of the decisions. Hazel had picked out the house, which had needed some renovations. Hazel had included Linc in discussions, but he'd deferred to her wants and needs. Natalie knew how little input she'd had in any life decisions in her first marriage, so she just loved how Linc asked her how she wanted things.

Probably why Hazel had fallen in love with him. He knew exactly what she needed. And that made Natalie love him, too.

Once she got to the house, she rang the bell, smiling at the sound of barking dogs. Hazel appeared at the door not long after, shushing the dogs and enveloping Natalie in a hug.

"I'm so glad you're here. Lunch is just about ready."

After Natalie loved on the pups, they all ran off behind Hazel, so she gathered her tote bag and followed Hazel into the kitchen.

"Something smells good."

"I'm baking bread. I also made a flavored tea. Does that sound good?"

"Sounds perfect. And you didn't need to go to the trouble of making bread."

"It's not trouble at all."

Hazel poured a glass and handed it to her, then took a sip from her own glass. Natalie took a seat at the island and watched as Hazel prepped kale and put it into the salad bowl, along with red quinoa, sliced dates, almonds, and a few other ingredients.

"Let's go sit at the table," Hazel said, bringing the bowl over and setting it in the center. "I'll get the bread."

The salad looked amazing. Hazel put dressing on the table, then added the bread that smelled so good it made Natalie's stomach rumble with hunger.

"It's a citrusy dressing and should meld well with the salad," Hazel said, taking a seat. "I hope you like it."

"You're a superb chef, Hazel. I already know I'm going to love it."

She took a bite of the salad and made a low moan. So good. The bread? Even better.

"I could not live with you anymore," Natalie said. "I'd gain so much weight."

Hazel made a *psh* sound. "The salad is very nutritious and low in calories. Though I do agree the bread is killer."

Natalie tore off a piece, shoved it in her mouth and chewed, then took a sip of tea. "Worth it, though."

Hazel laughed. "So true."

They ate and talked about family things, mostly their mother, who was acting typically like . . . their mother. Loving. Annoying. In their business.

"She told me I need to get remarried as soon as possible because the children and I need a man to support us."

Hazel made a face. "That's antiquated and sexist as hell. What did you say to her?"

"Exactly what you said. I told her I didn't need or want a man to take care of me, that I could take care of both myself and my children just fine. Naturally, she disagreed."

"Yikes. I'm sorry, Nat. I know she comes from a good place, but good lord she can be a pain in the ass sometimes."

"Oh, you haven't heard the worst part yet."

Hazel's eyes widened. "There's more?"

"She told me she can set me up with men."

Hazel gave her a horrified look. "What? What men?"

Natalie shrugged. "I have no idea, and I don't care, since I don't plan to go out with anyone she suggests."

"She can be somewhat unrelenting, you know."

Natalie chewed thoughtfully, swallowed, and said, "Then I'll tell her I'm already dating someone."

"Are you?"

"Dating? Of course not."

"Why not? It's been a while since the divorce, Nat. You should get out there and have some fun."

"Surely you're not going to try and set me up with someone."

Hazel laughed. "I know better than that. You can choose your own guys."

"Thanks. Actually . . ." She pushed the salad around with her fork.

Sitting straight in her chair, Hazel asked, "Actually, what? Have you been seeing someone?"

"Not really. But I do have a date scheduled." She shouldn't tell Hazel about this, but now she'd blurted it, so it was too late. And, now that she thought about it, of all the people in her life, she knew she could trust her sister to be discreet.

"Ooh. Tell me all about it."

They cleared the dishes and put them in the dishwasher, then refilled their glasses and went outside so the dogs could run around. It was a nice day with a breeze, and Hazel turned the fan on under the shade of the porch, so they grabbed a seat at the table.

"Okay, so promise not to laugh when I tell you," Natalie said.

Hazel frowned. "Why would I laugh?"

"It's Eugene."

Hazel's brows shot up. "Linc's brother? Interesting. How did that come about?"

"We've been working on the design aspects of his new house, as you know. Plus he came over to the house the other night and brought some video games to play with the kids."

"Aww. Did the kids like him?"

"Of course they did, since he's like a kid himself. I don't know if you've noticed or not, but he's way younger than me."

Hazel cocked her head to the side. "He is not 'way younger,' Nat. He's a few years younger. And after being married to stodgy Sean, you need someone fun in your life. Plus, he's smart and charming and incredibly good-looking."

Natalie couldn't deny everything Hazel said about Eugene. She also couldn't hide her grin when Hazel referred to her ex as "stodgy Sean." That certainly described him to a tee.

"I don't know, Hazel. I'm dreading this date."

"Dreading it? Why?"

She didn't say anything. Just shrugged.

"Look," Hazel said. "If you're not ready, you're not ready. And if you're not feeling it with Eugene, then cancel the date."

"It's not that. The chemistry between us is crazy. Like, white-hot crazy. From the moment we met—oh God, he drove me batty with his jokes. I thought he was a jackass. But still, that attraction simmering under the surface is just wild and constant."

Hazel leaned back in her chair. "And all this hot chemistry is a bad thing."

"No, of course it isn't. But I can't let foolish lust get in the way of the plans for my future. The plans I've made for the kids and me."

"Okay. Tell me what you're feeling," Hazel said.

"It's just . . . I focused all my attention on Sean and the kids—to the point that I gave up everything me. I don't want to do that anymore."

"Natalie. You had everything you ever wanted before. A nice house, country club membership, amazing clothes, two awesome kids. I wonder what it is that you want now."

Natalie gathered her thoughts before answering, because Hazel had presented a good question. "From the outside, it must have seemed like I had the perfect life. It wasn't. For the most part, I felt separated. Alone. Don't get me wrong. I love my kids and watching them grow is incredibly fulfilling. But my life with Sean was lonely. He had his friends and his job and his interests, and most of the time, I was left on the outside. Even the friendships I cultivated were surface in nature.

"And to Sean, I was nothing more than a prop on his arm whenever it suited him. The people we hung out with were always his friends, never mine." She took a deep breath, trying to hold the tears back. "I was miserable, Hazel. And all I want now is to be happy."

"Honey." Hazel grasped her hand. "I want that for you, too. So go grab some of that happiness."

"I don't know."

"You don't have to marry Eugene. Just go have some fun. God knows you deserve that."

Natalie breathed in, then let it out on a heavy sigh. "You're right. Of course. I'm getting ahead of myself. I just didn't expect to have all these . . . feelings so fast for someone. Only they're not feelings, of course. It's just unbridled sexual desire."

Hazel gave her a knowing smile. "That's not surprising, really. You've been repressed for so long. You should probably let loose and have some wild sex. Multiple orgasms will make you feel better."

"Hazel!"

"What? I know exactly what you're going through because I went through it myself. I pushed Linc away so many times when we could have gotten closer sooner. And as soon as I allowed myself to just let loose and have fun with him—that's when I fell in love."

Natalie frowned. "I have no intention of ever falling in love again."

"Then don't. Just do the fun part. You deserve it. God, Nat, you really deserve it."

For the first time, the "fun" finally entered her brain, and she realized Hazel was right. She did deserve it. She'd just have to control it. Because she did have freedom of choice. And her choice was to never give control of her emotions over to another man ever again.

But letting Eugene take her out and pay some attention to her?

Yes, she could do that. She'd put all her reservations aside and have a good time.

CHAPTER SEVEN

It had taken an extra week before Natalie gave Eugene the go for their date, but fortunately he'd been plenty busy with work. Since Natalie's ex had the kids this weekend, she'd told him she was free on Saturday. He planned a fun date for them and told her he'd pick her up around six thirty.

He showered and put on jeans and a T-shirt, his tennis shoes, and looked in the mirror, grinning. Yeah, he looked good.

He drove over to Natalie's house, passing his new house on the way, feeling that jolt of energy at the thought of moving in there someday soon. It was going to be awesome to have a house of his own. And he sure didn't mind that he'd be so close to Natalie.

He pulled into her driveway, and she came out the front door. He got out of the car.

"I would have come to the door, ya know," he said.

She shrugged. "I was ready."

"I'll say." He looked over at her tight dress. Her heels. Damn, she had a body, all curves and killer legs. Still . . . "You need to change."

Her brows rose. "Excuse me?"

"The dress might work, but how about you change into tennis shoes?"

"Where exactly are we going?"

"It's a surprise."

"In other words, we're not going to a restaurant for dinner."

"Nah. That's boring. I want you to have fun. You'll like it. Trust me."

She let out a frustrated breath. "Fine. I'll be right back."

She turned and headed back to the house. In five minutes, she was back out again, this time wearing light-colored capris and an off-the-shoulder blue top. And tennis shoes.

And still sexy as hell.

"I hope this outfit meets with your approval."

"The one you had on before was good, too. Next time I'll take you out to a fancy dinner so you can wear that tight dress."

She rolled her eyes. "What makes you think there'll be a next time?"

He laughed and opened the car door for her. "I'm overly confident." He got in on his side, put on his seatbelt, and they were off.

"How's your weekend going so far?" he asked as he pulled onto the freeway.

"Fine. If you like paying bills and doing laundry."

"Two of my favorite things." He gave her a lopsided grin.

"Really. Next time you come do mine."

"They're necessary evils, unfortunately. But at least you got them done, right? Now you have tonight and tomorrow free."

"I have tonight free. Tomorrow I grocery shop."

"Oh. Even more fun."

"Yes. My life is so glamorous."

He changed lanes, then gave her a quick glance. "You're doing the same things millions of us do on the weekends, Natalie."

"I know. It's just . . . I don't know. I'm in a mood, I guess."

"You're entitled. You have a lot to do, plus the kids."

"Mmm."

He could tell she wasn't happy. Maybe he should have altered his plans and taken her to a nice restaurant. Then again, maybe what he'd planned would be exactly what she needed.

Guess he'd find out soon enough.

When they got to the bar, he walked with her to the entrance, the raucous music blaring before they even got inside.

He opened the door and grinned. This was going to be fun.

"Well," she said as they made their way around the place. "This is interesting."

"I thought so. I hope you like it. We can sit at the bar and watch. Or play pool. Or bowl. Maybe go to the arcade. Even axe throwing."

She stopped and turned to face him, arching a brow. "Axe throwing?"

"I think you'd be amazed at how it helps get all your aggressions out."

"I'll definitely give that one some thought."

"And if this isn't at all something you're interested in, we'll go somewhere quiet, have dinner, and just talk."

"No, it's fine. I'm sure it'll be great. Like an adventure. So fun."

His lips curved. "You trying to convince me? Or yourself?"

"More myself. I'm sure you're very acclimated to this type of thing."

"First time here, actually. It looks awesome. You can order food from any area. Drinks, too. And speaking of drinks, what would you like?"

"Vodka soda for me."

"Okay." He led them over to a somewhat quiet zone where they could watch some people play pool. They grabbed a table and she sat. "I'll go get us drinks, and I'll be right back."

"Sure."

*T*his wasn't at all what Hazel expected. Though, to be honest, she should have known to expect the unexpected when she was with Eugene. The bar seemed fun, though she would have preferred a nice, quiet restaurant where they could talk and get to know each other better. But she was determined to have a good time tonight anyway.

She watched Eugene as he leaned against the bar, waiting on their drinks, and had to admit it wasn't a hardship to just stare at him. Dark jeans, button-down shirt, white tennis shoes, and all the dark hair and sexiness that seemed to naturally exude from him. He brought the drinks over and set them on the table, smiling down at her.

Flutters. That smile gave her flutters, along with the intensity of his blue eyes. She could get lost in them.

If she was into that kind of thing, which she absolutely was not.

"Thanks," she said, picking up the drink to take a long swallow. Its tangy warmth coated her throat.

Eugene took a seat next to her at the bar. He didn't seem to feel like he needed to engage her in constant conversation, which she appreciated. They watched the various activities going on around them, occasionally commenting to each other about a failed pool shot or ping pong. She had to admit that in this atmosphere it eliminated any sense of awkwardness or attempts at making polite conversation.

Not that Eugene ever had issues coming up with things to say.

"So, what feels good to you?" he asked.

She shifted to look at him. "Excuse me?"

"Games, Natalie. Feel like playing?"

Again she momentarily lost herself just staring at his face. Angles and planes and spectacular eyes. His hair had fallen across his forehead, and she itched to tangle her fingers in all that dark softness.

She resisted. Instead, she shrugged and said, "I don't know. It's been a long time since I've played . . . anything."

He leaned in and whispered in her ear. "You never forget how to play. You just have to get in there and do it."

His voice, low and seductive, made chill bumps pop down her arms while simultaneously heating her body from the inside out. She needed to shake off those sensations. She slid off the barstool and said, "Let's go toss some axes."

"Great. Grab your drink."

She did, and they wandered over to the axe throwing area, signing up for their time, which was an hour's wait.

"We should go get something to eat first," Eugene suggested.

"Sounds good to me."

They found a table and grabbed menus. Natalie liked that they had a varied menu, not just typical bar fare.

"What looks good to you?" Eugene asked.

"Not sure. Maybe a salad. Or flatbread. Though I'm interested in the fish, too."

"I like that you're keeping your options open. Me, too. I'm thinking a burger or a steak. Or, like you, the catch of the day depending on what it is."

When their server arrived he told them the catch of the day was halibut. Natalie ordered that since it would be accompanied by vegetables and wouldn't be overly filling.

Eugene ordered steak, which was great because he might share a bite with her. Then again, some people didn't like sharing. She supposed she'd find out.

"Ever tried axe throwing?" he asked.

"Can't say that's something I've ever tried."

He leaned back in the chair. "How about sports in high school or college?"

"Swimming and golf."

He nodded. "Both require a lot of skill and endurance."

She appreciated the compliment. "Thanks. How about you?"

"Baseball and soccer."

"I could see that about you. You have the body."

"Ohh," he said, grinning. "You've been checking out my body, huh?"

She rolled her eyes. "No."

"It's okay. I've definitely checked yours out. Would you like me to cite my favorite parts?"

"Absolutely not."

"Fine. I'll save it until after I've gotten you naked."

A flush of heat surrounded her. "That's presumptuous."

"Nah. Confident. We have chemistry, Natalie. It's only a matter of time until we get naked."

She leveled her gaze at him. "It's just dinner tonight, Eugene."

He gave her an enigmatic smile. "Just dinner. Tonight."

The way he looked at her was like . . . wow. No man had ever looked at her like he wanted to devour every inch of her. Eugene did. The thought of having sex with Eugene simultaneously turned her on and scared her to death. She could already imagine . . .

Well, it was probably best not to because it wasn't going to happen.

Not tonight, anyway.

No. Don't think that way. They weren't compatible in any way whatsoever. Why was she even contemplating the possibility?

Their food arrived, and Natalie was so wrapped up in her thoughts that she could barely stomach more than a few bites.

Eugene frowned. "Is the food bad?"

"No, it's excellent, really. Would you like a taste?"

"I'd love a taste." He leaned forward, and she scooped her fish onto her fork, sliding some between his lips. "Mmm. It's really good. Would you like a bite of my steak?"

Watching him take a bite of her food was a sensual experience she hadn't expected. "Sure."

He sliced a bite-size piece of steak, then held his fork to her lips. She couldn't help but make eye contact with him when he slid the fork between her lips, all her nerve endings focused on his eyes, the way they darkened as he slid the food into her mouth.

She barely tasted the steak, which she presumed was good. All she could think about was his mouth. Her mouth. Tongues. Kissing. Holy crap.

"Good?" he asked, his voice deep. Husky. Sexy as all hell.

She cleared her throat and nodded, needing a sip of her cocktail before she could answer. "Yes. Very good."

She managed to eat half her halibut and vegetables, fully concentrating on her plate of food instead of looking at Eugene. Satisfied she'd eaten enough, she polished off her drink, then smiled up at Eugene.

"That was so good."

"You're finished?"

She nodded. "I had a big lunch."

His phone buzzed and he picked it up. "We're due up at axe throwing."

She wiped the corners of her mouth with the napkin. "Perfect timing. Let's go kill it."

He paid the bill and led her around the corner and down the hall into the axe throwing room. They signed waivers, were given safety instructions, and then they headed to their assigned lane.

Natalie studied how far she'd have to throw that axe. Daunting. But she'd give it a try.

"I'll go first, if that's okay with you," Eugene said.

"Yes. Definitely."

She watched as he picked up the axe, the way he positioned it, the way he launched it toward the target. He hit just inside the bullseye.

"Wow," she said. "You're very good."

He leaned his body into hers. "Yeah, I am."

She laughed. "My turn."

She picked up the axe, felt its weight in her hands. Heavier than she thought it would be. She lifted her arm up, back, then threw, hoping she wouldn't end up throwing it against the side wall. Or, even worse, fling it to the floor.

It stuck. To the target. Bottom edge of the target, but she was on the target.

"Hell yeah!" Eugene yelled.

Natalie couldn't resist a small squeal of delight. "Okay, then. Let's go."

Since they had an hour in the booth, they took turns flinging the axe until her arm hurt. But she was determined to hit the center of the target. Eugene hit the center mark multiple times. She got close, skirting the edge of center twice. For her, a triumph.

They headed to the bar when they were finished. They leaned back to sip their drinks and watch the action in the other areas.

"That was exhausting," she said. "And exhilarating."

"You did good." Eugene laid his hand on her leg. "A couple more rounds and you'll hit center target."

She laughed. "I'll be lucky if I can move my arm tomorrow. But I have to admit, it was so much fun."

"Well, we'll give your arm a rest. How about go-karts?"

She leaned forward. "As soon as I finish this drink, prepare to lose the race."

He grinned. They ended up having another drink before spending the next hour racing each other—and several other people. Natalie couldn't remember ever laughing so much or feeling so free as she pressed hard on the gas pedal and drove so fast everything around her was a blur. She felt out of control, which so wasn't like her. Maybe that's what she liked so much about it.

They finished up and walked off the course. Being on solid ground again made her dizzy. Eugene slid his arm around her waist, tugging her body against his.

"You okay?"

"I'm awesome. That was so fun. What's next?"

"How about a breather?"

"Oh, I'm fine. Maybe another drink?"

She knew, on some slightly foggy level, that the few cocktails she'd had were probably more than enough. But she was having way too much fun to stop.

"I think I've had enough alcohol," Eugene said. "I'm thinking soda or water? Or maybe we go somewhere else for coffee and dessert? Take it down a notch and have some quiet time to just talk? What do you think?"

She sighed, a little dismayed that he'd ruin her happy high like that. Then again, she did like dessert. "Coffee and dessert sounds good."

When they got to the car, Eugene flipped through his phone, then they drove off. He drove them a few miles down the road to a restaurant that was apparently still open.

"They're supposed to have awesome desserts here." He looked over at her.

She shrugged. "Never ate here."

"Then it'll be a new experience for both of us. Come on."

He opened her car door, and wow, she was really wobbly as she got out. But Eugene was right there, arm around her as they went inside. She had to admit, she didn't mind the body-to-body contact at all.

Inside was dark, with low music playing. There was hardly anyone inside, but the hostess smiled.

"We're closing in forty minutes," she said.

"That's fine," Eugene said. "We're just here for a coffee and dessert."

The hostess grabbed a couple of menus. "Right this way."

They were seated at a table near the window. "Your server will be right with you."

Natalie opened the dessert menu. Oh, yum. There were several items she'd be very happy with.

"What are you thinking about?" Eugene asked.

"Cheesecake. Or maybe the tiramisu. You?"

"I'm thinking the molten chocolate cake. I've got a thing for chocolate."

"You order that and I'll have a bite, and I'll share mine with you."

"Sounds like a deal."

She ended up ordering the tiramisu, along with a decaf coffee. Their server brought their coffees, and she added creamer, then took a sip, sighing at the supreme pleasure of a late-night coffee. Normally she was water only after six p.m. because she had trouble sleeping. Tonight, for some reason, she just didn't seem to care.

Their desserts arrived and hers looked delicious. So did Eugene's chocolate cake. She took a forkful of the tiramisu, moaning at the slightly sweet, fluffy texture.

"Good?" Eugene asked.

"So good. Here, taste." She scooped some onto her fork and fed it to him, watching intently as his lips surrounded the fork. His tongue flicked over his lips, and she wanted to moan again, but held in the impulse. Barely.

"It's really good. So's this. Here." He gave her a taste of his chocolate cake, and it was deliciously decadent.

"Wow. I want to rub that all over me and—" Realizing what she was about to say, she averted her gaze and focused on her dessert.

"At some point I'll have you finish that sentence."

When she looked up, he had a decidedly heated smile on his face.

It had to be the alcohol that was making her say these things. Feel all these delicious sensations. And Eugene hadn't even kissed her. Had barely touched her.

How could you have foreplay without touching?

How could dessert be so sensual? Tasting each other's food, playfully feeding each other, enjoying the textures and flavors and laughing so easily, while knowing something intensely sexual simmered just under the surface.

Once they finished, Eugene drove them back to Natalie's house. The entire way home she wondered how she'd react when he put his mouth on hers. It was all she could think about, really.

He pulled into her driveway and turned off the engine. She

rubbed her sweaty hands against her thighs and blew out a breath as he opened her car door and reached for her.

"I hope you had fun tonight," he said as he walked with her to her front door.

She smiled up at him. "I did. Did you?"

His smile was filled with promise. "Yeah. I really did."

She pulled her keys out of her bag and unlocked the door, then turned to face him.

This was it. This was where the kissing would start. And after that . . .

He picked up her hand, pressed a kiss to the top of it. "Goodnight, Natalie."

Wait. What? No make-out session on the porch? No pushing her inside to get hot and heavy? A kiss on the hand? That was it?

He walked away and got into his car. Mortified, she went inside, shut and locked the door, leaning against it, utterly confused.

What the hell had just happened? Or, rather, what the hell had just *not* happened?

CHAPTER EIGHT

*E*ugene took a break from the endless meetings that were a necessary but tedious part of his job. He stepped outside for a walk, letting the sun shine down on him.

It had been three days since his date with Natalie. He'd texted her the day after to tell her he'd had a great time. She'd replied with a polite Me, too, but that was about it. He smiled at that because he knew there'd been a lot more going on between them that night. But she'd been a little inebriated, and he wanted her clearheaded and certain.

It had taken everything in him not to kiss her. The chemistry between them was volatile. Like a sexual itch that crawled over and inside his body, refusing to let go.

He wanted her. And walking away from her last weekend had been the hardest thing he'd ever done. But he didn't want to be some fuckboy. Not with Natalie. He didn't know why, but there was something special about her. Maybe it was the fact that she had kids, and he wanted to be respectful about that. About her. He didn't really understand it himself. All he knew was that he wanted to reconnect with her soon.

His phone buzzed. He grinned when he saw it was a text from his brother Warren.

Just left court. Went against some
asshole.
Made me think of you.

He laughed and replied with: So you lost, huh? Feel bad for you. You should go get a drink and drown your sorrows.

Warren came back right away with: Hell no I didn't lose. Kicked his ass like I always kicked yours. That's why I thought of you.

Typical Warren. Always bragging. They'd done this one-upmanship with each other for years. Though he had to admit, his brother was a damn good attorney. He texted back.

Did you want something
specific?

Warren replied with: Nope. Just wanted to say hi. Call you later.

He shook his head and put his phone to the side.

Time for him to get back to work, too.

It was the most humiliating experience of my life." Natalie hated admitting that, especially to her sister, but she needed someone to talk it over with, and she trusted Hazel more than anyone.

"Why?" Hazel was in the process of grooming Freddie the dachshund, who stood patiently on a table out in the backyard while Hazel trimmed the hair around his feet. "Because you were slightly inebriated, obviously turned on, and he acted the gentleman and walked away?"

"No. That's not what happened. It was all one-sided, Hazel. It's all in my head. I feel ridiculous."

Hazel cocked her head to the side and shot her sister a look. "I seriously doubt it's one-sided. He was just . . . giving you space and time."

Natalie snorted out a laugh. "Please. He's a hot, virile guy. Obviously used to making moves. He made zero moves on me."

"Bullshit."

Natalie's eyes widened. "Excuse me?"

Hazel picked up Freddie, kissed the top of his head, and put him down on the ground. He happily scampered off to join the rest of the dogs. "I've watched him around you. He teases you. No guy does that unless he's interested."

"But—"

"Nat. He's interested. He didn't try anything because he didn't want to rush you. Excuse me for being blunt, but he doesn't consider you a one-time fuck. That's called respect."

The thought had never occurred to her. Her only thought—and granted, it had been an inebriated one—was that he wasn't interested.

"Oh. Maybe."

"Just give him another chance, okay? If he doesn't seem like he's into you after that, then let it go."

She took a deep breath, then let it out. "Fine. Also, if you're going to groom the dogs out here, you need a designated area, not

67

your back patio. Cuz that's also where you grill food, and swim, so that's gross."

Hazel laughed. "Okay. Well, I do sweep and vacuum up all the hair, but I agree with you. What do you suggest?"

She pulled her sketchbook out of her tote and took a look at the backyard. "We haven't really discussed back here yet, but I think you'd need something beyond the pool area. But definitely shady because you don't want to get sweaty, and you don't want the dogs to get hot. Plus you need access to water to bathe them." She jotted down notes. "Oh, and you'll need a bathing pool. Something to contain the animals, plus a designated table for grooming."

"Aww. You're so smart, Nat. You think of everything."

"Probably not everything, but give me some time to wander the property back here and see what might fit. Then I'll do up a proper sketch for Linc to build something for you."

Hazel laughed. "I'm sure he'll love that."

Natalie shrugged. "He loves you. You know he'll do it."

"Yeah. He will."

Natalie noticed the sparkle in her sister's eyes when she talked about Linc. She was so in love it was ridiculous.

Natalie had thought she was in love once. No, she had been in love. Sean and she had been good at the beginning. They'd had similar ideals for their future. The only problem was Sean had been the only one who'd realized all his goals, while Natalie had only been able to achieve one of hers—to have her two beautiful children. But her professional goals? Those had been put on hold in order for Sean to achieve his. She hadn't even realized it had happened until year after year, Sean had asked more and more of her but had given nothing back.

Her dissatisfaction was partly her fault, though. She hadn't sat down and talked to Sean about how she felt, what she wanted. She'd allowed herself to be completely swept up in his life, fulfilling all of his dreams, and somewhere along the line, the future she'd envisioned for herself had totally disappeared.

Not anymore. Now she had her kids, and they were settled and happy. She had a job she loved. She had goals, and she wouldn't allow anyone to disrupt her goals for her future ever again.

However, that didn't mean she wasn't allowed to have some fun. Like her sister said, she was overdue. And it was high time she indulged.

So she'd test the waters with Eugene and see what happened.

CHAPTER NINE

After an intensely busy week, Eugene was more than ready for the weekend. He wrapped things up at work, then decided to stop by and see how Linc and his crew were doing on his house. Of course, he didn't need to worry because the reno was going great, and he was impressed by how efficient his brother was.

Not that he'd tell him that.

"How's the new job going?" Linc asked.

Eugene looked down at Linc, who was busy pulling up the crap flooring throughout the house. Since there were several workers assisting him, there was dust flying everywhere. "The job's amazing."

Linc didn't even look up. "Wasn't talking about the job, though it's good that's going well. I was asking about you and Natalie."

"Nothing much to report there. We had one date."

"And?"

"And, I'm taking things slow with her."

Now Linc stood, wiping his hands as he regarded Eugene. "Why?"

"Why am I taking things slow?"

"Yeah."

Eugene shrugged. "Because it's Natalie, and she's just stepping back into dating. I don't want to rush her."

Linc pondered what he said, then nodded. "That's thoughtful. I hope you two have fun together."

He liked that Linc didn't pressure him for details. One, because he didn't have any, and, two, because he wasn't about to give any. He liked Natalie. They'd had fun together the other night. He also knew she had a lot of responsibilities, and he didn't want to push her too hard too fast. Though holding back from kissing her had been damn difficult.

She'd been such a good sport about his choice of venue for their first date. He'd have to take her someplace really nice next time.

"Wanna go and have some lunch?" he asked his brother.

Linc swiped some sweat from his brow. "That sounds like a great idea. Let me wash up and I'll be ready to go."

They ended up at a bar that also served food, which suited both of them just fine.

They each ordered a beer and a burger.

"You're moving along pretty fast on the house," Eugene said after taking a long swallow of his beer.

"It's easy when I have people to help me. And the house is in great shape. It's mostly cosmetic stuff."

"I'm glad to hear that. How long do you think it'll take to finish?"

Linc thought for a minute before answering. "Probably six to eight weeks—maybe a couple more depending on material delivery."

"Not bad. I'm looking forward to having a home office I can really dig into."

"You seem to really like what you're doing."

Eugene leaned back in his chair. "Yeah, it's kind of surprised me how much."

"Really? Why? Isn't it what you wanted?"

"The job was too good to pass up, for sure. But was it my dream to be able to design a theme park ride? No. Never. I'm a game designer."

Linc nodded and took a swig of his beer. "But then the opportunity of a lifetime came up. I know you. You'd never pass up the chance to do something you've never done before. Still, I thought you had talked about starting your own company. What happened to that?"

Eugene shrugged. "I thought about it, and that could still happen somewhere down the road. But the more I learn now, the more I can put into a business of my own, right?"

Linc sighed. "You're right, of course. It's less risk at this point, and you're developing knowledge you wouldn't be able to have on your own. Not this quickly, anyway. It's a smart move, Eugene."

He was used to arguing with his brother, not being patted on the back. This was new. "Thanks."

His phone buzzed. He pulled it out, smiling when he saw a text from Natalie.

Birthday party for Christopher this
weekend. Do you want to come?

He grinned and texted back: I'd love to. Send me the details.

She texted back with the day and time, and that it would be at the housing development's clubhouse.

"Something—or someone—just put a big smile on your face," Linc said. "I'm guessing Natalie?"

He looked up from his phone. "Yeah. Her little guy is having a birthday party this weekend, and she invited me."

"Oh. Big stuff, being invited to share in her kid's celebration."

"You think so?"

"Hell yeah. Most moms are very protective over their kids, especially where boyfriends are concerned."

"I'm hardly her boyfriend. We had one date."

Linc smiled at him over the rim of his beer. "Must have been a memorable one, then."

For Eugene it was. For Natalie? He wasn't sure. Then again, he had an invite to Christopher's birthday party. So maybe she really did like him.

He'd find out on Saturday.

73

CHAPTER TEN

*B*alloons, check. Tablecloths and napkins, check. Gifts, check. Cupcakes, plates, forks, and gift bags, check, check, check, and check. Pizza, to be delivered. And all the rest, maybe check.

"I know you're running through a list in your head," Natalie's mother said. "I printed a checklist out for you several days ago, if you recall. If you didn't use it, that's on you. Besides, I have things well in hand."

Resisting the urge to snap at her well-meaning mother, Natalie turned and smiled. "Of course I used your checklist. I'm just . . . double-checking everything."

Hazel pushed through the doors of the clubhouse carrying gift bags. "Oh, it looks amazing in here, Nat. Christopher is going to go bonkers."

"Thanks. Hopefully Sean will actually deliver him and his sister on time."

Her mother frowned. "Why are the kids with Sean when it's your weekend?"

"Because it's Christopher's birthday, and Sean asked if he

could spend half the day with them. He said they were going to have pancakes and a mini party this morning."

"Aww, that's sweet. And very nice of you, Nat," Hazel said. "I'm sure Christopher loved being able to spend time with his dad on his special day."

Natalie hadn't wanted to give Sean any time with the kids. But that was her relationship with him, and Sean was trying to do better about carving time out of his schedule to actually be with his kids. And he'd asked for only a few hours on the morning of Christopher's birthday. She'd have to be a royal bitch to deny him that.

"We should clear an area for the kids to run amok," Hazel said.

"There's a playground right outside." Natalie motioned with her head to the area where the playground stood.

"Oh, I see," Hazel said. "They'll all love that."

"And, even better, they can scream and yell and it'll be outside."

"Right. Like they won't also do that here."

Natalie laughed. "You're probably right about that, Mom."

Hazel rubbed her back. "It's all going to be fine and Christopher will have a blast. Now let's get this place decorated."

Her sister was right. It was time to settle in and get ready for this party. She was going to make it the best party Christopher ever had.

The door opened and she saw Linc come in, followed, surprisingly, by Eugene.

"We ran into each other in the parking lot," Linc said, carrying bags. "I guess we both showed up early to help."

Eugene came over to Natalie, smiling at her, making her lose all focus. "The more hands the better, right?"

Why was it that his mere presence made her neurons cease firing? "Uh, right. Thanks for coming."

His grin also made her tingle in all her feminine places. "Wouldn't miss it. Where are the kids?"

"With their dad. They'll be here soon."

He stepped closer. "Where do you want me?"

She lifted her gaze to his, her thoughts running amok as his question rolled around in her head.

Where did she want him? On top of her. Underneath her. Behind her. Pushing her against a wall. Hell, she wanted him inside of her in any way she could get him.

The room got hotter and she shook her head to shake off the sex thoughts. "How about you put the tablecloths on for a start?"

"You got it."

After he walked away, she finally took a breath.

Hazel tipped her head over Natalie's shoulder. "Can't breathe around him, huh?"

"Shut up. And don't let Mom know that I'm going out with him. You know how she is."

"Oh, believe me, I know."

Speak of the devil, she walked right over and entered their circle. "Who's that young man spreading the tablecloths?"

"That's Linc's brother Eugene," Hazel said. "He just moved here recently for work."

Mom eyed Eugene, then nodded. "It's nice that he's here to help."

"Well, he's—" Natalie gave her sister a wide-eyed look, so Hazel nicely pivoted. "He's just a great guy, and Linc's his only family here, so Natalie thought to invite him."

"Aww." Mom patted Natalie on the arm. "Aren't you sweet?"

"Thanks, Mom." Natalie tried to get her pounding heart under control and went about decorating the clubhouse. They had just gotten the gifts set up when guests began to arrive, along with Sean and the kids. She went outside to greet them, and the kids ran into her arms for a hug.

"It's my birthday!" Christopher gave her a hug and a wide grin. "Daddy got me a go-kart!"

She cast a disparaging look at her ex. "A go-kart?" She watched Sean pull it out of the back of his SUV. "Tell me that's not supposed to go to my house."

"It's not like I can keep it at the condo, can I?"

She rolled her eyes. "Sean. That is the most—"

"Hey, little dude," Eugene said as he walked outside. "Happy birthday." He held out his fist and Christopher bumped it.

"I got a go-kart!"

Eugene grinned. "Whoa. You did? So cool."

"Eugene," Natalie warned. "I was just explaining to Sean—"

"Hi. I'm Eugene Kennedy."

"Sean Parker." They shook hands and then launched into a very excited conversation about the go-kart, to include her five-year-old son. Disgusted, she turned on her heel and stormed into the clubhouse.

"What's going on out there?" Hazel asked.

"Sean. He bought a go-kart for Christopher."

"Really? That's kind of cool."

Natalie frowned. "What? It's dangerous. He's five, Hazel. Not fifteen."

"I don't know. It looks appropriate for his age. Sean bought him a helmet to go with it. And he'll have a lot of fun driving it around the cul-de-sac. And Cammie can drive it, too."

Natalie groaned and walked away, went to the window where all of Christopher's little friends were gathered around the go-kart, shouting excitedly. Sean, Eugene, and Linc stood around grinning like a triplet of asinine fools.

Ugh.

Obviously it was some kind of conspiracy. Couldn't everyone see that her baby boy had no business riding around in that death trap?

When everyone piled inside, she decided to push away thoughts of the evil machine and focus instead on Christopher's party. They played games, had pizza, let the kids run around on the playground, then had cupcakes. By the time they cleaned up and she took the kids home and unpacked the car, she was utterly exhausted, and the kids were on an epic sugar high, but at least they were outside. All she wanted to do was hide in the bathroom and cry.

And then the doorbell rang and she wanted to kill whoever was on the other side of that door.

She opened the door, surprised to see Eugene there.

"Why are you here?" she asked, knowing her words came out bitchy, but she was just so tired.

He held out a bag. "I stayed behind to chat with Linc and I

noticed you left this behind at the clubhouse, so I thought I'd deliver it to you."

"Oh. Thank you."

He handed the bag to her. "Well, you look tired and I'm sure you have a lot to do, so I'll let you go."

With a sigh, she realized she was behaving terribly. "Would you like to come in? The kids are outside running amok. I'm sure they'd love to see you."

"Are you sure?"

"Yes. I'm sure. We're going to have hot dogs and macaroni and cheese for dinner. Nothing fancy."

He shrugged. "Sounds good to me. Thanks."

After spending an hour hanging out with the kids and with Natalie outside, it became clear that Natalie was utterly exhausted. He couldn't blame her. It had been a long day, and kids would go and go until you forced them to sit still for five minutes. He'd been an active kid himself and never allowed himself any downtime because as soon as he sat still he might fall asleep.

He took over grilling the hot dogs from her and suggested some veggies to toss on the grill as well. Maybe the kids wouldn't jump on the veggie train but Natalie had smiled at that idea, so he grilled them both while she made the macaroni and cheese. She hollered for the kids to have their baths while he finished off grilling, and then they came out looking fresh and freaking adorable in their pajamas.

"Did you have a good birthday party today, Christopher?" he asked as they all gathered at the table to eat.

"The best. I got lots of presents and my friends came to my party."

After setting applesauce on the table, Natalie took her seat. "You had lots of friends there."

"And Jack has a birthday next weekend and I'll get to go to his party."

"Fun." Natalie gave Eugene a tired smile.

After dinner, they cleaned up while Natalie told the kids to get books and get in their beds.

He laid the dish towel on the counter. "Mind if I read to them?"

She gave him a questioning look. "You. Want to read to them."

He moved into her, his shoulder brushing against hers. "This might surprise you, but I do know how to read."

She shoved her shoulder against his. "I know that. But we have a bedtime routine. And they abuse it every chance they get."

"Okay. Tell me about it."

"They get one story each. They'll try for more along with trips to the bathroom and glasses of water."

"I think I can handle it. Why don't you pour yourself a glass of wine and put your feet up."

She kept giving him incredulous looks. "You really want to do this."

"I do."

She shrugged. "Fine. Call me when you're ready to surrender."

He laughed and headed down the hall to Christopher's room.

Christopher was sitting up in his bed, his covers tucked

around his hips. A stuffed dinosaur sat next to him. God, the kid was cute.

"Where's Momma?"

"She's . . . busy, so I'm going to read to you tonight, if that's okay."

Christopher nodded. "Okay."

"Great. What are we reading?"

Christopher handed him an awesome-looking book about some amazing dragon and his adventure, so they settled in to read. From the kid's constant yawns, he figured he wouldn't get to the end of the book before he was asleep.

He was so wrong. It took four books, one trip to the bathroom, and several sips of water resulting in another trip to the bathroom before Christopher finally fell asleep while they were talking about his go-kart.

Okay, so maybe he didn't have it all in hand.

Camryn, on the other hand, was sweet and smiley and said it was her job to read to him. She read three chapters of a book about a little girl detective that was really kind of cute. He was disappointed when she said she was tired and ready to go to sleep.

"Thanks for letting me read to you, Eugene," she said, her little face earnest and oh so sleepy.

"I want to know how the rest of it comes out. Maybe you'll read to me again soon."

"Maybe. Goodnight."

That was a definite dismissal. "Goodnight, Cammie."

She told him to turn her colorful light globe on, which he did before he turned off the overhead light. Then he popped his head in and checked on Christopher. He stared down at his pink-cheeked little face and felt a pang of something he'd never felt before.

These kids were adorable for sure.

He wasn't at all ready for kids, figured he wouldn't be for a long time.

But Natalie's kids were easy to like.

He made his way downstairs. "You were right. That took a—"

Natalie was on the sofa, curled up in a sleeping ball.

There was that flood of warmth again. Eugene smiled and walked over to pull the blanket from the back of the sofa. He covered her and started to leave, then thought about it for a second before taking a seat on the sofa next to her, picked up her feet and laid them in his lap. He picked up her untouched glass of wine and took a long swallow before taking out his phone to check his emails.

Natalie woke, her back and neck aching. She frowned and blinked her eyes open to realize she was lying on the sofa. And, not alone, apparently.

Eugene was asleep, sitting up, his head lying against the back of the couch. And her feet rested in his lap.

Wow. She must have really passed out hard last night. But why was Eugene still here? And, more importantly, what time was it?

She grabbed her phone to see it was four a.m., immediately breathing a sigh of relief. The last thing she wanted was to have to explain to the kids why Eugene spent the night.

She sat up and ran to the bathroom to pee, making an ugh face as she looked in the mirror. Wow, her hair was a wreck, and she hadn't even washed off her makeup.

Whatever. She needed coffee more than she needed to look pretty. But it wasn't even time to get up yet. First, she needed to get Eugene out of her house.

She made her way to the living room to see he was awake and stretching. She made her way to the kitchen and turned the coffee maker on, poured water in, and slid a pod in the slot, breathing in the smell of the coffee as it poured into the cup.

He groaned. "Oh, my freakin' back."

"You fell asleep."

"Yeah. Sorry." He got up, went down the hall and into the bathroom.

Okay, calm down, Natalie. The kids wouldn't be up for hours so there was no reason to panic. Eugene would leave, and she'd go wash her face and get in bed.

Eugene came back in. "Sorry. I meant to only sit there and finish your glass of wine and make sure the kids stayed asleep. Guess I fell asleep, too."

"That's okay," she said, handing him his cup of coffee. "Thanks for staying. Though I'm sure your body is regretting sleeping sitting up."

He took a couple of sips of coffee. "I've slept in worse positions. Your couch is comfortable."

"It is. Anyway . . ."

"Yeah, I need to go." After another long swallow of coffee, he laid the cup on the counter.

She walked him to the door, regretting that he couldn't stay, that they couldn't tumble into her bed together and cuddle. And do other things together.

"Thanks for coming to Christopher's party."

"It was fun. Everything with you is fun." He leaned in and brushed his lips across hers. "Talk to you soon."

Her breath caught and she momentarily lost the ability to speak, so all she could do was nod. He smiled and walked to his car.

He'd kissed her. Not a deeply passionate kiss—just a brief brush, but enough to set her body on fire, to make her want more.

So much more.

CHAPTER ELEVEN

Natalie's desk was filled with wallpaper samples. Too many. In fact, if she sat, she wouldn't be able to see over the piles of wallpaper. This was not good.

"Digging the wallpaper, huh?"

She looked up and saw her boss, Delilah Lawrence, leaning against the open doorway.

"My client. Elizabeth Jones."

"Oh. Now I understand. Sorry about that. I normally would handle Elizabeth, but I'm booked. She does have trouble deciding, doesn't she?"

"That's an understatement. First she wanted to paint the dining room, but then decided to wallpaper. Then it took a week to decide on the texture. Once we got through that, we started browsing samples. We've looked through all the books, but she can't decide on stripes or flowers or the three types of birds that made her happy, so now she's thrown all those out, and we're starting over. Oh, and now she wants to add wallpaper to the entry."

Delilah laughed. "I'm sorry. She's a very difficult client, but I promise you that if you make her happy, she'll give you a lot of business. Not only her, but her friends as well."

"Good to know, because I'm drinking a lot of wine at night."

"I know that feeling. Other than that, how's your schedule looking?"

"Great. I picked up a new client on Monday who wants to re-design their living room and guest bath. She's given me a very healthy budget."

"Excellent. You've just jumped right in and made a name for yourself here, Natalie."

Natalie looked up from her planner. "I have?"

"Yes. I'm impressed. I think you're going to do great things."

"Wow. Uh, thanks, Delilah."

"Just the truth."

"Hi. Sorry to interrupt."

As if her shock over Delilah's compliment wasn't enough, seeing Eugene peek his head in her office nearly knocked her off her chair.

"Eugene." She cleared her throat of the squeak that eked out. "What are you doing here? Uh, excuse me. I mean, how nice to see you." She stood. "Delilah Lawrence, this is Eugene Kennedy, my, uh, client."

Delilah raised a brow, clearly not buying the client part. "A client, huh? How nice to meet you, Eugene."

Eugene shook her hand. "Thanks. Natalie is doing a great job with the design of my house. Though right now my brother is wrecking it and putting it back together, so it'll be a bit before it's an actual house. But Natalie has awesome ideas."

"Indeed she does. I'll leave you two to talk. Very nice meeting you, Eugene."

"You, too, Delilah."

After Delilah left, Natalie came over to him. "What are you doing here? We didn't have a meeting scheduled."

"I wanted to ask you out to dinner this weekend, if you're free."

"You have a phone, you know. You could have texted me."

He picked up her hand. "But then I wouldn't have been able to see you, and I wanted to see you."

She looked out the window of her office to see Delilah pretending to concentrate on something in the center room while simultaneously sneaking glances at her and Eugene.

She jerked her hand away. "We can't do—this—here."

"Then let's do—this—on our date."

"Fine. I'll let you know when I'm free. Now go away."

"Sure." He swept his hand alongside her neck, drew her face closer to his, and kissed her. This time, he actually kissed her, his lips moving over hers subtly, the kind of teasing kiss that made her reach for his arms, feeling the flex of his biceps under her hands.

He pulled back, his eyes dark with desire, while her heart violently pummeled her ribcage, making her short of breath. She slid her hands across his chest, wishing they were anywhere but here right now. She wanted more. A deeper, more passionate kiss, the kind with tongues and hands roaming and lots of moaning and groaning. But they were here and they couldn't.

"You have to go," she whispered.

"Yeah. I'll see you soon."

He walked out, waving to Delilah, who smiled and waved. As soon as the door closed behind him, Delilah hurried her way toward Natalie's office. Natalie braced herself for the lecture about inappropriate behavior.

Instead, Delilah leaned against the doorway and fanned herself with the file folder in her hands.

"Natalie. Damn, girl."

Natalie exhaled. "Yeah. He's . . . something."

"What he is is hot. And sexy. And apparently yours."

"He's not mine. Not exactly. He's my sister's boyfriend's brother."

Delilah shot her a look. "He kissed you, Natalie. He's a lot more than your sister's boyfriend's brother. He's your guy, and, may I say, congratulations."

"I am not dating."

"Who cares about dating? Strip him naked and have your way with him. Or vice versa. Enjoy the hell out of that man."

She wanted to argue about the semantics of the whole thing, but why bother explaining what she and Eugene were to each other? Did it even matter?

It did not. She'd received enough encouragement to know that it was okay to have some sexual fun with Eugene. And after that kiss? She would not deny herself any longer.

She had a kid-free weekend, and she intended to spend it with him.

CHAPTER TWELVE

Y ou don't have to keep stopping by. I do know what I'm doing."

Eugene cracked a smile at Linc's sniping. "Are you sure? Because that cabinet looks crooked."

With a sigh, Linc laid down his drill and turned to face his brother. "Since when did you become a contractor? Because the last time I looked the only thing you know how to do is play games."

"Hey, I know how to do all this stuff."

"Is that right? Good. Then put up or shut up."

Oh shit. He knew he could only push Linc so far, but it was fun getting under his skin, and Linc got irritated so easily. Now he either had to back off or dig in and help his brother hang kitchen cabinets, something he most definitely didn't want to do.

Rolling his eyes, he helped Linc hang the upper cabinets. Of course Linc made him hold the heavy cabinets while he drilled the screws in, making Eugene drip with sweat.

"Too hard for you?" Linc asked, pausing, drill in hand, while Eugene held on to the cabinet.

"Just fucking do it," he said.

Linc laughed. Asshole.

After they finished the uppers they got the lower cabinets in place, then put on the cabinet doors.

They both stood and stared at their work.

"Looks awesome," Linc said.

Eugene swiped away the sweat from his brow. "Hell yeah it does. We did all right."

"Yeah, we did. Thanks for the help. You saved me half a day's work."

"That means you can take me to lunch, then."

"I already ate a sandwich before you got here."

"That was hours ago. And I haven't eaten. Plus, you're probably hungry again anyway."

Linc rolled his eyes. "Fine."

They found a pizza place not too far from the house, ordered a large pizza and a couple of beers.

"You did great today," Linc said, taking a long swallow of his beer.

"Thanks. I have to admit it was fun to get sweaty and do some heavy lifting. I can see why you enjoy it."

"Yeah, it makes me feel good. I like putting things together, creating something with my hands. Kind of what you're doing with the new job, huh?"

"Yeah, sort of."

"Not sort of. Exactly. How's that going?"

"It's going good. It's like putting puzzle pieces together. Similar to the games I've designed, only more three dimensional, more of a real-world experience. It's definitely different from anything I've ever done."

"You sound more excited about this job than you have in years."

"Thanks. It's something new, for sure, and that's always exciting."

"Speaking of new and exciting, how are things going with Natalie?"

He fortunately didn't have to answer that question right away because their pizza arrived, and despite Linc telling him he'd already eaten a sandwich, he dove in with both hands to grab a slice.

Figured. His brother always ate the most. Eugene had to fight Linc and Warren to even get a bite of food when they were kids. Fortunately, he had his mom to slide him extra slices so he wouldn't starve.

The pizza was excellent. Eugene could have eaten the whole thing by himself, which was why he was happy his brother shared it with him. Now he wouldn't have to work out so hard at the gym.

"I think we were talking about how things were going with Natalie," Linc said after he signaled for the server to bring them another round of beers.

"Oh, right. It's fine. I'm still taking things slow."

Linc frowned. "Still? Why?"

He shrugged. "Because she deserves that. I don't have all the details but I think her ex held her back, and right now she's working her way into having a sense of freedom. The last thing I want to do is to stifle her."

Linc nodded. "That's considerate of you."

Eugene started to say something, then took a sip of his beer instead, trying to come up with the right words to express his feelings.

"I like her. I really like her. I don't want to screw it up."

Linc cocked his head to the side. "I get that. Seems to me you're handling things with Natalie . . . gently, right?"

"So far."

"Then keep doing what you're doing. And don't screw it up."

Eugene laughed. "Yeah, that's the plan."

CHAPTER THIRTEEN

*N*atalie decided to take the initiative this time and had invited Eugene over for dinner tonight. She was making lobster pasta, one of her favorites. She had already prepared a nice salad, which was chilling in the fridge. She'd bought bread from her favorite bakery.

There should always be bread.

She'd showered, shaved, buffed and puffed and put on lotion, dried her hair, put on makeup, and chosen one of her favorite sundresses, because after all that personal grooming, along with the precooking, she was hot as hell. Thank technology for good air-conditioning.

And now she was ready.

Ready for anything and everything that might happen tonight.

The doorbell rang, and she looked at the clock in the living room as she walked by, smiling.

Right on time, Eugene. Points for you.

She opened the door, fighting back the gasp as Eugene stood there in dark jeans and a tight white T-shirt that highlighted his amazingly sculpted chest and shoulders and, oh God, his abs.

"Hi," he finally said, breaking the spell.

She realized that while she was ogling, she'd left him standing on the porch. "Hi. Come in."

"Something smells good," he said as they made their way down the hall and into the kitchen.

"Lobster pasta."

He stopped and turned to face her. "You made lobster pasta?"

She laughed. "It's not like I went out and caught a lobster, Eugene."

"Yeah, but . . . I love lobster pasta."

She warmed all over, and this time it wasn't from the oven. "I hope you love this one, then."

"I know I will. Is there anything I can do to help?"

"No, but thanks. Would you like something to drink? I have wine, beer, and hard liquor."

His brows shot up. "Planning a big party tonight?"

She laughed. "Not tonight. It's just a party of two."

He gave her a heated smile. "I'm good with that. And I'll have a whiskey. Straight."

"Sure." She went to the liquor cabinet, which was high enough that she'd need the stepladder, so she turned to go grab it, only to discover Eugene right behind her. "I'll get it."

Now she was trapped between the counter and Eugene. While he reached up to grab the bottle, his chest and crotch pressed against her back and butt.

Oh God, it felt so good to have a man's body touching hers. And, suddenly, it wasn't important to get the whiskey or think about the salad. She turned around and pulled him toward her.

DESIGNS ON YOU

His mouth met hers in a fury of passion that made her moan with the need that she'd repressed for so long.

Now this—this was the kiss she'd been waiting so long for. His tongue slid inside her mouth and desire exploded within her, bringing forth a desperate need to be touched and kissed and everything delicious that would follow.

She pulled her mouth from his and murmured, "I need to take the casserole out so it doesn't burn."

Breathing heavily against her neck, Eugene whispered, "Yeah, you do that."

She moved away long enough to take the casserole out of the oven and put it on the top of the stove. Eugene had taken a seat on the sofa, his whiskey glass empty, his legs open and relaxed.

God, he was so hot. She grabbed her wineglass, took a long swallow, and headed toward him.

She climbed onto his lap and straddled him. He had just slid his hands under her dress when her phone buzzed.

"You need to answer that?" he asked as he teased her thighs with his fingertips.

She let out a low moan. "No." She leaned in and kissed him.

The buzzing stopped, thankfully. But then her voicemail beeped and the phone buzzed again.

She pulled back. "Shit. Sorry." She grabbed her phone, frowning to see the call was from her ex.

He'd never call her when he had the kids, unless—

She punched the button. "Sean?"

Her heated body went stark cold in an instant. "Is he okay? Where are you?"

95

She nodded as he gave her the information. "I'll be there as soon as I can."

She ended the call and looked up to find Eugene staring at her, a concerned look on his face.

"Christopher fell and has a gash in his chin. Sean's at the ER with him right now."

"Do you want me to drive you?"

She shook her head as she grabbed her purse and keys. "No, but thanks."

"Okay." He walked out to the garage with her while she popped the door open. "Let me know how he is."

"I will, thanks." She wanted to hug him, kiss him, thank him for being so understanding, but all she could think about was Christopher.

When she got to the ER, she gave her name to the front desk person, who directed her to the room where Sean and Christopher were.

She stood just outside the door for a second to catch her breath. Seeing her little boy lying in that bed, his eyes closed, nearly sent her to her knees. She closed her eyes and took a deep breath, then slid open the exam room door.

"They gave him something for the pain," Sean said, looking as worried as she felt. "He's sleeping. Since he hit his head, they want to do a CT scan, but he seems fine."

"Where's Camryn?"

"My mom and dad came and picked her up. No reason for her to be here."

She nodded. "Good. What happened, Sean?"

"I took the kids to the adventure park. You know, the one they really like."

"Right."

"Anyway, Christopher was doing the slide, climbing up backward, of course. I was watching him the whole time. I don't know if he tripped or slipped or whatever, but he fell off, hit his chin on the side of the slide, and then landed face-first."

"Oh no." She walked over to him and brushed his hair away from his scratched-up face. They had a bandage on his chin, so she couldn't see how bad it was.

She looked up at Sean. "Our poor baby."

"Yeah. Took at least five years off my life. I swear I was watching him, Nat."

"I believe you. Accidents happen."

The nurse came in. "We're going to take him to CT now. One of you can go. It won't take long."

"I will," Sean said, standing. "You should get something to drink and sit, Nat. You look pale."

He was right about that. She'd nearly broken every speed law getting here. "Okay. Thanks."

After they left, she found vending and grabbed a bottle of water, started to walk away, then stared at the machine for a minute. She hadn't eaten dinner and she needed her strength for Christopher, so she purchased an energy bar. She munched on that as she made her way back to the exam room, took a seat, and finished the energy bar, took a couple of swallows of water, then slipped the bottle into her bag.

And waited.

And waited, her heart pounding, her thoughts conjuring all kinds of terrible things. Like what if they found something on the CT? What if there was something terrible going on with her baby boy?

She shifted in the chair. No. She would not think the worst. She would not panic.

The doors slid open and they wheeled Christopher in, Sean behind them.

"Momma." Christopher's voice slurred, but he recognized her. That was a good thing. A very good thing.

Natalie got up and smiled over him. "Hi, baby. Did you get hurt?"

"I fell off the slide and cut my chin and hurt my face."

"Ouch." She smoothed her hand over his hair, watched his eyes drift slowly closed.

"It's the pain medicine," the nurse said, shifting kind eyes in her direction. "He'll be sleepy for a while." She adjusted his IV. "The doctor will be in shortly to discuss the CT and do the stitches on his chin."

"Thanks," Sean said, then turned to Natalie. "He's going to be fine."

"Right. Of course he is."

"Kind of like a rite of childhood, ya know? A fall? Stitches? Remember how I told you about the ones in my forehead?"

"You tripped over a brick and fell onto another brick because you and a couple of your friends were wandering in a construction zone."

He laughed. "Yeah. I was in so much trouble for that. But I still got ice cream, so . . . worth it."

She shook her head. "Boys."

"Yeah. Anyway, I was fine, and Christopher will be, too."

"I know. He just looks so vulnerable."

He reached over and grasped her hand. "It's just stitches, Nat. He'll be okay."

She looked down to where his hand clasped hers, realized how wrong it felt. She pulled her hand away. "Yes. He will."

Awkwardness hung between them like a thick fog. Fortunately, the doctor walked in at that moment.

"CT is totally clear," she said. "Let's do some stitches, shall we?"

Natalie breathed a sigh of relief, and she and Sean stepped out of the way as the doctor stitched Christopher's chin. She held Christopher's hand since he had woken up.

"You're being so brave, baby," she said, stroking his hand and his hair while the very awesome and gentle Dr. Weinberger put seven stitches in his chin.

Once finished, they did the paperwork and headed outside. Natalie bent down to give him a hug and kiss goodbye, but Christopher held tight to her. "Wanna go home with you, Momma."

Natalie started to tell him that he had to go with his dad, but Sean said, "It's all right. He needs his mom tonight. I'll bring Camryn home tomorrow at the regular time, if that's okay."

He was being so agreeable, so nice. She didn't know what to make of it, but she wasn't about to try and figure out Sean. Not right now. "That'd be great. Thanks."

Sean hugged and kissed Christopher. "You get some rest, baby boy. I'll call you tomorrow, okay?"

Christopher nodded. "Night, Daddy."

They got in the car and she got Christopher settled in his car seat. He didn't say anything on the ride home. She was certain he was exhausted.

"Momma?" he asked as they pulled off the highway.

"Yeah, baby?"

"Can we stop and get ice cream?"

There was her boy. She sighed in relief. "Yes, we sure can."

CHAPTER FOURTEEN

*E*ugene checked his phone for the fifteenth time.

Nothing.

He didn't know what to expect. It wasn't like Natalie owed him a text to let him know how her kid was. Christopher wasn't his, and he had no right to know. But still, he was worried. What if something had gone wrong? What if Christopher's injuries were worse? He hadn't texted or called because he hadn't wanted to bother her, but it was now Sunday afternoon, and he couldn't wait any longer.

"Fuck it," he finally said. "I'm texting."

How's Christopher?

He kept it short so she wouldn't have to read any worry in his text.

Surprisingly, she called. He punched the button.

"Hey. I'm sorry I haven't called."

"It's okay. Your kid was hurt and that's priority. Is he all right?"

"He's fine. Stitches in his chin and he has a scratched-up face, but otherwise, he's fine. They did a CT of his head and that was clear."

Eugene's heart stopped pounding. "That's such a relief. I'm so glad."

"Thanks. I'm so sorry about bailing on you abruptly last night. I owe you lobster pasta."

"Hey. It's your kid, Natalie. Your kids will always come first."

"Thank you for being so understanding." She paused, then asked, "Would you like to come over? It's just Christopher and me. Cammie is still with her dad until later tonight."

"No, that's okay. I'm sure you and Christopher want to be alone."

She laughed. "He's already bored and definitely tired of me hovering over him. He could use a distraction."

"I'd really like to see him. I was worried about him all last night."

"Yeah, I should have texted you, but the whole night was so overwhelming."

"Hey, Natalie. I understand. It's really okay." He could tell how much this had affected her. "Want me to pick anything up for you and Christopher?"

"No, but thanks. We're good."

"Okay. I'll see you soon."

They hung up and he made the drive over to Natalie's house. Despite her saying she didn't need anything, there was no way he'd show up without something for Christopher. He stopped at the store and picked up a cool-looking truck that had flashing lights and spun on its wheels. Hopefully Christopher would like it.

When he got to the house, he grabbed the bag and rang the doorbell.

Natalie answered, smiling. "Hi."

"Hi, yourself."

She led him inside. Christopher was on the sofa watching a kids' show on TV. When he saw Eugene, he grinned.

"Hi, buddy," Eugene said.

"Guess what? I fell down and hurt myself and now I got stitches." Christopher stuck his chin out for Eugene to see.

Eugene took a seat next to Christopher and inspected his chin. He had a bandage covering the stitches, but his face bore several scratches "Whoa. You're a mess. You look cool."

"I know!"

"How many stitches?"

"Uh . . ." He looked at Natalie. "How many, Momma?"

"Seven."

"Wow. You're so tough. And, you'll have a really awesome scar. I can't wait to see it."

"Me, too." He looked down at the bag in his hand. "What's that?"

"Well. When I heard you got hurt, I bought you a present."

His eyes widened. "You did?"

"Yeah. I thought this might help you feel better." He handed the bag to Christopher. He opened it and had the happiest look on his face. Eugene was glad he'd chosen right.

"Wow. Momma, look."

"I see that. It's very nice."

Eugene helped him get the car set up, and showed him how to use the remote to move the car and make the wheels spin.

"This is so cool."

"What do you say, Christopher?" Natalie asked.

"Thanks, Eugene." He was already halfway down the hall.

Eugene laughed as he watched Christopher disappear around the corner, wheels screaming, colors flying.

"Thanks for getting my kid a loud, annoying gift."

He moved close to her. "You're very welcome."

"Hey, I'm really sorry about bailing so fast last night. I never even gave you dinner. Or, anything else."

He turned to face her. "You're a mom, Natalie. Emergencies are gonna come up. I'm just glad Christopher is okay."

"I'm shocked you're so understanding."

He frowned. "Really? Why? I come from a family of three boys. One of us was always in an urgent care or ER. It's the price of growing up."

"I guess. Maybe I'll get lucky and Camryn won't end up in an emergency room."

He huffed out a laugh. "Hey, don't count out girls. They can play rough, too."

"Oh, thanks. That gives me so much to look forward to."

Christopher came down the hall, his remote-control car running ahead of him. "Hey, Eugene. Come play with me."

Eugene grinned. "Coming, buddy." He turned to Natalie. "If you'll excuse me, my friend wants me to play with him."

She shook her head. "Fine. I'll make us a glass of iced tea."

He played with Christopher for about an hour. He liked the

truck, then they played Legos for a while until Christopher started yawning. Eugene asked if they could read for a while, so Christopher picked out a few books. They sat on the floor, leaning against the bean bag chairs while Eugene read to him. Christopher sat next to him and laid his head against his chest, making Eugene's heart squeeze as they read story after story, until he felt Christopher go lax against him. He looked down and saw he was asleep.

It was just then that Natalie came in. The way she looked at him was indescribable. Kind of a combination of awe and . . . hell, he didn't know. It was some kind of sweet, maternal look, he supposed, and he was probably mistaking her looking at him. She was probably giving that warm look to her kid.

"Can you pick him up and put him in his bed?" she asked.

"Sure." He laid the book aside and pulled Christopher into his arms, got up, and laid him in his bed. Natalie turned off the light and they left the room.

"He still naps?" Eugene asked as they made their way into the kitchen.

"Not really, but sometimes he just needs quiet time or he gets overwhelmed and overtired. He's pretty much go, go, go from the time he gets up until he goes to bed, so a little downtime lets him recharge. If he falls asleep, great. If he doesn't, that's fine, too."

She handed him a glass of iced tea, poured one for herself, too.

Eugene took a long swallow. "He's a pretty awesome kid, Natalie."

"Thanks. I think so, too. I was thinking of making a very elegant dinner of hot dogs, applesauce, and chips. Maybe some fruit. Are you interested?"

JACI BURTON

He arched a brow. "Interested? It's my favorite food."

She laughed. "Sure it is."

"Seems kind of complicated, though. Anything I can do to help?"

"If you can handle the grill, I'll open the applesauce and bag of chips. When everything's ready I'll wake up Christopher, because if he sleeps too long I'll never get him to bed at a reasonable hour tonight."

He nodded. "I'm on the grill."

Eugene had expected a short visit, just to say hi and drop off the gift for Christopher. What he hadn't expected was lively chatter, the kid's exuberant laughter, and to have so much fun.

They ate food, then Christopher played with his new toy around the pool. He decided he wanted to go swimming, which Natalie said wasn't allowed until after his stitches came out, so Eugene suggested they dip their legs in the pool instead. He found a couple of sticks, and they pretended to be fishing. Of course Christopher knew nothing about fishing, so Eugene explained how it would be when they went fishing for real, but for tonight, they'd have to pretend to catch the toys floating at the top of the pool. Christopher giggled and listened to Eugene talk about all the types of fish they were going to catch. Even Natalie seemed enthralled listening to Eugene tell stories of deep-sea fishing, though when he suggested a fishing trip, she shook her head violently and made it clear she had no intention of getting on a boat and going fishing. Ever.

That had seemed rather definite.

Eventually Christopher began to yawn, so Natalie dried him

off and got his pajamas on. They all sat in the living room to watch a movie. Christopher fell asleep after thirty minutes.

"Should I put him in bed for you?" Eugene stood.

"No, I've got him. I'll leave him on the sofa for a bit to make sure he's fully asleep."

"Okay. I'm going to head out."

They both headed for the door. Natalie turned to face him, and that familiar tension that always seemed to surround them curled through his body.

"Thanks for staying," she said, taking a step forward.

He knew if he kissed her, if he pulled her into his arms, he'd want more. And that wasn't going to happen tonight.

So instead, he brushed her cheek with a kiss. "I had fun. Thanks for letting me hang out. I'll call you tomorrow."

She smiled. "Sure."

She closed the door, and he headed out to his truck. A car was pulling up as soon as he got to the driveway, giving him pause. He recognized Sean, Natalie's ex, so after he got out Eugene waited, wanting to make sure Natalie was going to be okay. Then he saw a little girl climb out of the back seat and he grinned.

"Hi, Eugene," Cammie said.

"Hey, Cammie. How's it going?"

"Good. Did you know my brother got stitches?"

"I did. Pretty cool, huh?"

"Yeah. I haven't gotten stitches yet."

"Good for you. You're too pretty for stitches."

She laughed. "I'm gonna go see Mommy. Bye, Eugene."

"Bye, Cammie."

Sean said, "I'll be right there, honey."

"Okay, Daddy."

He went over and held out his hand. "Hi. I'm Eugene Kennedy, a friend of Natalie's. We met a couple of weeks ago at Christopher's birthday party."

Sean gave him the once-over. "Right. So you're dating my wife?"

So that's how this was going to go. "You know, I don't think that's any of your business. Anyway, nice to see you again, Sean."

He walked away, not wanting to get into an altercation with Natalie's ex-husband. Eugene pulled out of the driveway, lingering as he watched Sean go to the door, deciding to wait it out in case something went sideways. Natalie and Sean talked for a few minutes, and it was clear Sean wasn't happy, but Natalie stood her ground. Finally, Sean went back toward his car and got in, started it up, and backed down the driveway, so Eugene drove off.

Well, that was awkward, but probably couldn't be helped.

He just hoped Natalie was okay with it. The last thing he wanted to do was add more stress to her life, especially now, when things between them were just starting to get good.

He'd call her tomorrow to check on Christopher and see how she felt about everything.

CHAPTER FIFTEEN

He said what?"

Natalie sipped her iced coffee. She'd been pissed off since her conversation with Sean the other night. She'd tried to let it go, but it stuck with her, and the more she thought about it, the angrier she got. So she'd asked Hazel to meet for lunch. Hazel couldn't do that, said she had a few errands to run, but she said she'd bring coffee over to Natalie's office, which Natalie happily agreed to.

"He said that I had no right to bring a man to, and I quote, 'our home,' while the kids were there."

Hazel reared back in shock. "I assume you told him to shove his opinions up his ass."

Natalie snorted a laugh. "In similar words, yes. I told him the house was mine based upon our divorce agreement, so he had no right to tell me who I could have there. I reminded him we are divorced now, so my personal life is none of his business. Then he tried to tell me that I couldn't parade a bunch of men around our children, to which I told him that Eugene was one guy, and I wasn't parading anyone around."

"Oh, that's rich, coming from him."

She frowned. "What do you mean?"

"It means that Linc and I ran into him and some extremely clingy woman when we went out to eat pizza last week. And your kids were with them. I mean, it was obvious she was his date. Or his girlfriend or something. They were—how do I put this—very close. The kids didn't seem to care, but still, hello, pot, meet kettle."

"So." She picked up her coffee and took a long sip, pondering the info she'd just gotten from Hazel. "In other words, he can bring our kids around his dates, but I'm not allowed. That is some serious bullshit."

"Indeed."

Now she was even angrier. So angry, she wanted to drive to the hospital where he worked and scream at him. But that would be a bad look, and Natalie would never do that, anyway. Still, she and Sean needed to have a conversation, and sooner rather than later.

Right now, though, she needed to push it to the back of her mind, or it was going to eat her up. She changed the subject so they could talk about anything other than her ex.

"How's Christopher doing?" Hazel asked.

"He's good. The stitches don't bother him, though he's upset that he can't go swimming."

"That'll be over soon enough, though."

"Yeah, the stitches come out Monday, so I'm sure the first thing he'll want to do when we get home is jump into the pool."

"Can't blame him. Having a pool in Orlando is a necessity."

"No lie. Hey, I've got some preliminary plans drawn up for your backyard space. I can run those over tonight if you're not busy."

Hazel's eyes lit up. "Not busy at all. I'll let Linc know. Why don't you and the kids come over for dinner?"

"Sean has the kids tonight, but I'll be happy to come."

"Perfect. About seven?"

"Sounds great. Let me know what you're fixing, and I'll bring a side."

"You are working, and I've got all the food covered."

Natalie pointed a finger at her. "And you have a job, too, so I can provide a side dish. Or two, even."

"Fine. I'm making a casserole. And you make amazing salads."

Feeling triumphant over her victory, Natalie smiled. "Consider it done."

They finished their coffees, and then Hazel hugged her and left. Natalie had to do the final touches on a home office this afternoon. The homeowner, Clara, was awesome, and their collaboration had been tons of fun. By the time Natalie finished, Clara was ecstatic and told her she couldn't wait to start working from home in her gorgeous office.

Natalie couldn't blame her. The design was modern but efficient, and everything that Clara needed was within her reach. Plus, now she had tons of cabinet storage so everything could be put away at the end of the workweek. Since Clara had been working in her kitchen, this was a night and day difference. She'd have privacy to do her job, and Natalie knew how much that meant.

She finished with Clara and stopped at the office to drop off her work things. Delilah was already gone for the day, so Natalie drove home, heading into *her* home office.

She smiled at the beauty of it.

After her divorce had been final and Delilah had hired her at the design firm, the first thing Natalie had done had been to convert Sean's office to hers.

Sean had always called the office his sanctuary, the one place—according to him—where he could dictate his reports, work on his calendar, and get his schedule set up for the next day or the next week.

Whatever. He'd gone in there to hide, play games, or watch sports, since he'd put a big-screen TV in there. He'd forbidden the kids from going in there, saying they might ruin his documents or films or whatever.

Sean was full of shit.

She'd taken that room down to the studs, repainted it a lovely cream color, put up built-ins and a very nice desk. She'd added several potted plants because greenery was cheery, and added shutters to the two big windows. She'd also put in a sofa and a couple nice, soft chairs. That way the kids could come in and hang out whenever she was working.

Her kids were always welcome, no matter where she was.

She made some notes on Clara's space for final invoicing, went through her emails, delighted to see one from a prospective new client who'd been recommended by a former client, which always made her happy. She made a note on her to-do list to call the prospective client first thing in the morning. Then she tucked everything away and closed her office door.

She made an arugula salad and slid it in the fridge. She loaded the dishwasher, cleaned the kitchen counter, put away a few things the kids had left out, then headed upstairs to change.

She took off her dress and shoes, washed up, and walked into her closet, deciding on shorts and a sleeveless top. It was always casual for dinner at Hazel and Linc's, which suited her just fine. She slipped into her sandals, then touched up her makeup and pulled her hair up with a clip.

It was only May, and it was already brutally humid. Now she felt a lot cooler. Then again she was inside where it was air-conditioned, but at least when they went outside she wouldn't feel like she was totally melting.

She decided to slice up some fruit and made a tangy but sweet dip, then put all the stuff in her car and drove over to her sister's house. She frowned when she saw the SUV in the driveway.

"No. It can't be," she whispered to herself. Hazel would have warned her.

But who else could it be?

She grabbed the food out of the back seat and went in through the open garage door. The sound of her mother's voice made her cringe.

Well, crap.

There she was. Her mother, looking impeccably put together, as always. She wore crisp capris, red flats, and a button-down shirt that looked as if it had been starched within an inch of its life. Her medium-length auburn hair curled at the ends, utterly resistant to Florida's brutal humidity.

She plastered on a smile and walked into the kitchen. "Hey, sis. Hi, Mom."

"Hello, Natalie." Mom didn't get up from her spot at the island, so Natalie went over to give her a peck on the cheek.

"I didn't expect to see you here," Natalie said, then added, "What a nice surprise."

"Well, Paul is out of town, and I was talking to Hazel earlier, and she mentioned you were coming over. She suggested I come, too, since I was all alone. Isn't that sweet of her?"

"So sweet." Natalie traded looks with Hazel, who gave her an apologetic shrug.

"Would you like some sangria?" Hazel asked. "I made a fresh batch."

"I'd love some." Natalie put her stuff in the fridge, then grabbed the glass from her sister.

"Where's Linc?" she asked.

"Oh. He's outside with Eugene. He stopped by, so he's staying for dinner, too."

She managed to choke out what she hoped was a rather bland, "Eugene's here, too?"

"He is. Problem?"

She shook her head. "No. Not at all." Now she'd have to make sure her mother didn't catch on to . . . whatever was going on with Eugene and her. And why was Eugene here every time she came over? Did he live here or something? Ugh.

"Where are the children, Natalie?" Mom asked.

"They're with Sean tonight, Mom."

"I see." Her mother lifted her chin and took a dainty sip of her drink. "It's still a shame about the divorce. So hard on the kids."

"The kids are doing fine, Mom. Sean and I make sure they get plenty of time and attention."

"But still, their home is broken."

Natalie rolled her eyes. "Mom. Come on. This isn't the fifties. People get divorced. It's not the end of the world. Our children will adapt and thrive. Sean and I might not agree on a lot of things, but as far as our children, we're in sync."

Mostly.

Her mother shrugged. "Whatever you say."

Which was her mom's way of tuning her out. "Whatever is right. I'm going outside to say hi to Linc and Eugene."

Despite the blast of heat and humidity that greeted her when she opened the back door, she was happy to be away from the icy chill of her mother's judgmental attitude.

"Hey," Eugene said, getting up from his chair. "I didn't expect to see you."

"I was surprised to find out that you were here, too."

He wrapped his arm around her and hugged her. Her first instinct would have been to ask for distance so she wouldn't have to explain yet another thing to her mother, but right now she was pissed off at her mom, and if she could irritate her a little more, that would be ideal.

But then Linc hugged her, too, and then the dogs surrounded her, causing her to have to kneel and pet the pups, including some dog she'd never seen before. The new pup was on the medium side, with dark, curly fur. She—yes, it was definitely a she—was very fluffy and oh so affectionate. She had a very prominent underbite, which, surprisingly, only made her cuter.

While she was petting the new member of the dog family, Hazel and their mom came outside.

"Who's the new dog, Hazel?" Natalie asked.

"Oh. That's Grizelda. She was an emergency surrender I picked up a few days ago. She's a real peach. Sweet and affectionate and she loves the neighbor's kids. You should bring Cammie and Christopher over to meet her."

"She is very cute. And the kids have been asking for a dog for so long." Natalie was not a dog person, and Sean had always been a firm no-pets person. But getting used to being around Hazel's dogs had almost—almost—changed her mind.

"A dog is the last thing you need, Natalie," her mother said, taking a seat near the fan outside.

Count to ten, Natalie. That's what she and Hazel always told themselves whenever their mother got on their last nerve.

Like now.

Natalie smiled up at Hazel. "Okay if I bring the kids by tomorrow to meet her?"

Hazel beamed a smile. "That sounds perfect."

She caught the disgusted glance her mother sent her way. In return, she sent her a warm smile.

She'd spent years with a man who had constantly told her what to do. And what she couldn't do. She'd damn well not go backward and allow her mother to do the same.

This was her life now, and she was the one who was going to make decisions. No one was managing her life for her anymore.

She followed Hazel and her mom inside, the dogs following. Her mother's consternation over all the dogs was Natalie's private joy tonight. She was especially brightened by the fact that Grizelda seemed taken by her, spending all her time right at her ankles. Which meant, of course, that she had to constantly bend down to give her love and affirmation.

"I think she loves you," Hazel said.

She looked up at her sister. "Shockingly, the feeling might be mutual."

Hazel cast a smile her way. "You know, sometimes you just get hit by the love bug. There's just no avoiding it."

Natalie let out a surprised laugh. "I guess so."

Eugene came inside to grab a couple of beers. On his way past, he knelt down to pet Grizelda, then looked up at Natalie.

"Getting a dog, huh?"

"Maybe. I don't know. I'll bring the kids by to meet her, and we'll see how it goes."

"Kids and dogs are like peanut butter and jelly. It's a done deal, babe."

As soon as the word "babe" spilled out of Eugene's mouth, Natalie shifted her gaze to her mother, catching yet another of her patented disapproving looks. Deciding to ignore her mom for the rest of the evening, she gave Eugene a dazzling smile.

When Linc and Eugene came inside, Hazel put the dogs in their playroom and then finished things up in the kitchen. Natalie tossed the salad and added dressing, then brought out the fruit and dip as well. They took everything over to the table and everyone sat.

The food smelled incredible. Hazel had baked bread—of course. Hazel lifted the lid and everyone simultaneously inhaled.

Natalie looked over at Hazel. "This smells amazing. What is it?"

"It's a caprese chicken casserole. Chicken and pasta in a cream sauce with tomatoes and basil."

"Yum," Linc said. "Let's eat."

They did, and Natalie was in heaven. The food was so delicious she had to try hard not to shovel it into her mouth.

"This is amazing," Eugene said in between bites. "Can I come over for dinner every night?"

"Thank you," Hazel said. "And, no."

Eugene laughed.

Then everything went quiet as everyone just ate the remarkable food.

"Hazel's been putting some of her meals on social media," Linc finally said.

"You have?" Natalie looked over at Hazel. "I haven't seen it."

"I started a new account just for cooking. I'm creating some videos where I do recipes for simple and also more complex dishes. I'm getting kind of a following." She finished with a shrug.

"Hazel, that's very exciting," Natalie said. "You'll have to give me your account info so I can follow you and tell everyone I know about it."

"Thanks."

"I would also like to know about it," their mother said.

"Sure, Mom. And, thank you."

"She's also writing a cookbook."

Hazel's fork stilled in midair as her gaze shot to Linc. "Dammit, Linc."

He gave her a sheepish smile. "Sorry. I didn't know it was a secret."

"A cookbook?" Natalie asked. "Hazel, this is awesome. I want details."

"I will definitely fill you in and give you all the links." She continued to eat, but stopped when she realized they were all staring at her.

"What?" Hazel asked.

"It's a big endeavor to write a book," Eugene said. "But after tasting your food, I can see why you'd do it. You should own your own restaurant."

"That's what I've always told her," Linc said.

"You are pretty impressive," Natalie said.

"It's a huge endeavor, Hazel," her mother said. "But your food is very good."

Hazel blushed. "Come on. It's not that big of a deal."

"Actually, it is. I'm very proud of you, Hazel."

Hazel's eyes widened. "Thanks, Mom."

Even Natalie was shocked by her mother's praise of Hazel's endeavor. She didn't offer it up easily, or often. Or at all, for that matter.

"Okaaay, now that you've all embarrassed me to death, who wants dessert?"

"There's a dessert, too?" Eugene asked. "This could possibly be the best night of my life."

"Dude, you need to get out more," Linc said, then, when Hazel gave him a side-eye, he added, "I mean, yeah, Hazel makes phenomenal desserts. It is the best night of your life."

All Natalie could do was laugh. Watching the brothers interact was truly a high point of her night.

At least so far.

After dinner, Mom had to make an exit, claiming that she had an appointment early in the morning on a house closing. They said their goodbyes to her and then gathered back at the table for Hazel's incredible strawberry shortcake dessert that was fresh and delicious. Linc cleared the table and told Eugene to help him do dishes, which he did without a word.

"Huh," Natalie said.

"What?" Hazel asked.

"Does that happen often?"

"Does what happen?"

Natalie inclined her head toward the kitchen.

"Oh." Hazel took a sip of her wine and smiled. "Indeed. Linc said I do almost all the cooking, so it's only fair that he handle the cleaning up after."

"Wow. Sean never once stepped foot in the kitchen unless it was to get himself a drink. Most of the time he'd want me to do that for him, too. And he never once washed a dish because he worked and I was at home doing—and I quote—'nothing all day long.'"

Hazel wrinkled her nose. "Bastard. And look at where he is now. Not married to you anymore. Too bad for him, huh?"

She smiled. Yeah, too bad for him.

Her gaze wandered over to where Eugene and Linc stood side by side at the sink, talking and laughing while they put leftovers away, rinsed dishes, and loaded them in the dishwasher. Then Linc took the dogs outside while Eugene washed pots and pans.

"Those two are a whole other breed," Natalie said.

"Not really. They're just the type of men we deserve."

She pulled her gaze away from Eugene's amazing forearms and onto her sister. "You know what? You're right. We do deserve them." Not that Eugene was hers, but she did deserve the kind of man who shared household duties equally.

Every woman should have that.

And more. So much more.

While the guys were on seconds of dessert, Natalie splayed her design scheme for the backyard on the table. After the guys finished, Linc came over, along with Eugene.

"I like this here," Linc said, pointing to the oasis of shade trees and the pergola with misters Natalie had designed on the east side of the house. "It stays cooler, and the dogs will really enjoy hanging out there on hot summer days."

Hazel nodded. "I agree. And I love the way you added more lush grasses in that area. The dogs will love that."

"I wanted to put the dog shower near the door here," she said. "That way if someone gets muddy, it's easier to hose them off and dry them before they come into the house. But you can change that if you want it somewhere else."

"No, I think that's a smart idea," Hazel said, studying the drawings. "But could we move the splash pool farther back? Say to the left of the rocks on the west side?"

"Sure." She made notes about the adjustments. "Anything else?"

"Can we keep these and study them a while?" Linc asked. "It might take a day or two to let everything sink in."

"Of course. Give it at least a week. I'll check back with you then. And call me if you have questions."

Hazel smiled. "I'll call you either way."

They visited awhile longer, then Natalie said she was going to head out. Eugene left at the same time, so they walked outside together.

"I like your plan for the backyard," he said as he stopped beside her car.

She leaned against the door. "Thanks. I like it, too."

They looked at each other, neither of them saying a word. All Natalie had to do was reach out for him, take that step. But for some reason she didn't.

"Okay." He pushed off the car. "Anyway, I guess I'll—"

"Wait." She turned to look at him. "Come home with me."

He arched a brow. "Are you sure?"

"Yes. No. I mean, I don't know. Yes."

His lips curved. He picked up her hand in his. "A little conflicted?"

"I guess. But not in the way you think. I want some time alone with you. But I'm not sure I'm ready to—"

"To . . ."

"Come on. Don't make me say it."

"If you can't say it, Natalie, then you're definitely not ready for it. I think I should just go home. I don't want to force you to do something you don't want to do."

He didn't seem upset at all, while she was very upset. With herself.

He started to pull his hand away, but she grabbed on to it. "Wait. I'm . . . scared."

Now he frowned. "Of me?"

"No. I . . ." She looked around. "Look. Can we have this conversation somewhere other than my sister's driveway? Like at my house?"

"Okay. I'll follow you home."

She nodded, got in her car, and started to drive, trying to calm down her rapidly beating heart.

They'd talk. They'd just talk. And she'd tell him what she was afraid of.

As soon as she figured it out herself.

CHAPTER SIXTEEN

*E*ugene was worried that maybe he'd stepped into something that he couldn't handle. Natalie was obviously conflicted, and he should have said no when she asked him to come over. She needed time to decide what she wanted.

Then again, it also wasn't his place to tell her what she should do or how she should feel, either. She invited him over, and maybe she just wanted to talk, so that's what they were going to do.

He pulled into the driveway at Natalie's house, waited until she drove into the garage. Then he parked and got out. She was waiting for him next to her car, so he walked into the garage. Without a word, she turned and headed toward the door leading into the house, so he followed, opening the door for her.

She waited while he closed the door behind him. He figured she was going to turn on the lights and they'd go into the kitchen, she'd brew some coffee and they'd talk. Instead, she backed him against the wall and pressed her body against his.

He inhaled the sweet lemony scent of her skin as she rose up to whisper, "Kiss me."

Oh man, he really wanted to. But first—"You said you were afraid."

"Yes. And, no."

"You're not afraid of me, are you?"

"Of course not. I meant . . . of this. I don't want to get attached. I mean . . ." She drew in a breath and let it out. "I don't plan on getting attached. I don't want you to, either."

"Okay."

She shook her head. "I need you to understand that this is just sex. I'm not looking for a relationship. And my kids are always going to be my priority."

She was undulating against him while she laid down her hard-and-fast rules. Kind of hot. "I get that. I'm on board, Natalie."

"Okay. Now kiss me."

His entire body went tight with desire. He wrapped his arm around her and pulled her to him. And when he kissed her, it was like lights exploded inside his brain, zapping his nerve endings like fire.

She tasted sweet and sexy, and in the dark, he focused on the way her hands mapped his body. Across his arms, over his chest, and down his abs, lifting his shirt up to slide her fingers across the seam of his jeans. His breath caught as she rubbed his cock through his jeans. He was no novice at this but damn if Natalie didn't make him feel like he was. His throat had gone dry, his heart pounded, and if she continued to rub his cock like that, this was gonna end before things got started.

He pulled back, swept his fingers across her perfect jawline, wishing there were lights so he could search her face, see what she was feeling. Because he sure as hell felt a lot.

"Let's go to my room," she said while at the same time rubbing her entire body against his.

He slid his hands alongside her ribs, brushing the fullness of her breasts. "You keep doing that and we won't make it to the bedroom."

"I don't care where we do it," she whispered, her voice slightly out of breath. "I just want to get naked. And get you naked."

He definitely wanted that. "How far away is your room?"

She grabbed his hand and moved at a fast clip to the room at the end of the hall. She kicked off her sandals and shimmied out of her clothes, compelling him to shed his clothes, too, which he was more than happy to do. When she was down to her bra and panties, she reached for him, pulling him toward the bed. They climbed on, and he lay next to her, sweeping his hand over the silken softness of her stomach. Moonlight spilled in through the windows, casting Natalie in a soft glow. Like some silvery goddess, her dark hair spilled across the white pillow, making her look more than a little ethereal.

"Don't stop now," she said, taking his hand and sliding it over her breasts.

He looked down at her. "Satin. And hot pink. With matching panties. You are a constant surprise, Natalie."

She slid her leg over his, sliding her foot along his shin. "You have no idea. It's been a long, very long time for me, Eugene."

He shifted, pushing her onto her back. "Then I'll make this very, very good for you."

———

*N*atalie had never been bold, not sexually, anyway. But tonight, with Eugene, she was. Kind of surprising, actually, and more than a little hot. Yay for her.

She'd initially invited him to the house to have a conversation with him about her reservations regarding taking their relationship to a more physical place. Instead, they hadn't stepped more than two feet into the house when she'd attacked him.

Because she had needs, and she wanted him, and on the drive home she'd realized that she was an adult woman who was entitled to have a sex life.

Now here she was, with Eugene in her bed, and she could barely breathe as he undid the clasp of her bra, bending to kiss the top of her shoulder as he pulled the strap down her arm. His lips moved along her collarbone to the swell of her breast, his tongue mapping a trail across her skin, which had suddenly become incredibly sensitive.

He pulled the bra off of her, casting it aside, somewhere. She didn't know, didn't care, because his hand covered her breast and his lips surrounded a nipple. And then he licked and sucked, and she arched her back off the bed because the sensations were just so, so good.

He lavished attention on her breasts, and then her stomach, teasing her with his mouth while he removed her panties. Then he blazed a hot trail of kisses toward her sex, using his fingers and tongue until she heard herself begging out loud for release. He kept on for a very long and extremely talented amount of time.

127

Such a mind-blowing experience. She tried to think of when she'd had this much attention paid to her clit—hell, that he'd actually found her clit and knew what to do with it was a revelation. A definite first for her.

This all felt so new. And maybe that's because it was Eugene, and he made her feel worshipped and wrapped in sensual pleasure unlike anything she'd ever felt before.

"You make me feel . . ." The sensations intensified, making words more difficult, but she could explain to him with her movements against his hands, his mouth. "So good, Eugene. Give me more."

He murmured unintelligible words against her sex, then licked her, over and over until she came. And, oh, did she ever come. She let out a shudder and cry while her body spasmed with a glorious orgasm.

She barely had time to come down from that incredible high before Eugene had her wrapped in his arms. "You ready for more?" he asked, his lips sliding across hers with tantalizing promise.

She reached for him, teasing her nails across the solid muscle of him. "Yes. More."

He slid on a condom, and then he was there again, his body covering hers, his cock slipping inside of her. She let out a gasp.

"Okay?" he asked.

She raised her knees and lifted until he filled her completely, until she felt she was part of him. She reached up to sweep her fingers over his face. "Oh. More than okay."

And then they moved—together, and Natalie felt every inch of pleasure. That spark that had lain dormant for far too long. Now it sprang to life with renewed force and she embraced it with her whole being.

"You know what it feels like being inside of you, Natalie?" he murmured against her. "Hot. Like molten fire, making me want to come. Come with me, Natalie."

The utter joy of being joined with Eugene like this brought her right to the edge. His low, sexy words as he moved within her took her right over, making her tense, shudder, and clutch him closer to her as she rode that wave of ecstasy.

She collapsed against the bed, feeling the warmth of Eugene's body leave her when he got up and disappeared for a minute. Then he was right there, pulling her against him.

"I'm sorry," she whispered.

He swept his knuckles gently over her cheek. "For what?"

"I was so self-absorbed and into my own pleasure, I have no idea if you came or not."

He let out a hard laugh. "Trust me. I did. And it was good. Really good."

She smoothed her hand across his chest, then pushed on him so he lay on his back. She rolled over on top of him. "Same here. So good, in fact, that I'm requesting a repeat performance. Only this time, I'm on top."

"Hmm." He swept his hands across her back, then lower. "It's a sacrifice, but I'll allow it."

Then he cupped his hand behind her neck and pulled her down for a kiss, and she was once against lost in him.

CHAPTER SEVENTEEN

*T*he best part of game design was having an opportunity to test drive, so to speak, a new creation. Only this time it wasn't a new game, but a ride, which wasn't close to being ready. It would take the better part of a year and a half—maybe longer—to make it ready. But they had the schematics and had designed preliminary routes and all the thrills. So right now they could at least do a virtual ride to make sure they were on the right track.

Eugene and his team went into the game room, got into their chairs, and put on the VR headsets.

"Okay, gang," he said. "Why don't we see how much of this we've gotten right so far. Let's hit it."

They ran through the entire ride about fifteen times. Eugene made voice notes about what looked good, and, more importantly, what wasn't working and needed fine-tuning. Fortunately he had an excellent team who also threw out comments and suggestions, so he added those to his notes.

The ride needed a lot of tweaking, which wasn't unexpected at this phase of the project. But, all in all, they were right on track, which was awesome.

After the test, he went back to his office and wrote up his notes, making design changes based on what they had seen on the VR run.

They still had so much to do, but now Eugene could visualize the way this ride would operate.

It was going to be kick-ass once it was done. This was where Eugene got excited like a child, already visualizing how much kids were going to love this ride. He had always felt the same way whenever he designed a game.

A ride, though? To be able to be there to watch families experience it? It was going to be a once-in-a-lifetime event. So much action, adventure, and nonstop thrills.

He couldn't wait. But, for now, there was more work to be done.

His phone pinged. He picked it up, smiling as he saw a text from Natalie. He'd told her he was going to have an intense next several days, but they'd been in touch via text and video chat.

Busy day?

He replied: Yeah. All good stuff. How about you?

She replied with a pic of herself with the kids and their new dog, Grizelda. Picked her up yesterday. Utter madness and joy at our house.

He laughed at the looks of love and happiness on all their faces. He texted back with: She looks like she's always been yours. You all needed a dog.

She replied a few minutes later: That's still up for debate. Can't deny she's very cute and cuddly. Come see her.

How could he pass up that invitation? He replied back: How about pizza tonight?

Sounds perfect. See you tonight.

She finished off with a heart emoji, making his own heart do a weird tumble in his chest.

Okay, yeah, he could just calm down. Sure, they definitely had fun together. And, as he learned the other night, the sex was outstanding. Plus, he really liked her kids.

So the problem was . . .

He frowned, refusing to work that problem through to its logical conclusion.

Or maybe he just wasn't ready yet.

So he'd just focus on pizza night and meeting the new dog.

That, he could handle.

*H*azel had called Natalie three times a day for the past two days, and had insisted on video calls as well, all to check on Grizelda.

"The pup is fine, Hazel," Natalie said. "She goes outside regularly, she has toys and food and water, and the kids play with her when they get home from school. We go for walks every morning and the kids run around with her nonstop. And then she takes a lot of naps in the bed we got for her. I've told the kids not to bother her when she's sleeping, and they're very good about respecting her sleep."

Natalie walked the phone over to where her furry baby was

currently curled up on the fluffy dog bed. "See? The kids are outside and the dog is inside napping. Happy."

Hazel sighed and smiled. "She does look happy. You're doing so well with her, Natalie."

Natalie turned the phone back to herself. "You sound surprised. Should I be insulted?"

"Of course not. Okay, maybe. I never took you for a dog person. For a while there you barely tolerated being in the presence of my dogs."

Not a lie. "You have a point. But that wasn't about your dogs. It was more me being stressed and unhappy. I barely tolerated my kids, let alone dogs. So I wasn't really myself." She thought about it. "I'm still not sure who 'myself' is yet, Hazel."

Hazel nodded. "I appreciate your honesty. And it's such a breakthrough for you to recognize that. Plus, you have a dog now. You're expanding your capacity to love, Natalie. That's a big deal."

"I don't know about that."

"I'm being serious. Being responsible for another creature— human or canine—is a major deal. During a time when most people would be introspective and focused on their own needs, you've decided to open yourself up to love. Both giving and receiving. That's huge."

Was it? She hadn't thought about it at all. "I think it was more of a case of instalove where Grizelda was concerned."

Hazel laughed. "Well, now, that I completely understand."

They talked for a few more minutes, then hung up since they were both busy. Since the kids were occupied outside kicking a ball back and forth to each other, Natalie took a seat at the table where she could keep an eye on them and opened her laptop to work on a few design projects.

She put the finishing touches on a project she'd been diligently working on since she first started back to work. It was a huge design, one that included a living room, dining room, and three bedrooms, along with a backyard redesign. She'd gotten to know the owners, Fred and Paula, a retired couple who'd lived in their home for over twenty years. Now that they had time to relax and recreate, they'd renovated the entire house, and Paula wanted it to have a design refresh. She had a keen eye for detail, which Natalie just loved. Working with a client who knew exactly what they wanted made her job so much easier.

She checked inventory and grinned when she realized that everything had come in and was ready to go. She should be able to finish the design next week. She shot off an email to Paula to schedule the install.

By the time she finished sending some emails to suppliers, Grizelda had woken from her nap and was whining at the back door.

"Good girl," Natalie said, opening the door for her. She walked out with the pup, who dashed out to join the kids. They were sitting in the shade under a tree, their heads touching. They were talking in whispers, no doubt plotting a world takeover. Or at least a takeover of the house.

But then Cammie and Christopher decided that rolling around on the ground with Grizelda was way more fun than a world takeover. The sounds of their giggles and the pup's happy barking were the sweetest music.

Her kids were happy. Her dog was happy. Her heart swelled with joy as she watched them.

But was she happy?

The thought shocked her.

She'd focused so much of her time and attention since the divorce on making sure the kids knew they were loved, that just because she and Sean were no longer living together, it didn't mean that anything would change in how they felt about the kids. It had been rough at first, but kids were resilient—much more than Natalie had been. Even though she'd been the one to initiate the divorce, it had still been hard. She'd had to learn a whole new way of living.

She'd never felt more alone than during that time. But even through those darkest days, she'd known she'd made the right decision. Because despite all the upheaval, for the first time in so many years, she'd felt a sense of rightness, of peace that she'd never felt before. And that calm had been worth all the mayhem.

But was she happy?

As she watched the kids and dog run the yard, she pondered the thought.

That daily tension from trying to be the perfect wife to Sean had evaporated. Now she could do whatever she wanted—within reason and childcare, of course. But knowing that she answered to no one but herself? That meant everything.

She loved her job, her clients, and the people she worked with. She had a new, much closer relationship with her mother and her sister, and those tightened bonds were so warm, so loving.

And then there was Eugene. And sex. Oh so hot sex that was

extremely nice and had definitely lowered her anxiety, while at the same time heightening all her senses.

So, yeah, right now, she was very happy.

And that was enough for now.

For now was all she could do.

*E*ugene balanced two boxes of pizza on one hand and a bouquet of flowers in the other. He used his elbow to push the bell at Natalie's front door, smiling at the sound of a dog's bark.

Natalie opened the door, and her bright smile was everything. Grizelda wound around his legs as he stepped in, her tail doing happy flips.

He bent down to give her lots of love as he looked up at Natalie. "She seems to be settled in and happy, huh?"

Natalie looked down at the pup. "It's like she's been here her whole life."

"Perfect."

"Eugene!" Christopher ran down the hall and launched himself at Eugene's legs.

"Hey, buddy," Eugene said. "What's up?"

"We found a turtle in the backyard yesterday. Mom didn't let us keep him."

"Oh, too bad. But that's because the turtle was probably traveling to his home in a pond somewhere, right, Mom?"

Natalie nodded. "That's right. Plus, Grizelda kept barking at him and wouldn't let him move."

"Ah."

They walked into the kitchen so Eugene could set the pizzas down on the island. "For you," he said to Natalie, handing her the bouquet.

She sniffed them and smiled. "Very sweet of you. Thank you."

Christopher flopped onto the floor. Grizelda immediately climbed onto Christopher's lap.

"This is Grizelda," Christopher said, absently running his hand over the dog's back. "She's our dog. We have to feed her and love her and take care of her. She likes balls and squishy toys."

Eugene kneeled down. "Having a dog is a big responsibility. I'll bet you and Cammie do a great job taking care of her."

"Yeah, we do. But mostly me."

"So not true." Cammie came in and sat next to Christopher. Grizelda hopped over to her lap and lapped kisses all over Cammie's face, making her laugh.

Christopher lay on the floor and the dog jumped on him, giving him kisses, too.

"I can tell that Grizelda has enough love for both of you."

"She's extremely affectionate," Natalie said. "And very gentle with the kids."

She went over to the cabinet and pulled out plates. "Kids, it's time to eat. Go wash your hands."

It was funny how two little kids could make sounds like an entire herd of buffalo as they ran down the hall.

Natalie pulled salad out of the fridge along with a bowl of fruit while Eugene laid the pizza boxes on the table.

"I think you did way more work than I did," he said.

She laughed. "This was easy and I don't have to cook tonight. You saved my life. Plus, the kids love pizza."

"I feel a little less guilty, then."

The kids came back, and he helped Natalie set up the kids' plates. He'd gotten one cheese and one pepperoni pizza, figuring those would probably work, which they did. Christopher liked pepperoni, and Cammie liked cheese, and Eugene could eat anything. Natalie opted for a slice of each. He piled salad and fruit onto his plate, and they all dug in.

The kids regaled him with talk of school and activities.

"We're both doing swimming lessons this summer, like we always do," Cammie said.

"That's what makes you both good swimmers," Eugene said.

"Yeah. Because someday I'm gonna be a lifeguard." Cammie paused to take a bite, chew, and swallow. "Or a scientist. Maybe a model."

He nodded, impressed with her thought process. "Those are all awesome careers."

"I'm gonna be a firefighter," Christopher said. "Or a race car driver."

"Both sound fun."

The salad was amazing, and the fruit salad was bright and delicious. The kids finished eating, took their plates to the sink, and ran outside to play with Grizelda. They put the leftovers away and cleaned up the plates.

Eugene leaned against the sink. "This was all so good, Natalie."

She smiled. "It's a pretty simple dinner. Plus, you bought the pizza, remember?"

"I remember. But you made salad and fruit. And it's more than I usually get. Single guy, ya know."

She pointed her finger at him. "That is no excuse. You know how to cook, right?"

"I can cook some things."

"And your new house will have an amazing kitchen," Natalie said, "both indoor and outdoor. Being a single guy is no reason for not being able to whip up incredible meals. Or at least decent ones."

He had been thoroughly chastised. "You're absolutely right. Once my house is finished, I'll start working on that."

She shrugged. "Why wait? You can use my kitchen and practice here."

Oh, now the gauntlet had been thrown down. "Sure."

"Seriously?"

"You offered. Did you think I wasn't up to the challenge?"

"I figured you'd turn me down."

He laid his hand over his heart. "Oh, the lack of faith."

She cocked her head to the side. "Yeah, I'm sure you're heartbroken. So you're going to cook for me, then."

"I absolutely accept your challenge. You just let me know when you want to do this and I'll be here."

She looked up, thinking, then said, "This weekend. Kids will be at Sean's."

"Afraid I'll poison them?"

"Not at all. I just want to watch you. Carefully. Can't have you burning my kitchen down."

"You're funny."

"I think so."

"Consider it done."

Now all he had to do was plan a meal, then figure out how he was going to cook it. "Then we'll be alone."

She leaned in closer. "Yes. We will."

He took a peek outside. The kids were busy with Grizelda, so he took the opportunity to brush his lips across hers. "Can't wait."

"Mmm. Me, too."

The weekend was just too damn far away.

CHAPTER EIGHTEEN

*O*ne would think that, for a single mom, kid-free weekends meant sleeping in, relaxing, and enjoying the quiet. Maybe reading a book. Taking in a yoga class.

Ha. Not so much. Or, at least, not for Natalie. She'd gotten up early Saturday to do laundry, drop off dry cleaning, and pick up things at the craft store because Camryn had a science project to do for class when she got home Sunday night. Natalie had mentioned it to Sean, thinking he might want to do the project with his daughter, but he claimed he wouldn't have the time. Whatever. She would handle it, just like she'd always handled it.

She thought about pushing grocery shopping til tomorrow, but then realized that Sunday was for laundry and cleaning the house, so she went ahead and did it, grumbling the whole time. After she put the groceries away she sighed in contentment. At least it was done now.

Then she realized her toenails were looking a little raggedy because, honestly, when did she have the time? And maybe it was an indulgence but—no, it wasn't. It was an absolute necessity. So she ended up getting both a pedicure and a manicure because, dammit, she deserved it.

She also stopped at her favorite coffee shop for an iced caramel macchiato, which made her supremely happy. Sean had always called her frivolous for spending unnecessary money on what he'd called "stupid frilly coffee drinks."

Sean could suck it.

She drove home and grabbed her coffee, walked inside her quiet, empty house. Correction. Not empty, because she was happily greeted by Grizelda, who apparently had chewed up one of her favorite white sandals and now presented it to her as a gift.

She picked up the shoe and sat on the sofa. The dog happily wagged her tail.

"Oh, Grizzie, what did you do?"

Tail wags and happy face. Natalie couldn't help but smile.

"Still a bit of a puppy, aren't you? Well, that'll teach me to leave my shoes out. And you obviously need more toys. And exercise." She swept her fingers through Grizelda's fur, rewarded with several dog licks to her hand. Then the pup circled and lay on top of her feet.

Okay, first, some exercise for Griz. She pushed herself out of the chair and grabbed the leash, rewarded with Grizelda's happy whines and fast-swishing tail.

They did a mile before the pup's tongue started hanging out the side of her mouth. It was ultrahumid today, which meant rain was probably on the way, so Natalie walked them home. Grizelda went straight for her water bowl and downed most of the water. At least the water didn't slosh over the sides onto the kitchen floor. Just a few drips from Grizelda's mouth, which was fine.

A year ago she would have freaked.

She freaked a lot less about the small stuff these days. She swiped up the water drops with a paper towel, then grabbed her iced coffee, plopped down in her chair, and took a sip.

Grizelda had curled up on one of the air-conditioning vents and was fast asleep with her stuffed bear. Natalie made a mental note to go to the pet store and get her more toys. After finishing her coffee, she set the cup on the table and laid her head back, letting her eyes close.

Perfect. At least for the twenty minutes her eyes were closed. But over the years she'd become a champion of the twenty-minute nap. She got up, stretched, and felt utterly refreshed, ready to tackle the rest of the day.

Since Eugene was coming over tonight, she had waited to shower. Now she did, shampooing and scrubbing and shaving and lotioning, followed by blow-drying and makeup-ing until she glowed. She stared at herself in the full-length mirror, giving her naked body a critical examination.

She was drawing ever closer to her thirty-fifth birthday. Still, she kept her body in shape—not by constant exercise, because no single mom had time for that. But she did take an occasional yoga class and then there was all the nonstop running after kids and their activities. Plus now she had a job that kept her active, too. And a very adorable dog who very much enjoyed walks.

But her breasts didn't droop—not that much anyway. And her

ass was still where it was supposed to be. She'd say she was still looking good.

More than good, actually. She looked amazing.

Now that she felt fantastic, she slipped on underwear and went into her closet and pulled out a sundress. It was a pretty navy with splotches of white flowers, comfortable, soft as hell, and had little bitty straps. It also showed off her legs.

After all, she had a date tonight. She looked at her watch, realizing he was due to show up in a few minutes, so she went into the living room, lit the candle, and turned on some soft music to help set the mood.

Not that she was planning a seduction or anything. Then again, maybe she was. Eugene was infinitely seduceable.

She took a seat and scanned her social media accounts, laughing at some of the memes, forwarding a few to her sister. She'd taken a very cute pic of the kids with Grizelda the other day so she posted it to her account, then checked the time.

Okay, Eugene was only ten minutes late. No big deal. She resumed scrolling, diving into a lengthy story that kept her occupied until she checked the time again.

Now he was thirty minutes late. Okay, she was worried. She texted him.

Are you okay? We said six thirty, right?

Taking a deep breath, she got up and went outside with Grizelda, who did her business and fruitlessly chased some birds. She checked her phone.

No reply.

Damn. She dialed his number, but after a few rings it went to his voicemail.

Maybe he'd gotten involved in something, and he was just in the shower. Still, he would have called or texted her to say he was going to be late.

Wouldn't he? Eugene didn't strike her as the kind of guy to just let her sit and stew in worry.

Would he?

Then again, how well did she actually know him?

Deciding to calm herself, she sent another text: Hey, we had a date tonight. Call me when you get this text so I know you're okay.

She'd leave it at that, refusing to worry about him.

Except that she *was* worried about him. But she'd hold off doing anything about it for a while longer.

She made herself a snack that she didn't even want to eat, ending up picking at some raspberries while wandering the house, periodically looking out the front window to see if he'd pull up in the driveway. In the meantime, dark clouds gathered, mirroring her mood.

Worry mixed with anger as one hour became two. She tried calling him again, and again his phone went to voicemail. Her stomach knotted, and she didn't know whether to be concerned or pissed off.

Finally she called Hazel.

"Hey, Nat," Hazel said. "What's up?"

"So I had a date with Eugene tonight," she started, letting it all spill out in what felt like was one breath. "He was supposed to come over at six thirty and he didn't show. I tried texting and calling and he's not responding and now I'm worried. Does Linc know where he might be?"

"Oh, honey, I don't know. Let me ask."

She waited, hearing the conversation between Hazel and Linc. Finally, Linc got on the phone.

"Natalie."

"Hi, Linc."

"Tell me what happened."

She told him exactly what she'd told Hazel.

"That's not like Eugene. He wouldn't leave you hanging like that. Let me try and get in touch with him and I'll call you back, okay?"

"Okay. Thanks, Linc."

Linc would find his brother. He had to. And when he did, Eugene would be fine.

And then she could yell at him for scaring the hell out of her.

I t's still not right, dammit."

Eugene and a few members of his team had run into a critical error, one they'd been working on since yesterday. He'd been at the office for over twenty-four hours, not even going home last night. He hadn't slept, and the only food he'd had was a couple of donuts and a half a sandwich. He was hungry, cranky, desperately needed a shower, and he was totally pissed off about the glitch that had ground their progress to a halt.

"It's like we get just so far and the program hits a wall." Heath, one of his programmers, dragged his fingers through his hair, looking as haggard as Eugene felt.

"There has to be an obvious glitch that we're not seeing."

"Maybe we need to wait for the rest of the team to come in on Monday. Fresh eyes and all."

Eugene shook his head. "There's no reason we can't fix this."

"You need some sleep. And a shower."

"Yeah, so do you. We'll stink up the place together until we figure this out."

They dove in until one of the security guards came in. "Sorry to bother you, but there's some guy at the gate claiming to be your brother."

Eugene frowned. "My brother?"

"Yeah. Says his name is Linc and says you're not picking up your phone and he wants to know if you're here or if you're dead."

Shit. "That sounds like my brother." He looked at the security stream and sure enough, it was Linc. "You can let him in, Roger, thanks."

Eugene turned to Heath. "I'll just be a minute."

"Take your time. I'm ordering some pizzas."

"Okay."

Eugene walked out of the design room where Linc would be forbidden from entering because of all the proprietary stuff in there. Roger escorted Linc to the lounge, where he greeted Eugene with a wrinkled nose.

"You look like shit," Linc said. "Smell like it, too."

"Yeah, we had a critical failure in programming, so I've been here since yesterday."

"You might try letting some people know that. Natalie was frantic. You two had a date tonight?"

"Oh no." He pulled out his phone and saw several text messages, multiple missed calls and voicemails. "I lost track of time. I totally forgot."

"She'll be thrilled to hear that. Anyway, glad you're not dead. Go home and take a shower. And call Natalie, okay?"

"I'll do that right now. Hey. Thanks, Linc."

Linc shrugged his shoulder. "It's what brothers do. I'm relieved you're not lying on the side of the road somewhere. I'd hug you but you smell."

Eugene laughed and signaled to Roger, who waited outside the door, to escort Linc out.

He punched in Natalie's number. She answered right away.

"Eugene?"

"Yeah. Natalie, I—"

"Are you okay?"

"I am. I'm so sorry. I got stuck at work. We had a major glitch with the ride, and I've been here with some of the team since yesterday. I just lost all track of time and I totally forgot—"

"You forgot. You couldn't just send a text to tell me you had to work and couldn't make it?"

"Like I said, I got involved."

"Uh-huh. Well, I'm happy to hear you weren't in an accident or suddenly ill or any of the other hundreds of things I imagined had happened that would have prevented you from answering my texts or picking up your phone when I called."

"Natalie, I—"

"You should get back to work. Goodnight, Eugene."

She clicked off, and the sound was like cymbals clanging in his ears.

Fuck. He'd screwed things up so badly. So not only was his work totally shit, so was his love life.

Great. Just fucking great.

CHAPTER NINETEEN

*D*elilah shook her head. "Men. They get into their heads about work. Or sports. Or a hundred other things, and then we slide on down to the bottom of their so called 'things that are most important to me' list."

"Yes, well, I don't ever intend to be put at the bottom of any man's list ever again."

"That's an excellent way of thinking, honey. Always prioritize yourself. And me. And your clients."

Natalie laughed. Delilah definitely had her priorities on straight.

She went over her checklist with Delilah to finalize the design on Paula and Fred's house. They were out of town for the next few days, which was perfect timing. Everything should be delivered to the house by late this afternoon, and she'd have two days to get the design in order. It was a huge order, and unfortunately, Delilah had a major design of her own to finish off for another client and would be unavailable to help her, which meant Natalie had to do this alone.

She'd already enlisted the help of her mother and Hazel, who said they'd take care of the kids and the dog while Natalie concentrated on getting her clients' house completed.

Delilah laid her hand over Natalie's arm. "You got this, honey?"

Natalie nodded. "I've totally got this. You don't need to worry about a thing. Paula and Fred are going to love everything."

"Oh, I don't worry about you and your design expertise. I meant personally."

She shrugged. "I'll be fine. I'm always fine."

Delilah gave her a half smile. "But maybe indulge yourself with a spa day after you finish this design, okay?"

"Definitely."

Natalie spent the rest of the day coordinating with the various vendors. She made her way to Paula and Fred's house to await the first delivery, which, fortunately, arrived promptly as scheduled. She was just about to dig into the first box when her phone buzzed.

It was a call. From Eugene.

He'd texted and called her multiple times over the course of the past few days, and she hadn't answered. Still furious with him for not bothering to send her one simple text saying he couldn't make it, she figured she wasn't important enough to bother with. And now, neither was he.

She let the call go. Except he called again. Which she ignored again. But then he called again.

Dammit. She thought about turning her phone off, but she

was waiting for delivery services to call and text, so she pushed the button. "Stop calling me."

"I'm not going to stop calling you until you agree to see me. We need to talk."

"No. I'm not going to see you, and we have nothing to talk about."

"Natalie. I'm sorry. I know I screwed up. Give me a chance to apologize."

"I'm working. I have a huge client and barely enough time to finish this design on time."

"Then let me help. We'll talk things out while you work."

She frowned. "What? No."

"I can be your manual labor. I'll do whatever you say."

She so wanted to hang up on him and never speak to him again, but she could really use the help. "Fine. I'll text you the address."

"Great. I'll be right there."

With a disgusted sigh, she hung up and texted him the address.

She'd use him to help her finish up this house on time, and then she'd tell him he was no more important to her than she'd obviously been to him.

And that would be the end of their relationship.

The thought of it made her stomach twinge, but it was for the best. The last thing she wanted was to allow him to hurt her, and what he'd done was a clear sign that falling for Eugene would hurt her.

No way was she going to allow that to happen.

*E*ugene had stopped along the way to pick up a cup of Natalie's favorite iced coffee, hoping the small token would at least entice her to open the door. Beyond that, he was going to have to do an enormous amount of groveling.

He'd been kicking his own ass ever since he'd been so in his own head about work that he hadn't bothered to check his phone. He just had to hope she'd forgive him.

He pulled into the driveway of the house.

Big damn house. Fancy, too. He got out of the car, grabbed the coffee, and walked up the steps to the porch to ring the bell.

After a minute, the door opened and Natalie stood there.

"Hey," he said, keeping it friendly and casual. "I brought you an iced latte."

She looked at the coffee, then back at him, taking the coffee from his outstretched hand. "Thanks. Come on, we have work to do."

At least she let him in, which he considered a small victory.

The floors were hardwood, at least wherever there wasn't marble, like the entryway. As he went in farther, he saw tall ceilings and so much light from all the huge windows.

"This place is outstanding," he said.

"Yes, it is."

He also saw boxes strewn everywhere and various people wandering around.

"Your crew?"

153

She took a sip of the coffee, then nodded. "A few installers for drapes and shutters. Otherwise, I'll be doing the rest of the décor."

"Okay, then. Put me to work."

Natalie figured that Eugene would spend all of his time just hanging out and doing nothing while she did all the work.

She was wrong. He'd hung pictures, put up shelving, arranged objects on said shelving over and over again until she was satisfied, and never once complained. He'd fluffed sofa pillows, bed pillows, and even dog bed pillows without making fun of the process or the outcome.

"The client has specific likes—and dislikes," she explained. "And two very cute but discerning Pomeranians."

"Which would explain the dog bed setup, right?"

"Yes. The client always gets what they want. Unless I can talk them out of it."

"Hey, you get paid if they're happy. And if they're really happy, you get referrals for even more business."

"You understand."

"Yup."

He walked around to see the place tastefully decorated. Not his style, but he could imagine the clients being extremely happy. It was colorful but not garishly so, with pale lavender colors and bold grays.

Natalie definitely had an eye for design. There were shelves with plants and knickknacks, but not so many that it was over-loaded. More conversation pieces and things that added texture to the place.

The art was outstanding.

"How do you choose the art?" he asked after he hung a beautiful modern oil with mixed colors in the entryway.

She studied the picture, and he didn't know if she thought it was crooked or if she just liked the art. "I have long conversations with the clients before the project starts. We go over their likes and dislikes. Some people dislike art entirely and only want family portraits adorning their walls. Others like bare walls."

"Ugh. That's kind of sterile."

"Right? Anyway, Paula and Fred love colorful art, something that tells a story that every viewer can interpret on their own. So no people or faces or objects, just impressions."

He looked at the myriad of colors and shapes in the art in the foyer. "You have a good eye. This is some cool shit."

She laughed. "Thank you. Though the homeowners already had some fantastic art pieces. I just picked up a few more."

He turned to face her. "You're gonna do the same with my house, right?"

"You want art?"

"Well, yeah."

"So, no framed pieces of your video games?"

He snorted out a laugh. "Maybe in the game room. Nowhere else."

She nodded. "We'll discuss what you like. We can go shopping at some of the art shops so you can peruse in person. Or, you can do that on your own and tell me what you like."

"I'd rather we do that together. If you want to."

With every step in their conversation, she felt that icy resolve melting, and she didn't want it to. So, instead, she lifted a shoulder. "You're the client. Whatever your preference."

"Natalie." He moved in closer. "Can we take a minute and talk?"

She didn't want to talk. She was still angry. And hurt. But she'd told him they could have a conversation, and he had worked his ass off all day.

"Fine. We'll take a short break." She turned and walked into the kitchen, reached into the cooler she'd brought and pulled out two bottles of cold water, handing one to him. They took seats at the kitchen table.

Eugene scooted the chair within an inch of hers, their knees touching. Just the simple touch of his knees to hers sent a jolt through her.

Ridiculous.

"Natalie. I am so sorry about what happened. I could make excuses and tell you that when something goes wrong with game design everything other than fixing it gets pushed to the side, but that's no excuse. It was a terrible thing to do to you and I know it must have hurt you to think that I blew you off."

"I was worried about you. I know I have no right—"

"You have every right. We had plans and I didn't show up. And when you texted and called, I didn't respond. If our situations had been reversed, I'd have panicked. I'm so sorry I put you through that, and I don't blame you for being angry. I know you don't trust me, but believe me when I tell you this has been a wake-up call. It won't happen again."

She blew out a breath. "I appreciate the apology."

He picked up her hand, reading her hesitation. "But?"

"But . . . I don't know. I've already had years of not being a priority in someone's life. I'm not fond of repeating that."

"Give me a chance to show you that you are important to me. Let me make up for this."

Part of her wanted to shut him down, to tell him whatever it was between them was over. But the flame between them still burned hot. And his apology had felt sincere. Plus, he looked so damn hot right now in his dark jeans and black-and-white button-down shirt with the sleeves pushed up over his muscular forearms that all she could think about was climbing on his lap and rocking against him until he threw her to the floor and . . .

Wait. She was working. And this wasn't even her house.

Banishing those thoughts, she stood. "We'll give it another shot."

His lips curved. "Okay. But for some reason that felt like a job interview."

He had a point, so she raised up on her toes and curved her hand around his neck, pulling him down for a blazing-hot kiss. He wrapped his arm around her and drew her against his rock-hard body, making her want to climb all over him.

Damn. Why had she kissed him? Why had she started this when she knew they wouldn't be able to finish?

Before she lost herself completely and they ended up on her

clients' very polished kitchen floor, she pulled herself away from Eugene's very delicious mouth and body, taking in a deep breath and grounding herself back in reality.

"Sorry," Eugene said, dragging his fingers through his lush hair.

Honestly. Did every movement he made have to be such a turn-on? She needed to get rid of him.

"I have to get back to work."

He cleared his throat and took a step back. "Right. Sorry. What do you need me to do?"

"I need you to leave so I can concentrate on said work without wanting to get naked and then get you naked."

His lips curved. "Okay, then. So . . . when can we pick this up again? Because I'd really like to see you." He smoothed his hands down her arms. "And touch you. I have much more apologizing to do."

She quivered in all the right places. "Sean has the kids Thursday night. You could come over. Or we could go out."

"I'll be happy to come over. Or go out. You choose."

"I'll text you then."

"Okay."

She walked him to the front door. He bent and brushed his lips across hers.

"Thursday," he said.

"Right." She closed the door behind him, then sighed in utter sexual frustration.

She pushed off the door and grabbed her phone, checking off what she'd accomplished from the to-do list.

Thanks to Eugene's help, she didn't have much left to do. Which meant she'd be out of here earlier than expected. She'd planned for a long night, so she'd gotten a sitter for the kids.

Free night. She grinned and texted Hazel.

> How would you feel about dinner and a spa night with your sister?

Hazel texted back a few minutes later. Sounds perfect!

Natalie booked the spa reservations, then made plans with Hazel to eat at their favorite Italian restaurant.

It was going to be a perfect night.

CHAPTER TWENTY

*E*ugene's plans with Natalie for Thursday never happened because her ex had suffered some kind of dental emergency, which meant that he couldn't take the kids that night. Natalie had apologized profusely, but Eugene had told her it was no big deal, and they could do something together another night.

In fact, the company he worked for was doing an event that weekend for all employees along with their family members. Since it was an amusement park, he figured the kids would enjoy it, so he asked Natalie about going on Saturday with the kids. He invited Hazel and Linc as well.

Surprisingly, everyone said yes, so they were all set to meet today at his house. He'd ordered a car that would fit everyone comfortably.

Hazel and Linc arrived first.

"I am so excited about this," Hazel said. "Linc is, too."

"Less than Hazel," Linc said. "I outgrew amusement parks years ago."

"Trust me," Eugene said. "You're going to enjoy this."

Natalie drove up, and Eugene saw the kids waving excitedly. He went over and helped them get out of the car.

"We're going to the park!" Christopher nearly bounced out of his tennis shoes.

"Yeah we are."

"I'm gonna have cotton candy today," Cammie said. "And ice cream."

"I like cotton candy, too," Natalie said, greeting him with a warm smile.

He really wanted to hug her. Kiss her. Feel her body against his. But currently there were four sets of eyes staring at him, so that wasn't going to happen.

Fortunately, the car pulled up, a sleek, black, and very roomy extended SUV. They got the kids set up, then everyone else climbed in.

There were drinks—nonalcoholic, unfortunately, but that's what they were going to deal with today. The kids were excited and exuberant, and they sang and watched the TV in the limo, so that helped pass the time.

Eugene looked over at Natalie. "It's going to be a long day. How's Grizelda going to handle it?"

"Oh, she's over at my house," Hazel said. "Hanging out with my herd."

"And was very excited to play," Natalie said. "I'm only hoping she'll want to go home with us when we pick her up tonight."

Hazel laughed. "Trust me, by the time the other dogs wear her out with play, she'll be more than ready to go home for some quiet snuggle time."

"I don't think hanging out with the kids is considered quiet."

"Aww, my sweet niece and nephew know how to snuggle their puppy, don't you?"

The kids were so focused on whatever show was on that they completely ignored Hazel.

Once they got to the park, Eugene showed his pass at the private entrance. They were all given VIP wristbands that would allow them to bypass any lines. They would also be able to eat free at all the restaurants.

God, he really hoped they all had a good time. Especially Natalie. Though he knew the park would be fun for the kids, he wanted Natalie to relax and have some fun, too.

Of course the first thing the kids wanted to do was ride one of the rollercoasters. Natalie grimaced, no doubt ready to give them the unfortunate news. Cammie was tall enough to ride but Christopher wasn't.

"I've got a great idea," Eugene said to the kids as they walked along. "Let's do this new ride. It's dark and kind of spooky, but still a lot of fun. What do you say?"

"I wanna do it," Christopher said.

"Me, too," Cammie said. "I'll hold your hand, Christopher, so you're not scared."

Eugene's heart squeezed at Cammie's sweet gesture. Having siblings was everything. He looked over at Linc, who frowned.

"What?" Linc asked. "You need me to hold your hand?"

Eugene laughed. "I'll try to be brave."

Surprising him, Natalie walked up next to him and took his hand. "I've got you. Just in case."

An even bigger surprise was Cammie taking his other hand. "We've both got you."

"Me, too," Christopher said, nudging in between Natalie and him to take Eugene's hand.

Linc came up behind him to whisper in his ear. "Cute family, dude."

He wanted to shout out that this wasn't his family, that it was all fun and games with Natalie and him, but he couldn't, because her kids were involved. And, like it or not, he'd gotten involved with her children, too.

Besides, the way he was surrounded by Cammie and Christopher, with Natalie taking Christopher's other hand? It felt like a family.

His family.

He waited for the familiar panic, that need to bail when things with a woman felt a little too close for comfort.

That feeling didn't come. Maybe it was because the kids were talking nonstop and his brother and Hazel were there so it felt more like a gathering of friends and family.

Yeah, that's what it was. A gathering. Of friends. Not family. Certainly not his family.

But it could be, if that's what you wanted.

Yeah, but it's not what Natalie wanted. And they'd both agreed their relationship was just for fun.

Christopher tugging on his hand drew him out of his wayward thoughts. He took in a deep breath and let it out, clearing his head.

They got on the ride and Natalie grabbed his arm. He looked over at her and saw she was a little pale.

"You okay?"

She gave him a faint smile. "Oh sure. I'm fine. Can't wait for this."

He wasn't sure how he felt about her answer. Maybe she was nervous about the kids and the ride. And maybe he should have chosen a milder ride. Too late now, though.

He thought it might be a little scary for Christopher, but, surprisingly, he was the one who laughed and screamed the loudest. Cammie enjoyed it, too.

Natalie, on the other hand, buried her head in his shoulder the entire time, refusing to even watch after the first jump scare. She gripped his arm so fiercely that he lost feeling in his hand. He put his arm around her and squeezed her tightly to his body.

After the ride was over, Christopher and Cammie jumped out. Hazel noticed how shaken Natalie was, so she grabbed the kids.

"Let's go get some cotton candy," she said, then turned to Eugene. "We'll be right over here."

He nodded and helped Natalie out of the ride. "How about something cold to drink?"

Her hand was shaking as she took his hand. "The kids."

"Hazel and Linc have them. Let's go sit down."

"Okay."

He took her to a nearby food and drink stop, taking Natalie inside. He sat her down at an empty table and went up to the counter, ordering two lemonades. He set the cup down in front of her.

"Drink," he said.

She picked it up and took a sip, then another. "Mmm," she said. "It's cold and sweet. Thanks."

He took a couple swallows, too. "Yeah, it's good."

After a couple more sips, she sighed. "I don't know what came over me. It went dark, then it got scary, and I freaked out."

"It happens."

"Not to me it doesn't. Well, I take that back. I used to have nightmares when I was a kid. Horror movies would terrify me. And the dark. But that was a long time ago."

He shrugged. "You'd be surprised how something can trigger those memories. Obviously today's ride did."

"I guess. Maybe the dark and that fucking creature jumping out at me."

"Sorry. I should have never—"

"You didn't know. I didn't even know."

"But I should have thought. I mean, Christopher is too young for something that intense."

She frowned. "Was he upset?"

"Actually, no. He laughed."

"Well. Good for him. I guess he's braver than his momma."

He rubbed her back. "I think you should give yourself a break. We all have our fears."

"Oh right. And what are you afraid of?"

"Clowns. And those rooms with all the mirrors. Freaks me right out."

"Huh. Well, that makes me feel marginally better."

"Good." He wound his fingers with hers. "It's okay to be afraid of things, Natalie. It's not a sign of weakness."

"Thank you." She finished her glass of lemonade. "I guess we should join everyone else."

"Sure." He stood and turned to leave, but she grabbed his hand and tugged him close.

She stepped into his body, and he wrapped his arms around her. "Thanks for holding on to me."

He sighed and laid his chin on top of her head. "Always."

The next ride was more adventure based, with some pretty awesome graphics. Eugene made some mental notes while also paying attention to Natalie, who grinned and squealed with enjoyment, so he was relieved about that. She seemed to be fully recovered from the trauma of the first ride, thankfully. Then the kids wanted to go on a water ride, and since it was hot out, no one complained about that, even when they got drenched. They dried out by walking around, stopping for pretzels along the way.

After two more rides, Christopher and Cammie both wanted lunch, so they stopped in one of the themed restaurants where it was dark and cool. The kids enjoyed the characters while the adults sat back and chilled.

"This was a lot more fun when we were kids," Hazel said, taking a long swallow of her iced tea.

"The parks were smaller then." Natalie rolled her neck back and forth. "Plus we weren't watching kids back then. Just ourselves."

"Point taken." Hazel sighed. "Growing up sucks."

"Oh, I don't know," Linc said, slinging his arm around the back of Hazel's chair. He slid his hand into her hair. "Being an adult has distinct advantages."

"Mmm, true. For example . . ."

"Hey, there are other people at this table," Natalie said. "Go get a room or something."

"Oh, could we?" Hazel asked. "Because I could use a massage. And a nap."

"You're all a bunch of lightweights," Eugene said motioning toward where the kids were giggling and laughing as they watched the ducks parading around in the pond that circled various restaurants. "The kids aren't tired."

"Because they're kids, Eugene," Natalie said. "They have the energy of the sun."

Eugene laughed. "If you need a long break, I can take the kids on rides after lunch."

Natalie shot him a surprised look. "You'd do that?"

"Sure. I like the rides. The kids like the rides. What's not to love about that?"

Natalie wasn't about to let Eugene run amok with her children doing God knows what. She'd get them back in an exhausted sugar high and then she'd be up all night with them. But the fact that he offered to let her rest while he took care of her kids meant everything.

She had no idea what had happened to her on that ride. Some kind of flashback from earlier times? No clue. She wasn't about to delve too deeply into the whys of it.

But as she sat there and ate with Eugene by her side while her sister and Linc kept the kids occupied, she realized how he had instinctively seemed to know exactly what she had needed, how he'd held her, comforted her while she totally lost her shit. He hadn't once made fun of her or tried to force her to shake off whatever fear had taken hold of her.

"You're staring at me," Eugene said, taking her out of her thoughts of admiration for him. "Is there something on my face?"

She smiled at him. "Just your face. Which is quite handsome, by the way."

After a quick glance down the table at the kids, who were laughing at something Linc had just said, he picked up her hand and pressed a quick kiss to it. "Keep complimenting me like that and I might think you like me."

"Oh, don't think that." But she couldn't pull her gaze away from his beautiful face. The way he smiled at her—so hot, so filled with intent—made her wish they were anywhere but here.

Just then, there was a tug on her shirt. Cammie whispered in her ear that she needed to go to the bathroom, so she got up, and Hazel went with them.

After, while they were washing their hands, Hazel looked over at her. "Are you all right?"

"I'm fine. Why do you ask?"

"Because you seemed terrified on that ride earlier."

Natalie looked over at Cammie, who was busy applying a more-than-necessary amount of soap to her hands, all the while singing a Taylor Swift song to herself.

"Oh yeah, I was. No idea what happened. But it's all good now."

"Thanks to Eugene coming to the rescue."

She laughed. "I don't think that had anything to do with it. More like a cold drink and some sunlight."

Hazel gave her a knowing look. "Sure."

"Look, Momma. My hands are all clean."

"So very clean," Natalie said.

Cammie dashed out the door and ran toward the table, sitting in the chair next to Eugene. Christopher came over and climbed onto Eugene's lap. They got up and walked down the steps to get closer to the ducks. Natalie and Hazel took a seat at the table to watch them.

"Your kids like him."

She nodded at Hazel's observation. "Yeah, they do."

"That worries you."

Natalie turned to face her sister. "Of course it does. We're not exactly a couple. We're just—"

"Just what?"

"I don't know what. But I don't want to mess with the kids' heads. Or their hearts. What if they get attached? Look at them, Hazel. They're already attached. Eugene intends to move on once he finishes his project." She blew out a frustrated breath. "I should end things with him now."

"Or, you could just continue the way it's going and see what happens."

"At the risk of my kids' hearts?" She shook her head. "No, I don't think so."

Hazel laid her hand on Natalie's arm. "I know you're afraid, but—"

"Of course I'm afraid. For them. It's my job to protect them."

"Natalie, they're fine. They're going to be fine. Kids are resilient. And, another thing. What happens if things work out between you and Eugene? Wouldn't that be awesome?"

"I can't count on that. Besides, I'm not looking for a relationship. Just me and the kids is all I need."

"Okay. I agree that is all you need. But what about what you want?"

It was a valid question. What did she want?

"I want to be happy. Which means if my kids are happy, then I am, too."

"Look, sis, I get that Camryn and Christopher take priority in your life—at least for now. That's admirable. But you know what? If you're good, then they are, too. You know what I mean?"

"To a certain extent I agree with you. And I am content. I'm living life on my own terms."

Hazel grimaced. "That sounds less than ecstatic."

Natalie had to laugh. "Okay, so I made it sound like I was flat and miserable. That's not the case at all. Granted, when I was married to Sean I wasn't happy, wasn't doing what fulfilled me. Don't get me wrong, I love being a mom. Raising those babies satisfies me in ways I never thought possible. But I'm also okay being single. Alone and single, you know?"

"I do know. But that doesn't mean you have to stay in the house and *be* alone. Do you know what I mean?"

"Yes."

Hazel squeezed her hand. "So quit thinking so far ahead. Just enjoy what you have right now, honey. Eugene is good to you and you have fun with him, right?"

"Right."

"Then have some fun and quit worrying about what happens

tomorrow. You're fine and the kids are fine. And they'll continue to be. Okay?"

She nodded. "Okay."

They went down and joined the guys and the kids, who were much more interested in the ducks frolicking than in anything else they'd done so far today.

Go figure.

But they also got bored after a while and asked if they could go do some more rides, so they headed out, with the kids hanging all over Linc after he'd told them a string of seriously corny dad jokes.

"See?" Hazel said as they walked behind the guys and kids. "The kids like everyone. It's not just Eugene."

Hazel was right. She'd overreacted, which had probably been due to her growing feelings for Eugene.

She needed to chill and just have fun. And let things between Eugene and her cool a little.

Things between them had been intense. Everything had happened so fast. If she could calm down and just have fun with him, take it all at a slower pace, it would all be fine.

She could definitely do that.

CHAPTER TWENTY-ONE

Have you ever been to New
York?

Eugene sent the text and waited. He went back to work on the ride design, trying to figure out how to get around a particular problem his team hadn't been able to work out. After about an hour with no resolution, his phone rang. Seeing it was Natalie, he punched the button.

"Hey."

"Hey, yourself," she said. "No, I've never been to New York. Why?"

He pushed back from his chair and stood, stretching his back. "I need to fly up there for a couple of days to check out a game design company we might want to bring on to assist with this project. I thought you might want to come with me. We could do some sight-seeing, eat a lot of good food, maybe see a Broadway show."

"Oh. That would be fun. When?"

He told her the dates. "I have to be there on Thursday. I thought we could stay over the weekend and fly home Sunday."

"Sean has the kids that weekend. I'll need to see about the other days. When do you need to know?"

"It's in a week, so I'll need to make reservations. So, as soon as you can?"

"Okay. I'll see what I can do."

"Sure."

"And, Eugene?"

"Yeah?"

"Thanks for asking."

He grinned even though she couldn't see. "Always thinking of you. Of us."

She went silent for a few seconds, then said, "Talk to you soon. Bye."

He hung up and continued staring out the window, feeling that familiar warmth he always felt after hearing Natalie's voice. Getting away alone with her for a few days would be great, would give the two of them more time to get to know each other better. And have some fun, too.

Hopefully it would all work out.

Natalie buried herself in work, pushing down the aggravation from her conversation with Sean. She was flipping through fabric books with angry intent when Delilah walked into the room.

"Something piss you off about that book?" she asked. "Or just not finding what you're looking for?"

Realizing she was about to rip pages from a very expensive sample book, she smoothed her hands over the pages and gently closed it, then turned to Delilah with a smile. "No. Sorry. The book is amazing."

"Okay, so it's not design related. That's a relief." Delilah studied her. "I'm going to guess it's either the ex or the current boyfriend."

Breathing in slowly before letting it out on an exasperating sigh, she said, "Definitely the ex."

"Wanna talk about it?"

"No. It'll just make me angrier. But thank you for the offer."

"Sure, honey. If I might offer a suggestion, talk to someone about it. That always helps."

"You're right, of course. Thanks, Delilah."

"Hey, I have two exes and three kids. I know all about it. And I'm always available to chat."

After Delilah left, Natalie went back to work, this time without the anger, deciding to push it aside until . . . well, until sometime after work, at least. When she finished for the day, she was grateful to have tomorrow's work schedule front and center on her mind instead of her selfish ex.

But first, Grizelda had a vet appointment. She gathered up her things and drove toward home, grateful that Sean had the kids tonight so all she had to deal with was the dog.

Grizelda wagged her little tail with excitement when Natalie opened the door. She laid her things down and picked up the pup to give her some love. Her dark little eyes shined with adoration. Nothing like puppy love.

"It's good to see you, too, baby girl. And, guess what? We're going for a ride so the vet can give you a checkup. Hopefully there won't be any s-h-o-t-s."

The dog gave her a happy wiggle.

"Okay, let's take a quick walk to get some of that excited energy out."

She put on Grizelda's harness and they did a stroll over a couple of blocks, Grizelda happily sniffing every blade of grass. When they got home she took several gulps out of her water bowl. Natalie put her in the car and buckled her to the seat belt, and they were on their way.

When she got to the vet's office, she was surprised to see Hazel in there.

They hugged and sat next to each other in the waiting area.

"What's wrong with Gordon?"

Hazel looked down at the pug, who was comfortably sleeping on Hazel's lap. "He's got a bit of a cough. Given his age, I didn't want to take any chances so I want the doc to check him over."

"I hope he's all right."

"Me, too." Hazel reached over to run her hands over Grizelda's fur. "Is Griz okay?"

"She's fine. It's our first visit. I know she's spayed and has all her shots, but I just wanted to establish our relationship with the vet and make sure she's all healthy."

"Aww. You're a good mom, Natalie."

Her sister always knew how to make her feel good. "Thanks. Though if you asked Sean he'd tell you I'm the worst mother ever."

"Sean's a prick. What did he do now?"

"Eugene invited me to go to New York for a few days next week. It's Sean's weekend so no problem there, but I asked him if he'd keep the kids for a couple of extra days. He told me that I'm failing in my parental responsibilities in order to go off and have—and I quote—'an affair.'"

Hazel blinked. "What? He does realize you two are divorced, doesn't he?"

"Sometimes I wonder. Anyway, then he concluded by saying he's very busy and has all his days and evenings booked. And that next time I need to give him advance notice."

"I . . . don't even know what to say to that." Hazel shook her head. "I'm sorry you have to deal with him."

"Thanks. Me, too."

Hazel was called in for Gordon, so Natalie hugged her sister, and not too long after that the vet tech called her name.

"Okay, sweet girl," she said, scooping Grizelda up. "Your turn."

Of course, Grizelda was perfect, and Dr. Smith was amazing and took his time looking her over completely. They scheduled her next appointment, and she was on her way.

She stopped at the coffee shop for an iced mocha latte, and got a pup cup for Grizelda, who was so excited she nearly burst through the window of the drive-through. But she got oohed and ahhed on by the staff, and Natalie made a mental note to do this more often with the pup. The kids would get a kick out of it as well.

After they got home, Grizelda curled up on her bed and went right to sleep.

"That was a lot of excitement for you today, wasn't it, girl?" Natalie took her coffee and went to sit at the kitchen table, scrolling through her phone to read her emails, making sure nothing critical had come up.

The doorbell rang and Grizelda jumped up and barked, then ran to the door.

Natalie followed, checking the security through her phone to see it was her mom. Grizelda stood at the door, barking away. Some people might find that annoying, but a good guard dog sounded mean, and Grizelda definitely had that covered. Not that she'd bite anyone. She was a marshmallowy fluff ball. No one on the other side of that door knew that, though.

"Sit, Grizelda," she said.

The dog sat, but still at full attention, her focus fully on the door as Natalie opened it.

"Mom. What a surprise. Come on in."

"I know I should have called first," her mother said as she came in and bent to pat Grizelda on the head before moving down the hall.

Natalie followed behind.

"But I talked to Hazel," her mom continued, "and the two of us realized that something needed to be done."

"Something needed to be done about what?"

"Could I have some coffee?"

"Oh. Of course." She brewed a cup of coffee for her mom, then brought cream and sugar to the table where her mom had taken a seat. Natalie pulled up a chair across the table.

Mom took her sweet time pouring the cream and adding a teaspoon of sugar. Then stirring, stirring, stirring.

"Mom."

"Yes." She took a sip of coffee.

"What's this about?"

She laid the cup down. "Well. Hazel called me and told me about your planned trip to New York, and your horrible ex-husband's inability to care for his own children."

"Oh. That."

"Yes, that. Natalie, while you can't do much about Sean other than his contractual visitation obligations, you can always rely on your family. All you have to do is ask."

"If it was some kind of emergency or a work situation, I absolutely would, Mom. But you have a job and a life of your own. And this is just a fun trip. I can say no to Eugene."

"You're entitled to have a good time, Natalie, something that was sorely lacking in your marriage to Sean. I have a very flexible work schedule, so Paul and I will watch the children on the days Sean is"—she coughed for emphasis—"unavailable. And Hazel will watch your dog. Now make your plans with Eugene and go have a good time."

Her mother had always been so stern with her and so fond of Sean. Even after Natalie told her they were divorcing, Mom had been so certain it would be a mistake. Until Natalie had cried and spilled everything about how unhappy she'd been.

Her ex wasn't a monster. He just liked things his way, and her opinion had never counted. Her mom had been especially livid when Natalie had explained that she wanted more out of her life, and that she had given up her career to fulfill Sean's family-life ideals. It was then that her mother had decided he was worse than dirt. Her mom might come off as proper and old-fashioned, but

Natalie had been shocked to discover her mother was quite the feminist and thought no man should hold a woman back from her dreams.

"Okay. I'll go."

"Excellent." She took another sip of her coffee. "Now that that's settled, how about we go have a nice dinner? My treat."

"Mom, I'd love to have dinner with you. Where's Paul?"

She got up and waved her hand. "He's at the country club with the guys. I do have my own life, dear. And so should you."

Her mother was definitely right about that.

She might be opinionated as hell and often wrong about a lot of things, but it was a revelation to discover that her mom was always in her corner. She probably always had been, but Natalie had butted heads with her so much she hadn't noticed.

And that felt great.

CHAPTER TWENTY-TWO

*T*o be honest, Eugene was kind of surprised that Natalie had agreed to take this trip with him, especially since it was such short notice. But he was happy as hell she agreed.

He'd offered to pick her up, but she'd told him she had a bunch of stuff to do this morning so she'd meet him at the airport. They had a super early flight so he had no idea what she could possibly do before six a.m., but he didn't question it.

After he checked in, he grabbed a coffee and took his seat in the boarding area, sending some email instructions to his team here in Orlando. He'd only be gone four days, and he knew his team would be right on the ball as usual. They knew their jobs and they did them well, but he still wanted to follow up on a few items of a critical nature.

Heath emailed him back almost immediately: Calm down boss. Go have some fun. We've got this. We'll only have drunken office parties after hours and we promise to clean up after.

Eugene laughed.

"Something funny?"

He looked up to find the most beautiful woman he'd ever seen standing in front of him. Natalie looked amazing in long black leggings, a white tee, black cardigan, and white tennis shoes. Simple outfit, but her hair fell like shiny brown silk against her cheeks, and her lips sparkled crimson, making him want to grab her and mess up those lips with a hot kiss.

He got up and took the bag from her hands, slid his arm around her, and pressed a kiss to her cheek, not wanting to mess up those lips. Not yet, anyway. "Nothing funny. You look spectacular."

"Stop." She took a seat and he sat next to her. "Okay, don't stop."

He smiled and picked up her hand. "Ready to go?"

"So ready. When I tell you it was a lot of maneuvering to get all the chess pieces in place for me to take this trip . . . well, it was."

"I'm sorry. I wasn't thinking about your kids and the dog and your job. I should have been more sensitive to your obligations."

"Oh, the job part was easy. I'm not at a critical point with any of my design clients—including you. It was just the kids and the dog."

"Sean isn't taking them?"

"He is for his normal designated weekend. But not for today and tomorrow. My mom and Paul are watching them. I dropped them off last night."

Eugene frowned. "Why wouldn't Sean take them the extra days?"

"Honestly? I have no idea. He launched into some denigrating conversation about how it's my responsibility to take care of my children, and that he shouldn't have to give up the things that are important to him just because I want to jet off with my lover."

Eugene choked out a laugh. "What? Was he being serious?"

"Oh, he was definitely serious. He's very traditional in that way. The woman stays home and takes care of the kids. No career, no girls' weekends."

"So, no fun for you, then. He thought of you as basically just an unpaid nanny."

"Yes."

He took her hand. "I'm sorry. You must have been miserable."

"Actually, not at first. I know I'm making him out to be the bad guy, and from a feminist point of view, he definitely was that. But he was also kind and generous and loves his children. I think he's having a really hard time reconciling with the divorce and the fact that I didn't turn out to be the ideal wife he thought I'd be."

"Oh, too bad for him. And if he really loved his children he'd be thrilled to spend as much time with them as he could. Don't make excuses for him, Natalie. He's a jerk, and he needs to do some work on himself."

She sighed. "You're right, of course. But he's also the father of my children, and they love him. So all I can do is hope he realizes the mistakes he's made and corrects them."

Eugene realized he was stepping into something that wasn't his business and it was time to back off. "Of course. I have no right to interject my opinion."

She lifted her gaze to his. "No, you can feel free to say anything you want."

"And you can feel free to tell me to shove it, okay?"

"Deal."

"Now, enough about your ex. Let's talk fun plans for our trip. Anything you really want to do when we're in New York?"

He saw the way she relaxed, and he was happy about that. He made a mental note not to mention her ex again unless she brought it up and asked for his opinion. There were some things that were hot-button, don't-talk-about-it issues.

Ex-husbands definitely rated at the top of that list.

*T*heir flight into New York City went surprisingly smoothly. They grabbed their luggage and Eugene had arranged for a car to pick them up outside. Having never been to New York, Natalie gawked at everything as they drove into Manhattan.

Other than her and Sean's honeymoon in the Bahamas, she'd never been anywhere exciting. Or anywhere, really. She'd gone to college for fashion design at the University of Florida, hadn't taken any trips outside of the state while in school, so other than traveling throughout the state, and then her honeymoon, she'd been nowhere.

Until now.

Today it was cloudy and rainy. The city looked nothing at all like where she lived. Buildings butted up against each other as if they were the best of friends, and dark clouds hovered over each skyscraper. It looked ominous and utterly magnificent.

The car let them out at their hotel. She'd never seen anything so fancy. Decorated with subtle shades of bronze and dark gray, the lobby welcomed them in hushed tones. No toddlers running around screaming. This was a place of business, catering to business people. Natalie had to admit she didn't mind that at all. She loved her kids, but she gave a lot of herself to them. A few days away would be a nice, refreshing vacation.

Eugene got the keys to their room, and they took the elevator. He swiped his key across a pad, and the elevator started moving

"This place is nice," she said. "Fancy and quiet."

"The company booked it," he said. "So I imagine it's for frequent business travelers. Not exactly a vacay spot."

The elevator kept going until they reached the fifteenth floor. It opened onto an expansive lobby. At the desk, a guy wearing the hotel's uniform smiled at them.

"Your card, sir?"

Eugene handed over his card, and the man swiped it. "Mr. Kennedy, Mrs. Kennedy, welcome. My name is Michael, and I'll be your concierge. If you need anything such as show tickets, a car, directions, sightseeing tours, or dinner reservations, please call on me. Cocktails start at four p.m. with hors d'oeuvres. If there's anything else I can help you with, please don't hesitate to ask." He handed both of them one of his cards.

"Thanks, Michael," Eugene said, taking back his key. They walked to their room at the end of the hall, and Eugene opened the door.

"Whoa," Natalie said, stepping into what looked more like an apartment. A very elegant one, too. Very upscale, ultramodern, with a spacious living room, office, dining area, bar, and a separate bedroom. The bathroom had a luxurious tub and an oversize steam shower.

She walked back out to the bedroom, staring down at the amazing king-size bed.

"What do you think?" Eugene asked.

She turned around to face him. "I think your company treats you very well."

"I think so, too." He slid his arms around her. "Nice to be alone with you here."

She wound her hand around his neck. "I agree."

She brought his head toward hers, and he kissed her, his fingers tightening around her hips. Anticipation filled her as she ran her hands along his arms, feeling all that barely leashed tension coiled within his body.

His lips slid across hers, teasing and enticing as he tangled his tongue with hers. Desire enveloped her until all she wanted was to explore every inch of him.

She kicked off her shoes and pulled him down on the bed with her, rolling over on top of him. Just the feel of his body aligned with hers was a huge turn-on, ratcheting her need for him up another ten levels.

She rose up, squeezing his hips with her thighs. "You feel good," she said, sliding her hands under his shirt. "Your skin is warm against my hands."

"I like where you're sitting, but let's get some clothes off." He swept his fingers along her shirt, teasing them up underneath it. Her stomach rippled with that brief touch. And when he swept his hand under her shirt and cupped her breast, her nipples stood up and took notice. She wore a front-clasp bra, and he undid it in seconds. She removed her top and slid the bra off, anxious to feel his hands on her breasts.

And, oh, he was very good with his hands, teasing her nipples until her sex tingled with need and anticipation. She leaned forward so he could taste and suck, and she swore she was close to coming.

He flipped her onto her back, rising up to remove his shirt. He slid off the end of the bed, kicked off his shoes, then unbuckled the belt of his jeans, slowly sliding the zipper down as his gaze stayed on hers.

"This is a very good show," she said, focusing on his beautiful cock as he dropped his boxer briefs. "Do you sell tickets?"

He took his cock in hand and began to stroke it. "Only to a very select party of one."

She reached up with her foot to slide along his stomach, and lower, gently teasing his cock with her toes.

Suddenly her foot was grabbed and Eugene dragged her down the bed. He leaned over her and grasped the waistband of her leggings, pulling them down, then off. He climbed over her, nibbling at her hip until she giggled. He tugged her underwear over her hips, down her legs, circling them around his finger. He gave her a hot grin before tossing them in a nearby chair.

"Have I mentioned how beautiful you are naked?" he asked. "I mean, you look fucking awesome with clothes on, too. But like this?" He smoothed his hands along her thighs, spreading her legs. "Everything about you is beautiful."

"Your hands on me is what's beautiful." She lifted, asking without words for him to touch her.

He started with his hands, using his thumbs to circle and tease her sex, driving her wild with easy, gentle circles. And when she thought she might go wild from the sensations, he cupped her butt to tilt her up and put his mouth on her, using his tongue to lick and suck and drive her right to the edge of reason.

Unable to hold back from the deliciousness of his relentless hot, wet, swipes of his tongue across her clit, she came with a wild cry, grabbing on to the sheets for some semblance of reality.

When she could breathe again, she felt the kisses along her stomach and hip and smiled. She lifted her head. "You nearly killed me."

He looked up at her. "Sounded like it. I do know CPR, just in case."

She patted the side of the bed to summon him beside her. He crawled up and dropped down next to her. She rolled over on top of him, gliding her hands over his chest before dipping her head down to tease a kiss from his lips. She deepened the kiss, slipping her tongue into his mouth to slide along his, making her sex throb with reawakened desire. His cock was hard and pulsing underneath her and she rocked against it, rewarded by his guttural groan. When he grabbed her hips and rolled her back and forth over his shaft, that was all she could take.

"I brought condoms," she said.

"Me, too."

"Mine are closer." She climbed off of him and reached down onto the floor where she'd dropped her carry-on. Diving into the depths, she pulled out a box of condoms and tossed them onto the bed.

"A box." Eugene nodded. "I'm impressed."

"Shut up and let's get one on you."

He ripped open the package and applied the condom, which was damn sexy to watch. Natalie grasped his cock and slid down, taking her time to fill herself with his length and thickness.

"Mmm," she said, tilting her head back as she felt the pulses within her. She started to move, and Eugene moved with her, holding on to her as she rode him, giving herself pleasure, feeling Eugene's intensify as his grip on her tightened, and they rode their way into oblivion together.

Panting, she collapsed on top of him, her head on his chest as she listened to the rhythm of his heartbeat. He rubbed her back and there was no place else she'd rather be in the entire world right now.

"Pizza," he whispered.

She lifted her head. "What?"

"We should go out and wander. See the sights. Be tourists. Eat pizza."

That all sounded perfect. Just like the man underneath her. She wanted him over and over. But they were here to sightsee and eat. And have oodles of sex. Which they could do right now.

Then again, she was hungry.

"Yes, let's go have some pizza."

CHAPTER TWENTY-THREE

*E*ugene hated that he had to be in business meetings all day, but of course, that was the reason for the trip.

On the plus side, he was currently surrounded by design geniuses. They'd gone over his plans for the ride, and he'd outlined some of the programming problems that were giving him and his team fits. They'd suggested some awesome, time-saving solutions that would save them several weeks in the creation process and had pinpointed a few flaws in the programming. He could have kicked himself for not seeing where things had been going wrong, but he knew for a fact that a fresh set of eyes could help, and he'd been right. Plus, they had bonded over most of the games he loved, and a couple were fans of his work. What wasn't to like about that?

On their break, he grabbed his phone, smiling when he saw pics that Natalie had sent him. They'd had breakfast together in the hotel this morning, and he'd told her that Michael could set her up with some tours, but she wanted to go exploring on her own.

Now he saw that she'd done the Statue of Liberty tour and was headed to the Empire State Building. After that, she planned to do some shopping.

She hadn't seemed afraid to be off on her own exploring, which made him feel a little less guilty about being tied up in meetings all day.

Tonight, though, they'd have a nice dinner together.

He couldn't wait to see her.

Natalie had always loved shopping. But shopping here? A whole new experience. She tried not to overdo it, had gotten a few gifts for Camryn and Christopher, and had picked up a scarf she knew her mom would love. She'd found some "I ♥ NY" dog T-shirts for Hazel's dogs, which she knew Hazel would enjoy way more than a gift for herself, but she still bought matching shirts for Hazel and Linc. How cute would they all look in a pic together in their shirts? And she'd splurged a little on an outfit for herself. Eugene had told her he was taking her out to dinner. Sure, she'd brought plenty of clothes from home, but she could totally justify the new dress. She'd seen it at the shop and just had to try it on. And once on, it had molded to her body as if it had been made just for her.

It was like a sign that the dress had to belong to her. She couldn't say no. After all, she already had the perfect shoes to go with the dress.

When she got back to the hotel, she put all the packages away and hung the dress in the closet. She made herself a cold drink, then kicked off her shoes and put her feet up in the comfortable chair and called her mom to check on the kids.

"Shouldn't you be focusing entirely on having fun?" her mom asked.

"I am having fun. I went and did touristy things today while Eugene worked. Oh, and I shopped."

"Shopping is very exciting there."

"Yes, it is. How are the kids doing?"

"They're just fine. Paul and I took them out for pizza last night, then we came home and played games until bedtime. Tonight we're making tacos, and Christopher wants to build a fort in the living room. I'm putting Paul in charge of that."

"They love tacos. And games of all kinds. Make sure they put all the fort things away when they're done."

"Oh, no worries there."

"Thanks again for doing this, Mom. I really appreciate it."

"And I appreciate having time with my grandchildren. You should go away more often."

She laughed. They chatted awhile longer, then she hung up, took a deep breath, and let it out. Her kids were in good hands with her mom, and Hazel already told her that she and Linc were going to take the kids out on Friday night so Mom and Paul could have a break.

She was so grateful to have her mother and sister in her life, especially in light of her ex-husband not being as cooperative a parent as she would have liked. But she couldn't make him step up and take responsibility for his children with the enthusiasm everyone else had for the kids, so she'd make sure her kids were extra loved by her family.

The door opened and Eugene walked in, looking especially

delicious in a suit, though he carried the jacket over his arm, and the sleeves of his white shirt were rolled up to his elbows.

She warmed just looking at him, then got up and went over to him, curling her hand around his neck. "Hi. How was your day?"

His lips curved and he drew her against him. "It was good." He kissed her, a long, lingering kiss. "It's perfect now. How was your day?"

She stepped back and took his suit jacket to the closet to hang it up. "It was good. I had fun today. How about you?"

He went to the bar and fixed himself a cold drink. "It was productive. We got a lot accomplished and a few problems resolved."

"That's good." She took a seat in the living room, and he sat next to her.

"Tell me everything about your day."

She loved that he'd asked, that he was even interested. She gave him a rundown of all the fun she'd had sightseeing, shared some pictures she had taken, and told him about the gifts she'd bought for her family.

"They're going to love those," he said, running his hand along her thigh.

"I got a gift for you as well."

He gave her a curious look. "You did? Really?"

"Yes." She got up and went to the closet, bringing back a gift bag and handing it to him as she took a seat next to him.

"You didn't have to do this." He held the bag with both hands, but hadn't yet looked to see what was in it.

"I saw it and thought of you." She waited, but he still hadn't moved. "Open the bag, Eugene."

He did, pulling out the box. He looked at her and frowned, then opened the box and gave her a surprised look.

"I noticed you didn't wear a smart watch."

He shrugged. "Not really my thing."

"But I thought you might want one that just tells time." She held up her wrist to show him her watch. "I don't always like to have to look at my phone to see what time it is."

"This is . . . wow. It's really cool, Natalie." He took the watch out and slid it on his wrist.

Natalie had to admit that it looked sexy on him. A gunmetal gray, it was simple in design and utterly masculine.

"This is really cool," he said, staring down at the watch before looking up at her. "Thank you, Natalie."

He leaned over and brushed a gentle kiss across her lips.

"You're welcome."

He grasped her hand in his. "You surprised me. That rarely happens to me."

"You should get surprised more often." She lifted up and kissed him. "I'm going to go get ready for dinner."

"Okay. Me, too."

She went into the bathroom, smiling as she got dressed.

The night was starting out perfectly. And it was only going to get better.

CHAPTER TWENTY-FOUR

*E*ugene looked in the dining room mirror and adjusted his tie. The blue suit looked good. And the watch? Still a damn shock.

He'd gotten birthday and Christmas presents, sure. But an out-of-the-blue gift from a woman? He had to admit that was a first. That Natalie thought enough about him to choose something so personal made him feel . . .

Hell, he didn't exactly know how he felt other than really good.

"You look amazing."

He looked up and caught sight of Natalie in the mirror.

Whoa. He turned around and saw her coming toward him, wearing a short, cream-colored dress that showcased every single one of her incredible assets.

"Wow. You look . . . stunning."

"Well, thank you." She turned and reached for her bag before moving in front of him. Eugene didn't know whether to look at her amazing legs, the way that dress showed tantalizing hints of cleavage, or the way it cupped her incredible ass. But her knowing smile? The one that said she knew she looked damn fine? That was the killer, especially with her lips painted that irresistible shade of hot pink.

He teased his fingers along the column of her throat, down her arm, and took hold of her hand. "You sure about going out for dinner? Because I could get that dress off of you in about ten seconds."

Her lips curved. "Oh, we're definitely going out, and you can wait for . . . dessert . . . until later."

He heaved in a breath, let it out, and said, "If you insist."

They took a car to the restaurant. He'd made reservations at Le CouCou. He'd eaten there before on previous trips and the food and atmosphere were excellent.

"This place looks really nice," Natalie said as they were seated at a table against the wall. The server came over and offered up the wine list, asking if they wanted something else to drink. Eugene looked to Natalie.

"I'll have water for now, but I think I'll definitely want some wine." She looked to Eugene, who asked for the same.

He perused the wine list, then handed it over to Natalie.

"Choose something that looks good to you," he said.

"Okay."

She studied it for a few minutes, then sild the list back to him. "The zinfandel looks good. What do you think?"

He nodded and closed the list, ordering a bottle when their server returned with their water.

They looked over their menus and talked about all the items, whether they wanted appetizers or salads, and what they might be in the mood for.

"I'm thinking the Dover sole," Natalie said. "Or maybe the halibut. Though the sea bass looks good, too."

"So, you're ordering all three?"

She laughed. "No. I'll figure it out. What are you having?"

"The filet. Or the duck. Maybe the lamb."

"Now who's having trouble deciding?"

Their server returned, opened and poured their wine, then asked if they had any questions about the menu. Natalie surprised Eugene by deciding immediately on the sea bass, while Eugene went an entirely different direction and ordered the lobster. They agreed on an appetizer, and the server left to place their order.

Eugene lifted his glass. "To us, and this trip together."

She tipped her glass to his, her gaze locked to his. "To us."

She sipped her wine and licked her lips, and his gaze tracked her tongue, his stomach tightening as he thought about how warm and wet her tongue felt wrapped around his.

"This is really nice, Eugene," she said. "You didn't have to go so fancy."

"You deserve fancy. And a whole lot more."

"You've already given me a lot. Just being able to get away for a few days is so incredibly fun and relaxing. You have no idea."

"I'm glad you're having a good time so far." He picked up his wineglass and took a swallow, then set it down. "So. What are the plans for tomorrow?"

"I'm going to storm the fashion district."

"Uh-oh. Should I warn them in advance?"

"It's best they don't know I'm coming."

He let out a short laugh. "Okay, then. But, seriously, did you bring an empty suitcase for fabric?"

She shrugged and swirled the liquid around in her glass. "Everything can be shipped."

"You're very smart."

She took a sip of her wine and smiled at him over the rim. "Yes. I am."

"That means you have a list of what you want."

"Not really. I want to explore, see what's out there, what strikes me and I just have to have it. I've been meaning to reupholster one of my favorite chairs that my grandmother gave me, and I'm looking for fabric for it. I just haven't found anything that hits the mark yet."

"Mmm. So sometimes you look at a fabric and it just grabs you by the gut, and then you'll know it's exactly what you need?"

Her lips curved at his understanding. "Yes. That's it exactly."

He couldn't really appreciate the whole fabric thing, but what he did get was knowing when a thing was meant to be, that it just fit. It was a lot like his job, when he was designing a game and bits and pieces fell into place. That sense of rightness, of satisfaction, really hit his happy meter. Maybe it wasn't exactly the same as what Natalie was talking about, but he understood where she was coming from.

They enjoyed their appetizer and chatted about the kids. Eugene talked about his brothers, and he was struck by how easily conversation flowed with Natalie. Throughout their dinner, they never ran out of things to talk about, from family to work to their varied interests. He liked that they weren't exactly the same. That meant he had things to learn from her. It also didn't hurt that he could sit and watch her for hours, because she was so beautiful and animated and passionate when she talked.

"So then Mariah had the audacity to tell me that Cammie couldn't be in the same ballet class as her daughter because Bellamy had been dancing since she was six months old, which was the most ridiculous thing I'd ever heard."

Eugene swallowed the bite of lobster he had taken, then frowned. "Wait. Babies can't walk that early, can they?"

"Of course not. Bellamy might have been wiggling her butt then, but ballet? Please."

"Wow. Some moms are really . . . something, huh?"

She stabbed fish onto her fork and nodded. "Understatement."

"I can't imagine the bullshit you have to deal with being a parent. Not just arguing with your ex, but the one-upmanship from other moms, too?"

"Everything's a competition these days. It's exhausting. I feel bad for the kids who have friends with shitty overly competitive parents. Instead of letting them just have fun, it's a constant requirement that they be the best."

Eugene had no idea. "That sets them up for failure. Or at the very least resentment."

"Right? There's plenty of time for vigorous competition when they get older. Why not just let them have fun and make friends when they're little?"

"I don't disagree. So what's your solution to the ballet competition?"

"I talked to Cheryl, the owner of the ballet studio, to make sure she wasn't on the same wavelength as Mariah. She definitely wasn't. There are no tryouts, and they all go in the same classes by age group. They aren't separated by skill level until they reach middle school age, and even then, there are still beginner level classes for kids who are just starting out."

"Seems fair."

"It does, and I was relieved to hear that Cammie wasn't going to have to get competitive. Not yet, anyway. Not that my daughter isn't competitive. She's very fierce in that regard."

Eugene laughed and lifted his glass for a sip. "Hey, nothing wrong with wanting to win or be the best at what you do."

"True. And I'm fine with that. I just don't want either of my kids to be forced into something if they're not ready."

"I understand that. How about Christopher?"

"He's ready to tear it all down at a moment's notice."

Eugene laughed. "So, a little competitive, huh?"

"Very. He's looking forward to soccer season."

"I loved playing soccer. I wanna see Christopher play."

She gave him a curious look. "You would? I know he'd enjoy that."

"Good. Let me know when his games start."

"He's little, you know. They're not exactly what I'd call official games."

"I know," he said with a laugh. "More like bees buzzing around each other."

"Yes. Exactly like that."

After dinner, they headed outside and Eugene called for the car, which had been parked nearby.

"Feel good?" Eugene asked.

Natalie inhaled and let it out on a sigh. "I feel great. Thank you for a fantastic dinner. I've had a wonderful night."

He slid his hand over hers, entwining his fingers with hers, giving her a secretive smile. "Night's not over yet."

CHAPTER TWENTY-FIVE

Natalie looked down at their hands, then crooked a smile up at him. "Is that right?"

"Yeah. How about a drink? I know this unique, very quiet, very dark place that plays great music. But you have to be able to keep the place a secret."

"That sounds interesting."

"It will be."

When they got out of the car, Eugene slipped his arm around her and led her down a dark alley. She looked up at him and gave him a skeptical look.

"Is this where I find out you're a serial killer?"

He laughed. "Trust me."

"Say all serial killers right before they murder you."

He cracked a smile, then they headed up a set of stairs along a narrow hallway. She saw couples coming from the other direction, laughing with their arms around each other, and her excitement grew, especially when they walked up yet another set of stairs.

"Where are we going?" she asked.

"We're almost there."

There was a black door, and Eugene opened it.

Her eyes widened. She felt transported to another time as she was assailed by jazz music, opulence, glittering chandeliers, and amazing jazz music. They found plush seats at a table in the back and Natalie took a moment to catch her breath, her gaze taking in the ambience of this place called The Backroom.

"This is a speakeasy. Or modeled after one."

He slipped his arm around hers. "It actually was one in the twenties, frequented by all the usual suspects."

She shifted to face him. "Seriously?"

"Yes. They'd do"—he cleared his throat—"business here."

"Fabulous."

"I'll go get us drinks. What would you like?"

"Hmm." She thought about it for a few seconds, then said, "Vodka soda."

"You got it. I'll be right back."

He made his way over to the bar, and Natalie took the time to appreciate the tin ceilings, the opulent chandeliers, and the gorgeous art. There was music and some people danced right out in the aisles. She liked that no one seemed to pay attention to what anyone else was doing because they were completely involved in themselves.

Some dressed in twenties attire and others wore casual clothes, while there were some dressed like Natalie and Eugene. No matter what, it was obvious that everyone was having a good time.

Eugene came back holding drinks in teacups.

"Just like in the twenties," he said, sliding her cup toward her. "Or at least that's what the bartender told me."

She lifted her cup and took a sip. "Mmm, delightful. I'm going to have to do some research on these speakeasies. I know several clients who would love a secret bar room in their houses."

As they drank, she took in every corner of this place and even grabbed some pictures. At least until Eugene took her phone away.

"No work," he said, handing her phone back to her.

"Fine." She slipped it back in her bag, then continued to sip her drink. "This place is amazing. I knew speakeasies were out there but I've never been to one."

"I thought you might like it."

She leaned back against the chair cushion, drink in hand. "Oh, I definitely like it."

Two drinks later she was vibing to the jazz, watching people dance, and there was no doubt she felt good. Especially since Eugene continually rubbed her thigh, sending tingles of awareness throughout her nerve endings. She lifted her gaze to see him watching the dancers. Straight on, he was devastatingly handsome. But his profile? His straight nose and rugged jaw were things people wrote poetry about.

For her, though, he was simply a turn-on. Everything about him made her insides quiver. Then again, it could be the way his hand moved imperceptibly along her leg. Hardly noticeable to anyone else, really. But every time he shifted his fingers, it made her breath catch and her entire body quivered.

And he knew what he was doing to her because she saw the way his jaw would tighten, and then the corners of his lips would tick up ever so slightly.

Then he surprised her by standing up and holding out his hand. "Dance?"

Wow. "Yes."

She got up and slipped her hand in his. He pulled her tightly against his body, and she let the slow jazz fill her soul while his hands roamed over her back.

The combination of saxophone and this delicious man's touch wound around her senses, diving into her desires until all she could feel or sense was Eugene, the way his hands rested at the small of her back, his fingers dipping lower to tease the curve of her butt. And then he snaked his fingers up her spine, sending tingles of sensation throughout her nerve endings, making her nipples tighten, her clit quiver, until all she wanted was naked alone time with him.

She lifted her gaze to his and saw fierce desire in the stormy depths of his eyes. She was glad to know it wasn't just her.

"Ready to go?" he asked.

"So ready."

The ride to the hotel took forever, especially since Eugene's questing fingers teased underneath the hem of her dress. Bare fingers over naked skin, and they weren't alone, which made her hold in the gasps and moans she so fervently wanted to release.

Release. Yes, she needed that. So incredibly frustrating.

Eugene got out of the car first, held out his hand for her and gave her a once-over with his hot gaze before they made the slow, torturous walk to their room.

Once there, he slipped the key against the lock and opened the door, then closed it. She started to reach for the light, but he caught her wrist, raising her arm and pinning it against the door.

"No lights," he whispered against her ear, then slid his lips across her throat, using his tongue to blaze a trail down to her jaw, grasping her face gently before taking her mouth in a searing hot kiss she'd waited hours for.

She dropped her purse on the floor and finally let out that moan she'd been holding in, taking in his tongue and sucking on it with all her pent-up fervor. He pushed his body against hers, letting her feel how hard he was, how needy he was, and it drove her wild. He still had hold of her arm, so she tangled her fingers in his hair with her free hand, digging her nails into his scalp. He groaned in response and scraped his teeth along the column of her throat.

"Please," she said, not even sure what she begged for even though she knew exactly what she wanted.

Eugene kissed her again, a long, hot, mind-numbing kiss that made her legs weaken. He grasped her breasts and teased his fingers over the material of her dress to stroke her nipples. Despite the fabric his touch rocked her, and she wanted more.

But then he slid down her body, drawing one leg over his shoulder as he pulled her panties to the side. Before she could even think, his hot mouth was on her sex, licking and sucking until she thought she might die from the fiery pleasure of it.

This was what her wordless plea had meant. This was what she needed.

"Yes," she whispered, whimpering with the words that spilled from her lips. "Oh God, yes."

He hummed in acknowledgement against her as he did magical, delicious things to her with his mouth and fingers, making her writhe and explode against him, barely able to breathe through the cataclysmic explosions sparking through her body. She ached with the fulfillment of it, and yet still wanted more. She wanted Eugene to have more.

When she caught her breath she pushed against him and he released her leg.

And now it was her turn. She kicked off her heels and pushed his jacket off, and it fell to the floor. She lifted up to kiss him, tasting herself on his lips, feeling that desire spark up again as she dragged her nails down his chest and found his erection, rubbing the length of him that was straining against his pants. She undid his belt, his zipper, then dropped to her knees in front of him.

"Natalie."

Her name spilled from his lips in a hoarse whisper, making chill bumps raise on her skin. She tilted her head back to look up at him, barely able to see his face peering down at her in the dark.

"I like hearing you say my name," she said as she drew his pants and briefs down. "Let's see if I can make you scream it."

She took his cock in her hands, loving the steely hardness of him, the way he pulsed and pushed against her as she wrapped her fingers around the shaft.

And then she put her mouth around the head of his cock, flicking her tongue around the only soft part of him.

He groaned. She smiled and took him, inch by inch, until she had as much of him as she could. Then she pulled back, licked him, and did it all over again, using her hands as well.

She might not be able to see all that well, but she could hear just fine, and his raspy fast breathing told her he liked what she was doing. And oh, did it ever excite her to feel his movements, hear his breathing, to taste him and know that he enjoyed what she was doing to him.

And then he reached down to tangle his fingers in her hair. "Natalie," he rasped. "I'm gonna—"

He didn't finish the sentence but she knew from the way he tensed, the way he jutted his hips forward that he was close. She gave him more, all that he needed until he gave her the one thing she'd asked for as he let loose.

"Natalie!"

She held tight to him as he released, then slowly let him go. He held out his hand and lifted her up, kissing her lightly before righting his clothing.

"I don't know about you," he said, his voice soft. "But I need a drink."

"Mmm," she said, wrapping her arm around his. "Me, too."

"And then, how about we try out that tub?"

He hit the light above the bar and fixed them both a drink. She took a seat at the bar. "You do have work tomorrow."

He slid the glass across the bar to her, then smiled at her. "I can function on very little sleep."

"Good to know," she said. "Because I have several plans for us tonight. Starting with the bath."

He tipped his glass to hers. "I can't wait."

She took another long swallow of her drink, then slid off the barstool, coming around the bar to take him by the hand. "Then let's get started."

CHAPTER TWENTY-SIX

*N*atalie was arms deep in luxurious brocade and was the happiest she'd ever been.

Then again, there really was a lot to be said about having too much of a good thing. How was she supposed to decide on a fabric when everything was so gorgeous?

She laid the swatches on the table, using her critical eye to determine which ones were serious contenders and which ones she'd chosen just because they were pretty. It was obvious that some were too ostentatious for her living room. Beautiful, yes, but not practical. After starting out with about twelve fabrics, she narrowed it down to three.

She laid the finalists out on the table and stepped back, trying to decide which ones would look the best on her chair. How would they fit with the rest of the décor in the room, with the shape of the chair?

She walked past all of them, stopping to study, to touch, to imagine. But her focus kept going back to the striped and floral blue damask. Dark blue and gold, it would go perfectly with the blue sofa. Plus something about the fabric called to her. That was the one.

She ordered the amount she was going to need, gave them her address, and paid for the fabric and shipping, then happily headed out to another store, where she bought some amazing wallpaper that would look incredible in Eugene's game room. She'd never seen anything like it, and she knew Eugene would love it. In another store, she found some other unique looking fabric for a current client, then she stopped for a salad at an outside shop, sitting on their patio to watch people either strolling or hurrying by, depending on their destination.

It felt good to be here, to relax, to have this time to herself to shop and plan. Being alone with Eugene was a definite plus, too.

Her phone buzzed and she smiled, seeing the text from Eugene.

How's it going? Did you buy up all the
fabric yet?

She texted him back: Almost. Having lunch now. How's your day?
He replied with: Busy, but good. Can't wait to see you.

Her heart tumbled. What was it about him—everything about him—that heated her up from the inside out? She couldn't wait to see him, either, which both excited and worried her.

The last thing she wanted was to get too deeply involved with Eugene. Fun was fun, but his every touch ignited her fire, and she watched the clock, knowing she'd see him soon. Her relationship with him felt very . . . oh, what was the appropriate feeling?

High school. That was it. She felt giddy and silly, and she yearned to see him every moment of every day. She shouldn't feel this way. She was an adult with children and a job and responsibilities that should take priority over having some temporary fling with a younger guy.

She had no idea what to do about stopping these feelings, though. She'd never fallen so hard so fast.

No. She was not falling. She would not fall. This would not happen.

She took out her phone to check the time, put in her ear buds, then punched in Hazel's number. Her sister picked up after a couple of rings.

"How's it going?" she asked.

"It's good. I just had lunch outside. It's so incredible here. It's warm but not so humid you can't breathe."

"Sounds perfect. Have you been out and about?"

"Everywhere. Oh, Hazel, you would love it. People are outside walking their dogs all over the place."

"Now that I would love. Show me."

She transferred the call to FaceTime and threw away her trash, then got up and took her sister for a walk, mentioning a few areas she'd stopped at that she really liked. And, of course, since it was Hazel, she made sure to show her a few dogs that walked past.

"So adorable. Nothing better than a happy dog."

"Speaking of dogs, how's Grizelda?"

"One of the pack. She loves hanging out with the other kids." Hazel turned the phone around to show her Grizelda happily snoozing in the backyard with Penny the golden retriever. "They've been running amok all morning."

"Aww. Thank you so much for taking care of her."

"It's no problem. She's a very good dog, Natalie. She's warm and affectionate and so playful. I can see why you had instalove for her."

Yeah, she definitely had a problem with instalove. And not just the dog. "She has my heart for sure. So what's going on at home?"

"Not much. Mom is going to drop Cammie and Christopher off after school. Linc and I are going to take them to a kids' festival with face painting and rides and such, then after dinner we'll take them to Sean's. I already talked to him about keeping the kids through dinner and he was fine with that."

"I'm glad he didn't balk at it. He's such a stickler for a schedule."

"Yeah, I was surprised, too. Anyway, we'll have some fun with the kids and then they can go to their dad's."

"Thanks, Hazel. The kids will love it."

"Linc and I will love it, too. Now tell me everything you've been up to."

Natalie gave her sister every detail of her escapades so far, leaving out the intimate times she'd shared with Eugene, of course.

"Sounds like you've had so much fun. How are you and Eugene getting along?"

She'd entered the park, so she found a nice shady spot by a pond and took a seat. "Oh, we're fine."

Hazel arched a brow. "Fine? Really? That's all you have to say?

You get a fun getaway without kids or responsibilities, and you're with a hot man, and all you can say is that it's fine?"

She inhaled a deep breath, exhaled, and said, "Okay, actually, it's amazing. He's amazing. And that's a problem."

Hazel leaned back in her chair and took a sip of her coffee before asking, "Why is it a problem?"

"Because I've got my life in order. The kids are settled and have adjusted to the divorce, and I don't want to rock the boat."

Hazel didn't speak for a few seconds, and Natalie prepared herself for what was coming.

"So, what? You're supposed to just be alone and miserable for the rest of your life?"

"No, of course not. I just think that now might not be the best time."

"Okay. And when do you think the best time would be?"

She opened her mouth to pop out an answer, realizing immediately that she didn't have one. "I don't know."

"Could it be that you're just afraid of your feelings for Eugene, that maybe everything between you is happening so fast that you feel like your head is spinning, and you want the world to stop for just a minute so you can think?"

Natalie blinked. "Okay, wow. Where did that come from?"

"I had the same knock-me-out feelings for Linc. It was like they came at me out of nowhere, and I didn't know what to do with all these emotions, the wow-ness of it all. You know how I felt after the divorce. I wanted nothing to do with men or relationships. Look at me now."

"Well, that's different. I have children to consider."

"Point taken. You do have to tread carefully, but I can vouch for Eugene, and so can Linc. He's a good guy, honey. He's not going to hurt you or the kids."

"Logically, I know that. It's just . . ."

Hazel tilted her head and gave her a soft smile. "You're scared to put your heart out there again. You don't want it trampled."

"Yeah."

"Well, how about you take it one day at a time and see how it goes? It's not like he's asked you to run away and marry him, right?"

She let out a short laugh. "No, that definitely hasn't happened."

"Okay, then. So maybe you're putting the proverbial cart before the horse just a little?"

"Probably."

"Then go forth and have some fun, and if you develop feelings, or if you've already gotten them, let it happen. Holding yourself back from heartbreak means you hold yourself back from life. From love. And both of those are pretty awesome, Nat."

She felt the tension dissipate from her body. "Thank you, Hazel. I needed to hear that. I guess I worry too much."

"I've heard it comes from being a parent. And you're a very good one. I know you're looking out for the welfare of the kids, which is awesome. But you're entitled to have a life, too. And you have all of us to help back you up. You're not alone in this."

That meant more to Natalie than she could ever say. "Thanks. I appreciate you. And Linc. And Mom and Paul."

Hazel grinned. "We're your village. Now, tell me what's on tap for the two of you for the rest of the trip. Leave out the sex stuff, though."

Natalie laughed and then started talking. Leaving out the sex stuff, of course.

CHAPTER TWENTY-SEVEN

*E*ugene did a careful walk around his house, making notes of anything that wasn't coming along to his satisfaction. He had a great contractor, though, and there wasn't much that he had to nitpick. Everything was going well and he could already see how awesome this place was going to be.

The living room, dining area, and kitchen area were open and spacious, and he could already imagine the entertaining he could do there. Plus, the wide open doorway leading to the patio and pool area was a stunner. He couldn't wait to host parties outside.

Ned, the general contractor working with Linc, told him that he and his team should be finished with the renovations within the next few weeks, which was why Eugene had asked Natalie to meet him out here today. He wanted to know how soon she could be done with the design stuff so he could move in. He was so ready to get out of his temporary place and into this incredible house.

"Hey, are you in here?"

He pivoted at the sound of Natalie's voice. "In the kitchen."

She walked in and he smiled. After their trip to New York last week, they'd both been busy with work, and, of course, Natalie had the kids. So it had been a week since he'd seen her. There was something about her that took his breath away. Maybe it was the smile that lifted her lips whenever she saw him. A guy had to feel good about his woman being happy to see him, because he sure as hell was happy to see her.

"Hi," he said. "You look gorgeous." Which she did, in a black-and-white dress that hugged her upper body and flared out around her legs. She'd coupled it up with white sandals. Today, her hair was pulled back in a high ponytail, and all he could think about was the curve of her neck and how he wanted to put his mouth there, breathe in her scent, and lick his way across her body.

He blew out a breath. He definitely had missed her. A week was much too long to go without her.

"Thanks. You look hot as always."

Yeah, they could have some fun. Right now.

Ned came into the room, obliterating Eugene's fantasy. Ned shook hands with Natalie.

"Excuse us for just a few minutes, Eugene," Natalie said, as she and Ned wandered the house. They came back in a bit later, Ned nodding while Natalie talked. Then Ned left the room and she turned to him. "Ned's team is ahead of schedule. We'd better get started finalizing design plans."

"That's what I wanted to hear. I'm ready to go."

"What do you have that's on the way?" she asked.

He frowned. "What do you mean?"

"I mean furniture- and décor-wise. I assume you've had some of your things in storage."

"Oh. Nothing. I got rid of everything before I moved out here. It was all mostly older or borrowed or left over from college."

She grimaced. "Yikes. Okay, then. So you need everything. Furniture, dishes, pots and pans, towels. Things to hang on the walls. Everything, right?"

"Yup. Can you handle that?"

He figured she'd freak and he should have mentioned that to her earlier. But she surprised him by lifting her shoulder in a casual shrug. "I can if you'd like me to."

"I would like you to. It's about time I got grown-up stuff."

She laughed. "I'd say past time, but yes, I'll deal with it. Do you know what style you'd prefer?"

"Style? No. Just pick what you like and I'll like it, too."

She cocked her head to the side. "Eugene."

"What? I know game stuff. I don't know décor shit. That's your area of expertise, and you're very good at it."

"Décor . . . things, aren't the same as selecting what kind of dishes you like or what types of pots and pans you want to cook with. Or choosing a barbecue."

"Which will be built in." He scratched the side of his head. "Okay, I guess there are some things I need to pick out myself."

"Indeed. Let me get the appliance deadline date from Ned so we'll know when those are going to be installed. Then we'll go shopping for those, along with everything else."

He wrinkled his nose. "Joy."

She looped her arm in his. "Some shopping is fun shopping. We'll even buy you a lawn mower and a weed whacker, unless you plan to hire someone else to do that for you."

He frowned. "No, I'll do that myself."

"Okay, then we'll go buy you yard things."

"Now that does sound like fun. But first, how about lunch?"

"Do you always put your stomach first?" she asked.

"It complains the loudest, so yeah, it takes priority."

"Then, lunch it is."

*L*unch had been a good idea. Natalie had been hungry, and the grilled chicken salad and mango iced tea was exactly what she'd needed.

Eugene had a chicken sandwich and fruit salad. After they finished, they took their teas and drove to the appliance store. She had gotten the specs for the appliances from Ned so she knew what the max size parameters were for each item.

She waved off the salesperson who rushed up to greet them and told him she'd flag him down if they had questions, but otherwise she'd see him when they finished choosing their items.

"You're very good at that," Eugene said.

"At what?"

"Dismissing people."

She laughed. "I do this a lot. Trust me, it'll go a lot faster without George over there trying to push us to whatever gives him the biggest commission."

"Then you're in charge. Ma'am."

She laughed. "Okay, we'll start with the kitchen appliances. Fridge, stove, oven, microwave, and dishwasher." They wandered to that location, a shining heaven of stainless steel. She took a step back, giving Eugene a chance to look them over. She could tell right away that he gravitated to the dark stainless steel and shied away from anything shiny. She made a note of that.

She figured he'd point and say "That one," and they'd be out of there in ten minutes. Instead, he was thoughtful, discussed fridge space, and whether or not he'd need a convection microwave in case his mom came for Thanksgiving. Then he finally turned to face her.

"What do you like?" he asked.

"Me? It's not my house, Eugene. It's yours. You choose what you like."

"Yeah, but it's just me. And maybe it's not my forever house, but if and when I sell it, some family will likely buy it, so I'd want them to have something nice."

"Okay, then. Let's go."

In short order, and after a few suggestions from Natalie, Eugene had chosen all the appliances, including a fantastic washer and dryer. Of course then Eugene had to drag her to the lawn and garden section, where he choose a mower, trimmer, and more than a few lawn beautifying implements.

When they finished there, they were off to the furniture store.

"This place is enormous," Eugene said with a grimace. "This will take forever."

"Well, you got rid of all your furniture," she said, giving him a look. "All your everything, for that matter. So quit your whining and let's get moving. We have a big list."

They started with living room furniture. And while she was grateful appliance shopping hadn't taken long, she figured this would take up the rest of the day. She was surprised to discover that Eugene zeroed in on what he liked almost immediately, choosing a sectional and a couple side chairs along with end tables and a coffee table. The dining table had been equally easy for him to pick out, and then they'd moved to bedroom furniture.

Now he wandered a bit, taking the time to step back and examine each suite.

"Too big," he said to one as they walked by. "Not sturdy enough," he said about another. At the third set, he wrinkled his nose in distaste. "That one's just ugly. None of these are right."

She laughed. "Okay, Goldilocks. There'll be one for you that's just right."

He finally settled on a frame, dresser, and nightstands in black that suited his tastes. Natalie had to admit it had a sleek, modern look.

"With the right mattress, one nice and thick, it'll be one hell of a bed."

He grinned and put his arm around her. "Can't wait to try it out with you."

Her body tingled, making her heat all over. But she couldn't deny the idea of being the first to be in that bed with him made her want to hurry this along.

He had already ordered furniture for his office and had already arranged for the wiring and work product he'd need delivered from his company, so she wouldn't have to do anything in that room other than the wallpaper, flooring, and paint.

He picked out beds and dressers for the guest rooms, and they checked out.

"I'm done for," he said, tucking his credit card back in his wallet.

"We still have all the accoutrements to deal with," she said. "Pots and pans and dishes."

"Ugh." He dragged his fingers through his hair. "Do I have to?"

She could tell he was actually at the tipping point of not wanting to shop anymore. "If you trust me, I'll do the selections."

"I would love for you to do that for me. Thank you."

"Consider it done." She posted a note to herself to deal with it at the office tomorrow. "But for now, how about drinks?"

He looked at his phone. "You don't have the kids?"

She shook her head. "They're with Sean tonight. For the next three nights, actually. I told him he'd been lagging on being a good dad and that he was doing what I considered the bare minimum. I said he needed to step up and be responsible for the kids because I had some work things to deal with. And if he couldn't do that, then I'd ask for more child support and full custody."

As they walked out, Eugene cast a look of admiration her way. "Told him, didn't you?"

"I did. I'm tired of him walking all over me, thinking he can do whatever he wants and nothing ever changes. So I'm just not dealing with his bullshit anymore."

He stopped in the parking lot, turned, and grinned at her. "I like this feisty side of you, Natalie. Kick his ass."

Admittedly, it felt good. "Thank you. I like this side of me, too."

They resumed walking.

"Also, remind me not to piss you off," Eugene said as they slid into the car.

She couldn't help but smile at that.

"Do you have to go back to work today?" he asked.

She thought about it for a few seconds, then realized what he was asking. "No. I have some emails to deal with, but I can do that at home."

"Okay."

"What about you? Haven't I monopolized enough of your time?"

He cracked a smile. "I make my own schedule, and we're in a lull right now anyway while the physical design team creates some mock-ups to go with the programming."

"It's nice that you can take some time off."

"Oh, I'm still working, just at my own pace creatively. Which means it doesn't matter if I write code and review reports at three p.m. or three a.m."

"I see. And, when exactly do you sleep?"

He shrugged, then exited the freeway. "I get enough." He pulled into a restaurant and parked.

Natalie stared at the seafood place. "We're eating again?"

"Hey, we ate a light lunch and then spent five hours shopping. I worked up an appetite."

"I'm fine with eating."

They went inside and got a table, ordered drinks, and settled in to read the menu.

Eugene looked up at her. "I think I want a cast-iron skillet."

Natalie frowned and scanned the menu. "A skillet of what? I don't even see that on here."

"No, I mean, I want a cast-iron skillet."

"Oh. For your house?" She pulled out her phone and jotted it down. "Okay, I'll order one for you."

"Thanks. You know, I can do all that myself so you don't have to."

She was making a few other notations while she spoke. "It's not a problem. Plus, I'll bill you for my time."

He nodded. "As you should."

They ordered food and spent time talking about his house, about paint colors and furniture placement and when things would be delivered.

After the food arrived, Natalie gave him a direct gaze, pointing at him with her fork. "You should have a housewarming party."

He laughed. "Right now I don't even have a finished house."

"But you will soon enough, and it's never too early to plan a party."

"I don't plan or have parties. Or at least I've never done it before."

She lifted a shoulder while concentrating on her plate. "I'm a very good planner. I'll help you."

"And by help, you mean you'll plan the whole thing and be there with me, right?"

She lifted her gaze to his and smiled. "Yes, that's exactly what I mean."

She watched as his shoulders settled back in their normal

position, indicating the idea had made him tense. "Surely you're not afraid of hosting a housewarming, Eugene."

"Me? No way. And, hey, we don't even have to do it. I know how busy you are, Natalie."

She wanted to laugh but knew that wasn't the right thing to do. "A housewarming wouldn't be difficult, and I think it would be awesome to show off the house to your friends and family. You could even invite your mom and your other brother out from California. I'm sure they'd love to visit and see your place."

He didn't answer at first, and she thought maybe she might have overstepped.

"You know, that's not a bad idea. And I've been meaning to do a get together with my team from work. This would be an ideal time to get everyone out of the office and have some fun."

Relieved she hadn't gone overboard with her ideas, she smiled. "That's great. So you make a list and I'll make plans. Then, once the house is finished, we'll figure out a date that's convenient for you and for your family."

"Sounds good. And Natalie?"

"Yes?"

"Thanks. For the idea and for offering to help."

What was it that whenever Eugene cast a direct gaze at her, coupled with that warm smile, caused her to melt into a puddle of goo? She was no lovesick teen who'd never fallen for a guy before. She'd had men in her life. She'd been married and divorced. She knew the realities of love and heartbreak. Shouldn't she be immune to a man's charm? A man's smile? A man's sultry, utterly sexual scent that seemed to always turn her . . .

Okay, fine. She most definitely was not immune to Eugene. And that caused her a great deal of consternation.

No, not tonight. She was not going to overthink her relationship—or whatever it was—with Eugene tonight. They were having a perfect time together, conversation was flowing, she felt good. What she wanted was to spend the rest of the evening— the night—with Eugene. And she wasn't going to let negative thoughts interfere with that.

"Dessert?" he asked after their server removed the dinner plates.

She reached across the table and touched her fingertips to his. "Let's have dessert at my place."

*E*ugene teased his thumb over the back of Natalie's hand, feeling her shiver. Just the simplest of touches heightened his senses. And from the heated look in her eyes, she was as affected as he was.

"Yeah, we should go right now," he said, signaling for the server to bring the check.

They made their way out to the car, and he held the door for her while she slid in. A gust of wind blew her dress up, baring her thighs. She looked up at him and gave him a seductive smile, not bothering to smooth her dress down until he closed the door.

His cock tightened.

Not a good time to get hard. Not here in the parking lot.

He slid into the driver's seat and glanced over at Natalie, her hands balled into fists as she smoothed them over her dress.

"Tense?" he asked.

"You could say that."

He laid his hand over her leg, teasing his fingers along the hem of her dress and under, taking in her harsh inhale of breath as he moved his fingers upward. "Something I could help you with?"

She laid her hand over his and moved it upward, spreading her legs. "Yes."

He pulled his gaze away from her and onto the parking lot, which, while full when they'd arrived, had definitely lessened. Plus, their parking area distanced them from any other cars in the lot. And he needed to touch Natalie, now. He draped an arm over her shoulder, using his free hand to tease her sex through her silken underwear. She arched against his hand, silently asking for more. He was happy to give her whatever she needed, so he slipped his hand inside her panties and stroked her softness, circling the bud, driving himself to the brink while also taking her there.

His cock pounded and he wished they were somewhere where he could thrust inside of her until they both came, hard. But they weren't, and this was about giving Natalie release. His could wait. But not too long, so he swept his fingers gently around her clit until she let out a moan.

"More," she said. "More."

He took a peek out the front windshield to see all was clear, and then he slipped a finger inside of her, pumping while he used his thumb to tease her clit. Her breathing quickened.

"Yes," she said, grabbing on to his wrist. "Just like that. Don't stop."

"Oh, I'm not gonna stop, Natalie," he said, his voice just above a whisper. "I'm going to keep fucking you with my fingers until you come all over my hand."

She writhed against him and then shuddered, and when she came, she cried out. He took her mouth and kissed her, sucking her tongue into his mouth, absorbing her tremors as he continued to gently stroke her until she calmed. It took a few minutes, and he enjoyed the feel of her quaking against him.

He withdrew and she blew out a breath, raising her gaze to his. "Wow. That was good."

"I could tell. How about we head to your place now?"

Her gaze heated. "Yes, I'm ready to get home."

She smoothed her dress down and put her seatbelt on, as did he. The drive home was quiet, both of them sharing fleeting looks. All Eugene could think about was getting Natalie home and naked and in his arms. He really hoped she was thinking the same thing.

When they got to her house, he went around to her side of the car and helped her out, walking with her to the door. She turned around to face him.

"Well, I had a great time. Thanks."

He blinked. "Uh . . . sure."

She fished her keys out her bag and unlocked the door, then walked inside, giving him a teasing smile. "You're coming in, right?"

Blowing out a breath, he walked inside and shut the door. "You're a tease."

She dropped her purse on the table and stepped over to him, sliding her hands along his chest. "Oh, you have no idea."

Grizelda greeted them at the door. They both bent to give the pup some love.

"I'll take the dog out," he said. "Meet you in your room?"

She grinned. "Don't be long."

Natalie disappeared down the hall, while Eugene and Grizelda made their way outside. The night was cool, helping to clear his head from his and Natalie's heated encounter in the car.

Not that it helped to cool down his body any. If anything, the longer he waited for her, the more he wanted her.

Unfortunately, Grizelda wanted to play, bringing him her ball. Since she'd been alone for a few hours, he didn't want to bring her inside just yet, so he threw the ball several times, laughing as she happily pranced every time she brought it back. When Grizelda finally dropped the ball to go get a drink of water, he knew she was done, so they went inside. The pup grabbed her stuffed toy and stared up at him.

"Ready for bed, girl?" he asked.

She wagged her tail, so he headed down the hall, Grizelda staying in step beside him. The door to Natalie's bedroom was open so he walked in. Grizelda went right to her bed on the floor, and Eugene headed to the bed, where Natalie was curled up under the covers.

Naked. Hot. And sound asleep.

He smiled and swiped a soft curl away from her face. She looked peaceful when she slept. She looked beautiful, too. Hell, she always looked beautiful. And yeah, it had been a busy day, so he wasn't about to wake her. He walked around the house, made sure all the doors were locked and turned off the lights, then undressed and climbed into bed with Natalie. He pulled her back toward his chest. She wriggled her butt against him, making his cock twitch with painful awareness.

It was going to take a while before he'd be able to sleep tonight.

CHAPTER TWENTY-EIGHT

Natalie smiled down at the gorgeous man sleeping in her bed. She inhaled, releasing the breath on a quiet sigh. She could get used to waking up to Eugene's strong arms wrapped around her, his warmth surrounding her. And that face? That incredible body? No woman could do better.

She'd fallen asleep last night waiting for him, and instead of waking her, he'd cuddled her. What hot, worked up, no-doubt-sexually-frustrated man did that?

Eugene, that's who.

She'd woken this morning, let Grizelda out, fed her breakfast, and now the pup was busying herself with her toy in the kitchen. Natalie crawled under the covers, sliding her hand across Eugene's chest, then lower, over his abs, and lower still, circling her fingers around a very impressive erection.

"You up?" she asked.

He blinked his eyes open, staring down at her. "Very up."

She stroked him, slow and easy. "We didn't finish what we started last night."

He rolled over on top of her, framed her face in his hands, and kissed her, igniting the flame within her that had yet to extinguish since she'd met him. He rocked his hard cock against her sex and the reactions within her were instantaneous. She reached underneath her pillow and pulled out the condom packet she'd tucked in there.

"I'm ready now," she said, handing him the packet.

It only took a moment for Eugene to slide the condom on. Watching him made her quiver. And when he dropped down on top of her she welcomed him inside, wrapping her legs around him to draw him closer.

His groan was enticing. The sensations of him moving within her were so intense she felt enveloped, heated, desperate for the release only he could give her.

And then he lifted, gazed down at her with a soul-searing look that inflamed her and sent her right over the edge. She grasped his arms and catapulted into orgasm. He went right with her, the two of them embroiled in the passion of release.

Spent and satiated, she slid her foot along his calf, languishing in the afterglow. Eugene rolled over, taking her with him, then splayed his hands over her hip while easing his lips across hers.

"Do you have to work today?" he asked.

She stretched, enjoying the feeling of their bodies aligned. "I don't have anything pressing. What did you have in mind?"

He rocked against her. "Well, this—more of this, for sure. And then I thought we'd go out for something to eat. I'm kind of hungry."

She lifted and swung her legs over the side of the bed. "Food sounds fantastic. First, I need a shower."

"But . . ."

She turned and leaned over to press a quick kiss to his lips. "Yes, and sex. Definitely more of that. But let's get some food, okay?"

"Okay."

They both took quick showers, then got dressed. They drove over to Eugene's place so he could change into clean clothes, and they headed back out. It was still early so they decided on breakfast. Since Natalie knew all the places to eat, she chose a spot for them away from all the tourist locations. It was a small, quiet place with great food.

And it was busy, no doubt because of its reputation. After they were seated, their server brought them menus and they each ordered coffee.

"I don't know about you," she said, "but I'm starving."

"Huh," Eugene said while perusing the menu. "You must have worked up an appetite doing . . . something."

Her lips curved. "Yes. Something."

Their server brought their coffees, and she fixed hers how she liked it and took a sip, unable to resist the hum of satisfaction as the caffeine made its way through her system.

"Good, huh?" he asked, reaching for her hand to tease his fingers over her skin. She noticed he liked touching her. Judging from the way she reacted, her body liked it, too.

"It was exactly what I needed." Their gazes locked and for some reason whenever he looked at her—especially when he looked at her so intensely—it was as if they were the only two people in the room.

"Have you decided on what you'd like to order?"

She blinked and looked up to see their server smiling down at them.

Eugene smiled back. "You know what, we might need another minute."

They concentrated on their menus instead of each other so when their server returned, they could give her their orders.

Eugene took a sip of his coffee and set the cup down. "Before kids, what did you like to do on a day off?"

"Oh." That was so long ago she'd have to think back. "I was a different person then. I'd go shopping, hit the yoga studio, go to lunch with my friends, get a mani/pedi, kind of just . . . relaxing and fun things."

"And you don't do that anymore?"

"Well, sure I do. When I can fit it in. Normally when the kids are with their dad I get caught up on bills, clean the house, grocery shop, that kind of thing."

"Okay, then what would you like to be able to do?"

"Hmm." It was a good question. "I don't know. Let me think about it for a bit."

"Sure."

Their server arrived and set the plates down in front of them. Natalie's stomach grumbled as she inhaled the smell of everything delicious.

She had an omelet along with turkey sausage, toast, and fruit. Eugene, on the other hand, had bacon, eggs, and pancakes, the latter of which he smothered with maple syrup.

"Are you having pancakes with your syrup?" she asked.

He sliced off a piece of pancake and held it out for her. "Taste."

Unable to resist, she opened her mouth, and he slid the fork between her lips. The pancakes were soft and fluffy, the syrup sweet. After she swallowed, she said, "Maybe I should have ordered pancakes."

"I'm happy to share."

"I think I've got more than enough on my plate, but thanks."

"Okay, but if there's anything you want, just ask."

She tucked a bite of omelet in her mouth, thinking that comment over while she chewed. He'd asked her what she wanted to do or what she used to like to do during her free time before kids. What she'd told him was true. She'd do all this stuff to pamper herself or work on her body. It had been fun and frivolous and relaxing, but then again, she'd had zero responsibilities. Now? She had a lot.

Which didn't mean she couldn't take advantage of her occasional free days, right?

What would she like to do?

She looked up at him. "It's been ages since I've been to a baseball game."

Eugene arched a brow. "You like baseball?"

She nodded. "I love baseball. And, FYI, football and basketball, too. And hockey."

He gave an impressed nod. "You are sporty. And you were on the swimming and golf teams."

"Yes. But I love all sports. I tried out for the high school basketball team but I was, frankly, terrible."

He laughed. "Yeah, well, we can't be awesome at everything. I wanted to be a wide receiver on the high school football team. I played when I was little, but my apparently inept skill level didn't translate to the higher grades."

She offered up a sympathetic smile. "And there went your dream of playing for the NFL."

He shrugged. "I had to pivot and learn a different skill set. Good thing I was awesome at video games."

"Good thing. And now here you are, doing what you love."

He leaned back in his chair. "Yeah. It's a damn good life. And you're doing what you love."

"I am. Aren't we lucky?"

He reached over and entwined his fingers with hers. "So lucky."

She left to go to the restroom, checking her face and hair in the mirror after she washed her hands. She reapplied her lip gloss and went back out to their table.

"You're free this weekend?" he asked after she took her seat.

"Yes."

"Okay, then. How about we go watch a baseball game in Miami."

Her eyes widened. "Miami? I . . . I can't. I have Grizelda."

"I already checked with Linc and Hazel and they're happy to take Grizelda for the weekend. Now, would you like to go to Miami and see a game?"

Part of her was a bit irritated that he'd gone behind her back to make arrangements for *her* dog. Another part of her was excited at the chance to spend a fun weekend in Miami. And see a baseball game. These two sides of her were going to have to come to some sort of agreement and soon.

"Natalie."

"Yes."

"We don't have to go if you don't want to. It's just a suggestion."

She sighed. "I do have responsibilities, Eugene. I can't just drop and go like you can."

"I realize that. But this weekend you can, right?"

She hated that he was so smugly right. "I suppose I can."

He grinned. "Great. I'll make all the arrangements."

After the bill was paid, they headed back to her place, where Grizelda enthusiastically greeted her. "I'm going to take her for a walk," she said.

"Okay. I'm going to go pack. I'll be back to pick you up at say . . ." He looked at his phone. "At about one?"

She checked her phone. "That's fine."

"Okay." He came over to her and drew her against him, giving her a long, deep kiss that made her lean into him, grasping the fabric of his shirt. When he pulled away, she wanted to bring him toward her again, but now wasn't the time. Instead, she patted his chest and took a step back, creating the distance she needed.

She walked him to the door and opened it. "See you soon."

He smiled at her. "Yeah. Really soon."

She closed the door and looked down at Grizelda, her tail wagging madly.

"How about a nice long walk, little girl?"

Grizelda barked.

"I'll take that as a yes. Come on, let's go."

CHAPTER TWENTY-NINE

Eugene might have gone a bit overboard, but he desperately wanted to show Natalie a good time. They could have driven. It was only a three-and-a-half-hour drive, but he wanted to maximize their time in Miami, so he figured flying was the best way to go. And sure, chartering a plane was probably a bit much, but he knew a pilot who said he was flying a family down for the weekend, and they had two extra seats, so the cost wasn't bad at all. Plus they were able to avoid the crowds and potential delays, which made it totally worth it.

Eugene grabbed their luggage from the pilot, and then tipped him an extra hundred. "See you Sunday morning, okay?"

"You got it. Thanks."

"This was so unnecessary," Natalie said once they headed to the rental car counter. "You know I don't need all these bells and whistles, Eugene."

He turned to Natalie. "But think of all the hassle we avoided by doing it this way. Besides, in the end, it didn't cost that much extra. So just enjoy it, okay?"

"Fine. I will enjoy."

He leaned into her, and she gave a little laugh. The last thing he wanted was to upset her, so he was glad her mood could change so quickly.

They got the car and headed out onto the freeway, driving into Miami.

"It's so beautiful here," Natalie said as Eugene exited the highway. "And the views of the ocean are spectacular."

When he pulled into the entrance to their hotel, she gasped and turned to face him. "Here? Really?"

"I figured if we were going to stay in Miami, we might as well get some beach time."

The valet came and got their luggage, put it on a cart, and then Eugene handed over the keys to the rental while they went inside and checked in at the registration desk.

They took the elevator and Eugene slipped the card against the lock and opened the door.

"Oh. My. God."

Eugene seconded Natalie's comment. "That's a hell of a view, isn't it?" He laid their luggage down and walked through the room with her to the balcony, drew the door open, and stared out at the beautiful blue waters of the Atlantic.

"Wow. That's just incredible." She turned to him. "Thank you for this, Eugene. It's exactly what I didn't know I needed."

Her statement hit him like a warm squeeze to his heart. He didn't know how to react, so he gave her an easy smile. "It'll be fun, right? And we have tickets to the afternoon game tomorrow."

"Perfect."

"Which means it's warm, the sun is out, and we need to head to the water."

"I agree."

While Natalie was in the bathroom, Eugene grabbed his board shorts and changed into those along with a sleeveless tee. He dug out his sandals and slipped into them, then fished the sunscreen out of his bag. Now all he had to do was find his sunglasses and he'd be ready.

"Okay," Natalie said as she came out of the bathroom. "I've got a bag packed with my hat along with sunscreen, sunglasses, and lip balm. Oh, and a book to read. Is there anything else you want to put in it?"

All he could do was gape at her because she stood there staring at him, no doubt waiting for him to answer, but he was pretty sure he swallowed his tongue. She wore a red bikini that showed off her incredible curves, her long, long legs, and the swell of her breasts.

"You look so fucking hot."

She opened her mouth to say something, closed her mouth, then frowned and said, "Really?"

He stepped toward her and slid his arm around her waist, tugging her against him. "Oh yeah. Sure you want to go down to the pool?"

"I absolutely want to go to the pool. But just to let you know, I could get used to compliments like that, so thank you." She pressed her mouth to his, but only briefly.

Damn.

They headed downstairs and outside, and he had to admit, it

was pretty perfect. The pool area was large and the staff accommodating as they found chairs to sit in and ordered drinks. Eugene ordered a beer and Natalie ordered a vodka with pineapple juice.

He looked over at her and she shrugged. "I feel tropical."

"Tropical, huh? I guess our next trip should be to Hawaii. Maybe Jamaica?"

"Right. With all that spare time I have."

"Hey, you've got to make the time to indulge yourself."

She drew her sunglasses down her nose. "Uh-huh. Tell me that once you have a couple of kids."

"You make a valid point. However, if I may counterpoint, you don't have the kids all the time."

"But—"

He held his hand up. "I wasn't done. Or, we could take the kids with us somewhere. I'm sure they'd enjoy a nice vacation, too."

"Oh, and you can take all this time off?"

"Geez, you're a buzzkill," Eugene said with a wink.

She laughed. "I'm a parent. It's my job to be a realist."

He leaned over and trailed his finger up her arm. "It's okay to live a little, too, Natalie. Have some fun. Figure out a way to inject some joy into the daily drudge, ya know?"

"I suppose you're right." She stared out over the water, and he'd give anything to know what was going on in her head. Hopefully all good things, but he couldn't project his feelings onto Natalie. She was right in that they didn't live the same kind of lives. She had responsibilities that he didn't. He could come and go as he pleased, whereas she couldn't. He needed to keep reminding himself of that.

They were different in a lot of ways as far as lifestyle.

But she was here with him now, and that made him feel good. All he could do was try and show her a good time.

And maybe forget about real life for a little while.

Natalie was admittedly slightly buzzed and extremely relaxed. Who wouldn't be, sitting under the shade of her oversize umbrella, enjoying the pool and that spectacular view of the ocean?

She could get used to this. Ocean breezes, cocktails at the wave of her hand, and a gorgeous man asleep on the lounge chair next to her. She rolled over to give herself a better look at Eugene.

He lay on his stomach, his board shorts riding low on his back, sweat pooling there. She let her gaze roam along his upper back and broad shoulders, wanting to reach out and trace all that lean muscle, but she didn't want to disturb him while he was sleeping. Instead, she continued her visual appraisal of him, moving up to his strong jaw, straight nose, and wow, it was really too bad she couldn't see his amazing eyes, currently hidden behind his sunglasses. But at least she could watch the way his dark, thick hair blew in the breeze.

"You're ogling," he said, not even moving.

Taking a deep breath, she sighed. "I was."

He rose up and swung his legs over the chaise, drawing his sunglasses off. "Ready for a walk and a dip in the ocean?"

"Absolutely."

When he stood, his shorts rode low on his hips, showcasing that dip that she'd love to explore further—with her tongue.

Instead, she put on her hat and took his hand. They strolled along the water's edge, the waves lapping at their feet.

"Makes you want to live in a place like this, doesn't it?" he asked.

"Miami? It's very nice. And the ocean breeze is unparalleled. But Orlando is my home, where my kids were born. I've spent my whole life there."

He stopped, turned to face her. "Haven't you ever thought about living somewhere else?"

"Honestly? No, I haven't. I like where I live, Eugene."

"Hmm. Okay."

They resumed walking, and thoughts of that conversation stuck. Did he think she was boring because she never wanted to live anywhere else?

"What about you?" she asked. "I know your family lives in the San Francisco area, so that's your home. You plan to stay there?"

He shrugged. "Home is wherever I decide to make it, and family is always just a plane ride away. I mean, Linc's made his home here, and he's happy about it. My other brother, Warren, and his husband, Joe, are settled in California and don't intend to leave. But me? I don't know. I think I could live anywhere."

"Of course. That makes sense." It suddenly felt like a rock had settled in her stomach, though she didn't know why. Where Eugene lived shouldn't make any difference to her. It wasn't like they were in a long-term relationship. This was nothing more than a temporary hookup.

He slipped his arm around her waist. "But I do like Orlando. I could see sticking around there awhile. I did buy a house, you know."

She smiled at him. "Yes, I'm aware."

He backed her toward the waves, the water slowly climbing up her legs. "And this incredible designer is making it kick-ass awesome."

She reached for his arms so the waves wouldn't knock her over. "Will you write 'kick-ass awesome' in your review of my design services?"

"You bet." He leaned in and kissed her, his lips coasting over hers, teasing and tasting.

She was aware they were in public and that explained his gentle kiss. But she wanted so much more. What was it about Eugene that made her crave such deep passion? It wasn't like she'd never experienced hot sex before. Though maybe not the kind she'd had with Eugene. Or maybe it was just her reaction to this particular man. He brought out so many feelings in her, and she had to admit, there were feelings she'd never had. Excitement, overwhelming passion, and a sense of fun she'd never experienced before.

So much for this being just a temporary hookup. She was fooling herself if she didn't recognize it for what it was. She was starting to have feelings.

Ugh. Feelings. So complicated.

That needed to stop.

When the water covered them up to her chest, he grabbed her butt cheeks and hauled her up. She wrapped her legs around him and rode the waves. Rode him.

Oh, but she didn't want it to stop. She pushed against him and he slipped his hand between them. Their gazes met and it didn't matter to her where they were, only what she wanted.

The sounds of laughter close by jolted her. She dropped her legs, and Eugene let go of her. In an attempt to cool her heated libido, she swam away from him, letting the water and the distance cool her down.

She walked out of the surf and turned to look for Eugene. He followed a minute or two later, and just looking at him walking out of the water like some kind of wet merman god ignited that spark of desire all over again. She swallowed and lifted her chin, determined not to be affected.

"How about something cold to drink?" he asked.

She cleared her throat. "Yes. Cold. That would be great."

They rinsed the salt water off at the entrance to their hotel property, then made their way to their cabana. This time Natalie ordered a sparkling water and Eugene did the same. Once they dried off and reapplied sunscreen, they sat and sipped their drinks.

Eugene's phone pinged. He picked it up, frowned, then set it down.

"Do you need to check emails or make a call or something?" she asked.

He shook his head. "No. It can wait."

"Eugene. If it's important you should deal with it."

He looked over at her and smiled. "You're important, and I know how to prioritize my time."

"Just know I'm fine if you have work to do."

"I do have work to do. Just not today. Or tomorrow. I cleared my schedule and my staff is handling everything that needs to be handled. They send me updates on things I need to know about. That's what that message was. There's nothing urgent, okay?"

She sighed. "Okay."

"Do you think I'm slacking or something?"

She reached over and laid her hand on his arm. "No, it's nothing like that. It's just . . ."

She looked out over the water. "This is so different from my life with Sean. Everything with him was work first, family second. He thought his job was the most important thing in the world. He attended conferences and dinners, constantly working to make contacts that would build his business. In the beginning, I understood that it was necessary to build his practice. But after he was established, it continued. It was almost as if . . ."

She couldn't finish the sentence because that thought had lingered in her mind for years.

"Almost as if what?"

Turning to look at him, she said, "Almost as if he was more interested in his work than he was in the kids, or in me."

"And was that true?"

This time, she didn't hesitate. "Yes. It was one of the main reasons I divorced him."

"You and your kids shouldn't come in second to anything or anyone."

Her heart squeezed. "Thank you. That was my thought, too. That your partner and your kids should always be put first. Sure, sometimes work has to take priority, and I get that."

"I get that, too. But it shouldn't be all the time. If it is, then there's something wrong."

"Yes." She loved that Eugene understood, that he didn't think she was being unreasonable, which was what Sean had told her when she tried to explain she and the kids needed more of his time. They'd argued constantly about it, and she'd finally realized that they were never going to see eye to eye on something she considered so important. She could never make him see that being with his children was vital to his relationship with them. She wasn't sure he'd figured that out even now. But she had no control over that. So instead, she was determined to be enough for them. Plus they had her mom and Paul, and Hazel and Linc. And the kids seemed happy, which was all that mattered.

After they got warm, they took a quick swim in the pool to cool down, then dried off. They put on shirts and cover-ups and headed into the restaurant for a bite to eat.

Natalie got a lovely shrimp salad, and Eugene had a turkey sandwich. They sipped lemonade and iced tea while they ate. She was so relaxed but also had trouble pushing aside the guilt about not being at work or with her kids and her dog.

"I feel like I should be working, or at home with my kids," she said. "This is very decadent."

"Sometimes a break is good for you. Refreshes you for both work and parenting. Though I'm just guessing on the parenting thing."

He had a point. "I don't disagree."

"What would you do if you were suddenly rich?" he asked.

She swallowed a delectable bite of shrimp, then paused. "Oh.

Interesting question. I don't know. Pay off the house, put money away for the kids, donate some to several of my favorite charities, and then . . . well, I don't know. Probably put the rest away."

"You wouldn't upgrade your lifestyle in any way?" he asked. "You know. Trendy car, huge house, fancy clothes, and the like?"

She shrugged. "I'm pretty happy with my life the way it is. I can't think of anything else I want or need."

"That's boring. Reach for the stars and dream big here, Natalie. Tell me what you'd do if money were no object."

"Oh, I don't know. Maybe an SUV so I'd have more room for all my design stuff, plus all the kids' things."

He waited, and when she didn't say anything else he asked, "And?"

"And what? I don't lack for anything, Eugene. I have a nice house that has plenty of space for me and the kids. We're not hurting financially. Sean has set up a college fund for both the children. I have a job I love. We're good."

"Huh. Okay, then. You just want a bigger car."

She laughed. "Pretty much. Maybe a designer purse. Always wanted one of those."

"There you go. Something big just for yourself."

"And what about you? What would you do?"

"Oh, well. Huge house. Like seven or eight bedrooms, five or six bathrooms. But also a state-of-the-art game room that's on its own level with lots of room for various play."

"Of course."

"Hey, I not only design, I also play. It gets my creative juices flowing, ya know?"

"Sure. But an entire level?"

"Yeah. It allows me to stretch out, especially with VR."

She frowned. "VR?"

"Virtual reality." He stared at her. "You and I need to play."

She slid her hand over his. "Indeed we do."

He took in a breath. "Yeah, we definitely need to do that, but also, I need to broaden your gaming horizons."

"Oh wow, I'm not much of a gamer, Eugene. Unless it's *Ms. Pac-Man*. And I'm not into playing war games or racing cars."

"First, *Ms. Pac-Man* is a classic, awesome game. But you know what, there's a lot more to gaming these days than war or racing. Virtual reality can take you places you can only dream about."

She leaned back in her chair. "Really. Do tell."

"Mmm, it's better if I show you. Which I will when we get back home."

Sliding her fork onto her finished salad plate, she batted her lashes at him. "In the meantime, how about some actual reality?"

His eyes sparked. "I could go for that."

They finished up their meal and headed upstairs to their room. Once again she was struck by the unbelievable opulence. And that view was something she could get used to. She laid her bag on the chair and walked through the door to the balcony.

Even as high up as they were, she could still hear the crash of the waves. There was something so calming about watching the waves roll toward the shore, then back out to sea. Maybe she should have listed a house with an incredible view of the ocean as one of her must-haves should she ever become rich. Might as well go big, right?

A pair of warm arms wrapped around her as Eugene pulled her back against his chest.

"Hell of a view."

"It lulls me," she said. "Watching the water is so incredibly relaxing. All my tension seems to just disappear."

"Tense, huh?" He slid his hands up her arms to her shoulders and inward, massaging the tight knots that had seemed to take up permanent residence.

She raised her shoulders, leaning into the pressure of his fingers, the way he instinctively seemed to know where the tight knots were.

After a few minutes of him working on her shoulder and neck muscles, she felt soft. Melty. Needy in a much more elemental way. She pressed her butt against him, and he obviously felt the same need judging from the hard ridge of his erection pushing back against her.

He lifted her cover-up over her hips, sliding his fingers into her bikini bottom. She gasped, a shock of pleasure shooting throughout, then looked around to see if anyone was watching.

But who could be? They had a corner unit and no hotel across from them. Unless someone was on a boat with a telescope— highly doubtful—then no one could see. And right now, with Eugene's fingers sliding gently across her clit, she wasn't sure she'd even care. All she cared about was getting to her release, and Eugene was going to take her there.

After withdrawing his fingers, much to her disappointment, he flipped her around to face him, took her mouth in a blistering kiss, then slipped his hand inside her bikini once again, relentlessly stroking her sex until she gasped against his mouth.

"Oh," she whispered. "Yes, please."

"Come for me," he said, his voice deep, guttural, as if his need was as great as hers. "Come on."

She could barely catch her breath as she drew ever closer to orgasm.

And then she burst, crying out and shaking all over as her climax tore through every part of her. Eugene held her up when her legs trembled from the waves of pleasure crashing into her body.

She'd barely had time to settle before he turned her around, bent her over the chair in front of her, and jerked her bikini bottom off. She heard the tearing of the condom wrapper, and then he slid inside of her.

Her body pulsed and tightened around his cock, and she swore she could come again right then. But Eugene held still, waiting for her to adjust.

"Give it to me," she said, shocked by her demanding behavior.

But he only laughed, a gruff rumble before he began to drive into her, giving her a pleasure so deep it made her shiver all over. With each thrust, she grew ever closer to release. And when he gripped her hips and let out a low groan, she reached for her clit and began to rub, because she wanted to go with him.

"Fuck," he said, moving faster, and harder. So did she, and that was all it took for her to fall into orgasm, her body pulsing around his shaft. He pinned his hips to her and shuddered, and she held on while they both released.

Eugene pulled her up and wrapped his arm around her, turning her to give her a deep, tongue-filled kiss that stirred her, despite just experiencing two mind-blowing orgasms. They made their way back to the bedroom, where she undressed and stumbled into the shower to wash off. She wrapped up in the fluffy bathrobe.

"I'm going to grab us something to drink," Eugene said.

"Sounds great." Natalie climbed onto the bed and sank into the comfortable softness of the covers. Eugene came back a short while later and cuddled up behind her.

When she woke, the sun had set. The room was dark and all she heard was Eugene's soft breathing against her neck. Reluctantly, she got up to use the bathroom. When she came out, he was awake and lying on his back, smiling at her.

"Good nap," he said.

She climbed onto the bed and lay down next to him. "Excellent nap."

He rolled over to face her. "You ready to go out for dinner?"

"Mmm. I don't know about you, but I'm pretty comfortable here. How do you feel about pizza in bed?"

"I feel pretty good about it. How do you feel about pepperoni?"

She scrunched her nose. "How do you feel about sausage and mushroom?"

He did the same thing with his face. "I feel like we're about to have our first argument."

She laughed. "Okay, then. Let the fight begin."

CHAPTER THIRTY

*T*he door to the bathroom opened and steam poured out, along with Natalie, wrapped in the hotel's bathrobe, a towel on her head. How could a woman dressed head to toe in white fluff look so . . . hot?

Yeah, Eugene, you've got it bad for his woman.

No lie there.

"Just FYI," she said as she grabbed a tube of lotion from the dresser, "I'm taking that steam shower home with me. You can bill me for it."

He grinned. "Got it."

He'd intended to take Natalie out for a nice dinner last night. Instead, they'd ordered pizza and stayed in bed, watching movies until . . . well, hell, he couldn't remember what time they'd fallen asleep. They'd talked about anything and everything from their childhoods to college and best friends and enemies and first loves and heartbreak. Eugene couldn't ever remember being so open and comfortable with anyone. Natalie made it easy for him to tell her things he'd never told anyone. Maybe it was because she hadn't judged him for some of his stupid mistakes and admitted she'd made a few herself.

She'd told him they'd both been very young when they'd broken some hearts or hurt someone's feelings, and as long as they learned from it and tried not to do it again, then it was a good lesson.

She made him think, and that was a good thing.

They'd slept in, so after they got dressed, they headed downstairs to have a late breakfast.

"I don't want to eat too much," Natalie said as they took their seats in the dining area. "Need to save room for beer and hot dogs at the ballpark."

He laughed. "Yeah, that's all important."

"Not to mention nutritious."

They had coffee and ordered their food. Natalie took a sip and sighed, then immediately yawned.

"You stayed up too late."

She slanted a look at him. "And who's fault is that?"

"Yours. You talk too much."

She sputtered out a laugh. "Oh right. You gave me a blow-by-blow of your entire childhood. I even know who your second grade crush was."

"Hey, Tildy was the love of my life. We meant something to each other. At least until she stole my favorite pencil, crushing my dreams of us living happily ever after."

"No doubt thereafter clouding your view of women."

"Nah. Then there was Melissa in third grade, Amelie in fourth, oh, and then I took Heather to the sixth grade dance."

"Wait, wait," she said. "What happened to fifth grade?"

He shrugged. "None of the girls liked me then. I don't know what was wrong with them."

He winked at her and she rolled her eyes. "Okay, heartbreaker. I can see getting an in-depth look at your growing-up years will take even more time than I imagined."

He took his coffee cup and leaned back. "We haven't even hit my high school years yet."

She gave him an affected grimace. "Not sure I even want to know."

"Oh, come on. Surely you were popular. I mean, look at you. You must have had boys chasing you from early on."

"Hardly." She paused while their server brought their food. Then they dug in and started eating, and the conversation was momentarily halted. But Eugene hadn't forgotten, so once they had finished, he took a sip of water and put his empty plate to the side.

"What did you mean when you said, hardly?"

She frowned. "What?"

"I had asked you about boys being after you and you said hardly."

"Oh. I was awkward and painfully shy. Boys weren't interested in me and I wasn't interested in them. Not until high school, anyway."

"Really. No early crushes?"

"Nope. I was into book crushes."

"Huh. Who?"

"Oh. Well. Where do I even start? Nancy Drew. Mr. Darcy from

Pride and Prejudice. Also Elizabeth Bennett from *Pride and Prejudice.* Lestat from *Interview with the Vampire.* Meg Murry from *A Wrinkle in Time*, Jamie Fraser from *Outlander.* Aragorn from *Lord of the Rings.* I mean, I could go on for hours."

"It's good to have crushes, ya know."

She lifted her fork to her lips and paused, smiling. "Indeed, it is."

The way she smiled at him never failed to cause his stomach to tighten and his heart to feel swollen with . . . with something.

They finished eating and headed back up to the room to freshen up before heading out for the game. Natalie wore team-color capris and a short-sleeve shirt, along with tennis shoes. And she looked damned beautiful—like always.

"Very game appropriate," he said.

She walked over to him and slipped her hand around his neck, drawing him in for a kiss. After she pulled back, she said, "And you look hot."

He looked down at himself. He wore a T-shirt, jeans, and his kicks, so nothing special. But if Natalie thought he was hot, he'd make a note to dress like this more often.

Since parking was a nightmare, they'd ordered a car to take them to the stadium. They made their way to their seats along the first base line.

"These seats are amazing," Natalie said, looking around. "It's incredible here."

"Yeah, it's pretty cool, isn't it?" Eugene loved baseball. He'd always been a huge fan of San Francisco's team, but as long as it was baseball, he'd enjoy it. No matter what city he traveled to, if it was baseball season, he'd find time to go see a game. So he was excited for their plans today, even more so knowing that Natalie was also a fan.

As the stadium filled, he noticed Natalie eyeing all the women wearing the Miami team's jerseys and T-shirts.

"I'll be right back," he said.

She nodded, her focus on watching the players warm up.

He went to the concessions and sales area and surveyed the T-shirts. It didn't take him long to choose one that he thought Natalie might like. He paid and headed back to their seats.

"For you," he said, handing the T-shirt to her.

Her eyes widened as she lifted the shirt up to inspect it. "Really? Eugene, you didn't have to do that."

"But I wanted to. And you were salivating over everyone wearing theirs, so I figured you might want one."

"I did, in fact. Thank you." She leaned over to kiss him. "I'll be right back."

She hurried off and came back a short time later wearing the new shirt, her original shirt in her hand. "What do you think?" she asked, standing in front of him.

He sighed. The colors showed off her skin and hair and brought out the bright green in her eyes. "I think you're beautiful. Like always."

She slid into her seat and pressed her arm against his. "Now I'm game ready."

"Almost."

She frowned. "Almost?"

He signaled for the vendor selling beers, then shortly thereafter he dashed up to the concessions to grab them a couple of hot dogs. He handed one to Natalie and she grinned, holding the beer in one hand and the hot dog in the other.

"Dream come true, right here," she said.

"Hang on." He pulled out his phone and snapped a pic, then showed her the photo.

She laughed. "Perfect. Though, maybe . . ." She took his phone, leaned against him, and took a selfie of the two of them.

He looked at the picture, suddenly struck by how . . . perfect they looked together.

He waited for some warning signals to ping in his head at that thought.

But nothing came. So, instead, he sat back, ate, and drank, so ready for the game to start.

*N*atalie had the best time. Not only had Miami won with a walk-off home run, but she'd had two hot dogs, two beers, and now had a new T-shirt of her favorite team, thanks to Eugene.

After the game, it took a while to get a car and then fight through traffic, but Natalie was hyped up after the exciting finish to the game, so none of the waiting bothered her.

"Feel like hitting the beach when we get back?" Eugene asked.

Knowing they were heading home tomorrow morning, she wanted to maximize fun in the sun as much as they could. "I'd love that."

When they got back, they changed into their beach clothes, and Natalie wound her hair up into a ponytail, applied sunscreen, then put on her sun hat and sundress and slipped into her sandals. She came out to find Eugene in a sleeveless tee and board shorts, showing off all his delicious arm muscles.

She had to admit that having him all to herself these past few days was not a hardship. Then again, this was just fun and play. A dreamland that was nothing like her reality. A reality she was shortly going back to.

So just enjoy it.

Right.

They headed down to the pool and grabbed a cabana. Natalie grabbed her book and got comfortable on her chaise while Eugene decided to do a few laps in the pool. When a server came by, she ordered drinks for both of them.

Her phone buzzed, and she saw Sean's name and a FaceTime call.

This couldn't be good. Her stomach tightened, and she hoped nothing was wrong with the kids.

"Hi, Sean," she said.

"Hey." He was smiling, which was odd. "Nothing's going on so don't panic. Christopher misses his mom and wants to talk to you. So does Cammie."

Relief filled her. "Oh. Of course. Thanks!"

Within a few seconds, there was Christopher's sweet, chubby face. "Hi, Momma."

"Hey, sweet boy. What are you doing?"

"Daddy and Cammie and me went to breakfast, and then we went to see a movie, and then we went to Gramma and Grandpa's house. Now we're gonna go swimming."

"Wow. That sounds so fun. You've been busy."

"Uh-huh. And we played Uno with Gramma and Grandpa last night and then we had pie that Gramma made and Cammie and me stayed up late watching movies with Dad."

Her heart did a small leap at the thought of Sean spending quality time with his kids. "You did? That's great, Christopher."

She heard Camryn in the background, and then she and Christopher argued over the phone. Sean said it was Camryn's turn.

"I gotta go, Momma," Christopher said. "When you coming home?"

"Tomorrow. I'll pick you up tomorrow night, okay?"

"Okay."

"I love you, sweet boy."

"Love you, Momma. Bye."

Then she talked to Cammie, who filled her in on every single detail of their time with Sean, even though she'd already heard most of it before. But that was fine. While she was talking to Cammie, Eugene had come back and grinned as he listened in. When she finished, she told Cammie she loved her, and then spoke briefly again with Sean, thanking him for calling her so she could talk to the kids.

She hung up, sighed, and laid the phone down.

"Everything okay?" Eugene asked.

"Yes. Sean called and said that Christopher wanted to talk to me. Nothing urgent. He misses me."

"Aww. Of course he does. He's your baby."

She smiled. "Yes. And growing up way too quickly. They're

little for such a short period of time and then, poof, suddenly they're growing up and all independent. I just miss that baby stage."

"Do you want more kids?"

"Oh God no. I might miss them being babies, but the thought of going through all that again? The diapers, the crying, the sleepless nights? No, thanks."

"Huh. I'm gonna grab a drink. You want something?"

"No, thanks. I'm good."

He left and Natalie wondered if what she'd said had upset him in some way. But how could it? They weren't a couple, definitely not permanent. Besides, she was almost thirty-five and more than ready to be done having kids. Eugene, on the other hand, could make babies for . . . well, for a long time to come.

The thought of him having beautiful children with some other woman made her ache all over. Then she was irritated because why would she even care? His life was his, and once he was done with this project he'd be off to another one. Sure, they were having a good time right now, but that didn't mean they were in love or anything.

You sure about that, girl?

She shook off thoughts of falling in love. It wasn't going to happen. Not now. Not ever. She liked her life the way it was, focusing on her job and her kids. On herself.

Shouldn't she be allowed to put herself first for a change?

Eugene returned and plopped down on the chaise, flipped his sunglasses over his face, and sipped his drink while he looked out over the water. Natalie watched him, trying to find the words that she wanted to say, but unable to say them. Or maybe afraid to say them because their time together had been so idyllic, and if what she said destroyed this paradise they'd been living in, she'd be heartbroken.

But not knowing was killing her, so she had to know.

"Do you want kids?" she asked.

He shifted his gaze to her. "What?"

"You asked me if I wanted more kids, and my answer was pretty definite. Do you want kids, Eugene?"

He swung his legs over the chaise so he faced her. "I don't know. I like kids a lot. But having my own isn't something that's on my priority list. I guess I've always thought that when I meet the person I'm going to love for the rest of my life, that's something we'll decide together, ya know?"

"That makes good sense." It was such a mature answer, and she appreciated his honesty.

He came over to her chaise, and she shifted to make room for him. He lifted his sunglasses to the top of his head. "What's this about?"

"I don't know. Nothing, really. I'm being ridiculous."

He picked up her hand. "Talk to me, Natalie. There's nothing you can't tell me."

His words were so earnest, and when she looked up at him, she saw the same in his eyes.

"You asked about kids and I blurted about not wanting any more. I guess I feel like I hurt your feelings."

"You didn't hurt me, Natalie. The one thing I appreciate is honesty. And I'll always give it right back to you, and I was telling you the truth when I told you that I don't even think about having kids of my own."

He caressed his hand over hers, and the sensation was like a balm to her tortured feelings.

She laid her head on his shoulder. "I'm overthinking. I have a tendency to do that. Sorry."

"Nothing to be sorry about. You were considering my feelings, and I appreciate that." He pulled her back. "But let me tell you that I don't and never will think of you as a potential baby-maker. I like you for who you are and respect where you are at this point in your life. I like your kids a lot, too. I'm happy with the way things are between us, Natalie. Understand?"

She nodded. "Understood. And thanks."

They lay like that together for a while. And while she felt more settled about the whole kids thing, the one thing that still unsettled her was the fact that their age difference was still a prominent factor in their relationship.

They were still in two different places in their lives.

After a couple of hours frolicking at the pool, they decided they were hungry, so they headed inside to clean up for dinner. Natalie had shaken off whatever weird mood she'd been in earlier. The late-afternoon sex and an incredible orgasm probably had a lot to do with improving her outlook on life and everything in general.

Eugene told her they were going somewhere upscale for dinner, but not overly fancy, so she slid on a black sleeveless dress and silver heeled sandals, adding hoop earrings and a silver chain.

Eugene looked delicious in black slacks and a white button-down shirt.

"You dress up nice," she said as she stepped out of the bedroom.

He walked over to her, picked up her hand, and pressed a kiss to the back of it. "And you are stunning. Not just tonight, but always. Every day. No matter what you wear."

Damn if her heart didn't flutter. "You're very good at compliments, Eugene."

"I'm good at being truthful, Natalie."

With a sigh, she slipped her arm through his and they headed downstairs. They got a lot of looks walking through the lobby. She had to admit she enjoyed the attention of being seen on the arm of a spectacular-looking man.

A younger man, at that.

What a buzzkill. Her subconscious should really shut the hell up.

They drove to a restaurant near the ocean. Natalie was glad she'd dressed up because it was, indeed, upscale. Dark and atmospheric, the walls were adorned with rich wallpaper, and the tables were elegantly dressed. They were seated in a moody, romantic corner by the window with spectacular views of the ocean.

Their server brought them wine, and Natalie sat back and enjoyed the view.

"This has been fun," she said as she took a sip of the delicious cabernet.

"Trip's not over yet." Eugene took a swallow of wine and smiled at her. "There's still magic to be had."

JACI BURTON

She cocked her head to the side. "You know I don't need magic, right?"

"Why do you say that? Don't you think you deserve a little fantasy?"

"I don't know." She shrugged. "Maybe what I'm trying to tell you is that just a regular trip to the beach satisfies me. Everything doesn't have to be so . . ." She looked around. "Extravagant."

"Uh-huh. Why? Because you feel like you don't deserve it?"

Her earlier mood had returned, and she didn't understand why she was pushing this. "I guess because I'm afraid."

"Afraid of . . . what exactly?"

"I don't know. This has all been amazing. Relaxing. Beautiful. But it's not real life, Eugene. Not my life, anyway. My life is hectic schedules and kids and now a dog and trying to juggle all of it, and sometimes I don't do it all that well. My real life is not this idyllic fantasy where it's just the two of us wrapped up in each other."

"Of course you know that, and so do I. But you're entitled to get away and indulge every once in a while, aren't you?"

She started to object, then realized she was pushing against the whole idea of enjoying herself, of letting her guard down and just letting herself be, which was utterly asinine.

She rubbed her temple. "I'm sorry. I've been in a weird mood all day. I've enjoyed the hell out of this trip, and I think I'm being cranky because it's almost over."

He let out a soft chuckle. "Now that I understand. Who wants real life when you can have all this? If we were all gazillionaires, it'd be like this every day."

"I don't know." She took another sip of her wine, then said, "I think having an experience like this every once in a while makes me appreciate it more. I wouldn't want to be a gazillionaire. I'd take all this for granted."

They perused the menus, and when their server returned, they ordered.

Her phone buzzed. She picked it up, then slid it back into her bag.

"Anything important?" he asked.

"No. It can wait."

"Kids are okay?"

She nodded. "They're fine. That was work stuff."

He studied her, giving her a smile as he watched her tap her fingers on the table.

"What?" she asked.

"Are you anxious to get home? Get back to work?"

She didn't want him to think she was ungrateful for the trip. "Yes and no. I mean, I miss the kids, of course, and the last week of school is next week, so there are things that need to be done and I need to be there for them. I want to be there for them."

He gave her a smile. "Home means a lot to you."

"Home is my kids. My sister. My mom. I'm sure it's the same for you. Minus the kid thing, of course."

"Right." He shrugged. "I don't know. My home hasn't really been a single place since I left for college. I've lived all over since then, with occasional visits to where I grew up to see my mom and brothers. So I don't know exactly what home means anymore."

Her heart ached at his words. "That's sad, Eugene. Everyone

needs to feel like they have a home." She reached over and laid her hand over his heart. "A place where you feel it here."

He didn't answer, just looked at her.

Had she overstepped, said something that hurt him?

"Eugene, I—"

Their server brought their food, so whatever had been going on in his head was put aside—at least temporarily. Eugene seemed to act normally while they ate and shared bites of their food. She had salmon and he had lobster, and both were amazing. And it wasn't like conversation had stopped between them, but the emotional, more personal stuff had apparently been tabled. They'd rehashed their entire trip, picking out favorite things they'd done.

"I think for me it had to be the baseball game," Natalie said. "So much fun."

Eugene slipped a forkful of rice between his lips. After he swallowed, he said, "Gotta be the sex for me."

She sputtered out a laugh, then took a swallow of water. "You can get that anywhere."

"Yeah, but it's still my favorite thing to do with you."

She rolled her eyes. "Pick something besides sex."

"Mmm. Walking the beach. It relaxes me."

"So maybe that's your next living adventure."

"The beach? Nah. I like it, but it's more fun as a vacation."

"You're telling me you wouldn't want to live by the ocean."

"No, I really wouldn't. Beach areas are always touristy and I like to live somewhere quiet."

She leaned back in her chair and sipped her wine. "Oh, so you can make noise in your game room?"

"Hey, that's different. I'm in my own place in a soundproof room. Not bothering anyone. But if I want to sit outside, it's quiet. I enjoy the silence sometimes. The only sounds are birds, crickets, sometimes cicadas."

He looked over at her and found her staring at him, a look of disbelief on her face.

"Who are you?" she asked.

"What?"

"I mean, you don't strike me as a 'listening to the silence' kind of guy. You're more . . . how can I put this . . . a pool party blowout kind of guy."

He laughed. "Oh, how little you know about me, Ms. Parker. I can be very zen at times."

"Okay. Next full moon we'll zen it out in my backyard. Candles, crickets, the flitting sounds of mosquitos flapping against the pool covering, the whole ASMR experience."

His lips curved. "I'll bring my tortured soul."

She laughed. "You do that."

After dinner they had coffee, then paid the bill and walked out on the deck that paralleled the water. The night was warm, the moon was bright—though not yet full—and there weren't too many people walking the boardwalk, so it felt like just the two of them, all alone.

Eugene put his arm around her as they stood at the railing listening to the sounds of the ocean.

She liked that he didn't say anything, just leisurely rubbed his hand up and down her back. She leaned into him, stroking her hand along his chest. Suddenly she was in his arms, and his lips were on hers. The kiss heated up in a hurry and Eugene lifted his head to look down at her.

"I think we should take this to a less public place."

She smiled up at him. "So, the car, then?"

He laughed. "Hey, I'm game if you are."

She smacked his chest. "Let's go back to the hotel."

"Okay."

"And, Eugene?"

"Yeah?"

"Drive fast."

He nodded. "I'm on it."

CHAPTER THIRTY-ONE

*E*ugene was in the midst of an awesome virtual reality sequence when his phone buzzed. He decided to ignore it, until it buzzed again. He ignored it again because he needed to get through this section of the ride to make sure it was cohesive. But then his phone buzzed for the third time.

Dammit. He paused the VR and pulled off his goggles, checking the missed call log. Frowning, he saw all three calls were from his oldest brother, Warren. Hoping nothing was wrong with their mom, he punched the number and Warren answered immediately.

"Were you busy?" Warren asked.

"Yeah, I was. What's wrong?"

"Nothing. But I have news. Really good news."

Eugene grinned. "Tell me."

"Louisa is pregnant. We waited to tell everyone until she was well through the first trimester, so she's sixteen weeks now."

"Wow." Louisa was the surrogate Warren and his husband, Joe, had contracted to carry their baby. "Dude. That's awesome. Congratulations. How's Joe?"

"He cried when we found out the pregnancy test was positive."

"Oh, and you didn't?"

"Pfft. I never cry."

Eugene took a seat on the sofa in his office. "Bullshit. This is a big deal, Warren. I'm so stoked for you guys. Did you tell Mom? How did she react?"

"Oh, you know Mom. She's already out buying baby stuff even though it's early and we told her not to."

Eugene laughed. "Yeah, she'll be an unstoppable grandma, you know that."

"I do know that."

"Man, I'm gonna be an uncle. This is so cool." It was going to take a minute for that to sink in.

"Anyway, that's only the first part of my call," Warren said. "I have a deposition to do in Ft. Lauderdale next week, so Joe and I thought we'd fly in early and drive over to visit with you and Linc."

"Oh man, that'd be awesome. I'd love to see you guys."

"Yeah, it's real convenient that you and Linc live in the same city now."

"For now, anyway."

"Whatever, Eugene. Eventually you should consider settling down and staying in one place."

"I'll give that all the consideration it's due. So text me details on when you're gonna be here, okay?"

"Will do."

"And congrats again, bruh. Really excited for you and Joe."

"Thanks, man. Talk soon."

"See ya."

He hung up, then stood and paced his office while he texted Linc about Warren and Joe.

We're gonna be uncles!

Linc texted back. I know! So awesome. I'm stoked.

Ditto, he texted back to Linc. And Warren and Joe are coming to visit next week.

It took a minute for Linc to text back, but he said, Yeah. Hazel and I are excited. We'll have to get together to make plans. How about dinner tonight? See if Natalie wants to come.

I'll do that and let you know. After putting his phone down, he went back to work, then realized he hadn't asked Natalie about dinner. Instead of texting her, he called.

"Hey there," she said when she picked up.

"Hi. How about dinner at Linc and Hazel's tonight?"

"Hazel already texted me. I was going to call you, but you beat me to the punch. And, yes to dinner. I have the kids, so they'll be coming along."

"Perfect. I guess everyone's coordinating, so we'll talk later about time?"

"Sounds great. Have a good rest of your day."

"Okay. Lo . . . looking forward to it."

She laughed. "Me, too. Bye."

He'd almost blurted out "Love you" as if it were the most natural thing in the world. But it wasn't, and he didn't. Did he?

No. No, he didn't. Wait.

He dragged his fingers through his hair, letting what he'd

almost said sink in. Did he mean to say it or had it been just some kind of automatic response?

No. Absolutely not. And he wasn't about to do a deep dive into his feelings for Natalie right now, because he had work to do. He'd deal with his almost verbal fuckup later.

Much, much later.

CHAPTER THIRTY-TWO

Natalie stood at the door keeping a close eye on the kids as they frolicked with all of Hazel's dogs in the backyard, along with their dog, Grizelda.

"You do realize Linc and Eugene are out there, too," Hazel said. "They've got the kids."

"I know." They had all disappeared beyond the trees anyway, their laughter still ringing loudly.

"Then come over here and have a drink and update me on all your adventures."

She wandered into the kitchen and pulled up a seat at the kitchen island. She really wanted to talk to Hazel, to tell her about her feelings for Eugene. She was so confused lately and needed some guidance. Hazel handed her a glass of wine.

"Thanks. How are things going with you and with Linc?"

Hazel sighed and took a sip of her wine. "Honestly? Fabulous. I mean, even more wonderful than I ever could have imagined. I'm fostering, I love my part-time job at the restaurant, and now they want me to go full time."

"Wow. That's a lot. How do you feel about it?"

"I don't know." She took another swallow of wine. "I mean, cooking is awesome and I love it. But the animals need me. If I devote all of my time to the restaurant, then the foster will suffer and I can't have that."

Natalie leaned back. "I guess this is the point when you need to decide what's most important to you."

"The puppies are most important. They need me. Not only the ones who live here permanently, but also the ones I have to help find forever homes for. The more I'm here, the faster I can help them get settled."

"Okay, then. I mean, and don't take this the wrong way, but you don't have to have that job, Hazel."

She waved her hand. "I know. Linc can support me, I get that. But you know how I feel about not having my own source of income, because of what happened with Andrew."

"Of course. I totally understand Andrew taking all the money and you losing the house burned you badly. But you know Linc isn't like that. He's happy to take care of you financially so that you can take care of the animals."

Hazel sighed, then pulled over a charcuterie board for them to snack on. "I know that. He's offered to set up a bank account for me in my name only so I never have to be afraid to be without money. But I just can't, Nat. You know how important my independence is to me."

"I do, honey. Of all people, I totally do. Giving up my career to stay home with the kids made me feel—I don't know how to explain it. I mean, I don't regret it at all, and I wanted to do it. And I loved being with my babies. But at the same time . . ."

Hazel gave her a sympathetic nod. "You feel as if you lost a part of yourself?"

"Yeah. Kind of. But now it's all good, you know? I have the right balance that makes me happy. And that's how I want you to feel."

"That's the thing, Nat. I do feel good. I almost feel guilty about having the life I do, all things considered. The past year has been nothing short of amazing. I've fallen in love with a man I couldn't have dreamed up if all my dreams had come true. He's kind and funny and sexy and good-looking and smart and he loves me. And he loves the dogs and he supports all my dreams, no matter what they are."

"Yes, you got lucky in the love department for sure. But you know what, Hazel? You deserve to have everything you want."

Hazel gave her a big smile. "Thank you. And so do you. So tell me about your hot weekend in Miami."

"Oh. Well, we had so much fun." She filled in her sister on everything they did. Well, almost everything.

"It's good for you to get away, ya know. From kids and work and responsibilities. And let Sean take care of his own kids for a change."

"Yeah, he wasn't too happy about having to take extra time."

"Oh, too bad. He owes you. An extra couple of days with his own children didn't kill him, did it?"

She tried not to laugh, but instead picked up an olive and popped it in her mouth. After she washed it down with a swallow of wine, she said, "Apparently not. Cammie and Christopher even said they had fun with their dad. He took them to the park, to a movie, they had pizza night, even built a fort in the living room."

"Shocker of all shocks. That sounds like fun parent things."

"I know, right?" Natalie leaned forward. "Also, I think he might have a girlfriend."

"Really? How do you know?"

"Cammie said something about her dad having a friend over. She said she was fun and laughed a lot and played in the fort with them. Cammie said she's a teacher at their school but not in Cammie's grade."

"Hmm." Hazel spread cheese on a cracker. "Interesting. Maybe that has something to do with him being more involved with the kids."

Natalie lifted her shoulders. "It might. We'll see."

"I guess so." Hazel took a bite of the cracker.

"And, you know, sis, you can have it all. If you want to continue working lighter hours at the restaurant so you can devote most of your time to the rescue, then do that. If they don't go for it, then find a different restaurant to work at. That way you can continue to do all the things you want to do, and you'll still be able to put your own money away."

Hazel sat up straighter in her chair. "You know what? You're right. I know exactly what I want and there's nothing stopping me from getting it. I do want to continue cooking, but not full time because I want to mainly focus on fostering. So I will go back to the restaurant and tell them that while I appreciate their offer to go full time, I'm happier to work part-time. Then the ball will be in their court as to whether they keep me on or not."

Natalie nodded. "There you go."

"Problem resolved, sort of. At least in my head," Hazel said with a laugh.

"Hey, having that resolution in mind is more than half the battle, isn't it?"

"Yes." Hazel reached out and squeezed Natalie's hand. "Thanks, sis."

"You know I'm always here for you. Just like you've always been there for me."

They both slid off their stools and hugged.

"Love you," Hazel said.

Natalie squeezed harder. "Ditto." Now they had gotten Hazel's issues resolved, Natalie could tell her sister everything that was on her mind about her relationship with Eugene.

"Is this a happy hug or did something bad happen?"

Natalie turned and grinned at Eugene. "Happy hug."

"Okay, good. The kids are hungry and Linc wants to know if you want him to fire up the grill."

"Yes, definitely," Hazel said, then picked up the tray and took it outside.

Her conversation with her sister would have to wait until later. Natalie followed her and they all sat outside, snacked, and watched the kids run amok with the dogs. Or at least most of the dogs. Gordon, the pug, and Mitzi, the chiweenie, had skirted around the open door and made their way to their dog beds, tuckered out from playing with the kids.

"They're going to pass right out after bath time tonight," Natalie said.

"The kids or the dogs?" Hazel asked.

Natalie laughed. "Both?"

Linc grinned. "Hey, anytime you want to exercise your kids, the dogs are always agreeable."

"They do love Cammie and Christopher," Hazel said.

"The feeling is mutual," Natalie said.

"And soon we'll have Warren and Joe coming," Hazel said. "The dogs will love them."

"That's true," Linc said. "Have they said how long they're staying?"

Eugene shrugged. "I think a few days? I know he has a client deposition. Not sure how long that'll take."

"They can for sure stay here," Hazel said. "We have the room."

"I wish my new house were finished," Eugene said. "Though my rental has an extra bedroom, too."

Linc laughed. "Warren would think it was funny we were fighting over them."

"Which we will not be telling him," Eugene said.

"No. We absolutely won't. They'll stay here."

Eugene shrugged. "Whatever. Fine."

Natalie grinned as she watched the way the two brothers argued. She couldn't wait until next week when she could meet the third. Linc and Eugene sniped at each other like they were still kids, but there was underlying love there as well. Was it the same with Warren, or was there a different dynamic when the three of them were together?

She couldn't wait to find out.

CHAPTER THIRTY-THREE

*E*ugene had hustled to get caught up, making sure he could take some time off when Warren and Joe came to visit. And of course that meant they'd discovered some bugs in the ride's design matrix, which meant he'd put in some overnight hours debugging the program, which also meant he hadn't seen Natalie at all.

But they'd fixed the program, had done several run-throughs with no issues, and Eugene had even managed one excellent full night's sleep so he wouldn't be a cranky asshole when he showed up at his brother's house tonight to hang out with Warren and Joe.

He'd spent half a day at work to continue to check on the ride's progress. It was coming along, and the programming and design were now ahead of schedule, just like he'd wanted. After he left work, he stopped at the gym to work out the body stiffness from too many days bent over his computer, then went for a run, working out some of the frustration from spending all that time at the office. Nothing like fresh air and long strides to give him a brand new outlook. Now he felt energized.

A hot shower followed. He put on jeans and a T-shirt, laced up his tennis shoes, and stopped at the store to pick up flowers for Hazel since she was hosting, and, of course, flowers for Natalie because he'd missed her. He also grabbed wine, beer, and whiskey.

He was excited to see Warren and Joe. He was really looking forwarding to seeing Natalie. They'd texted and FaceTimed here and there whenever he could carve out a few minutes, but their talks had been brief and damned unsatisfying. She'd been totally understanding about his work situation, which he'd appreciated. It had given him the time to focus on what he'd needed to do without worrying he was hurting her feelings by not being there for her.

He arrived at Hazel and Linc's place, gathered up the booze and flowers, and went through the garage and into the house, per Linc's instructions.

Natalie was in the kitchen by herself. She turned when he entered and greeted him with her characteristic smile that never failed to brighten his day.

He laid everything on the counter and swept her into his arms and kissed her—deeply, passionately, as if that kiss was the satisfaction of a long, long craving that couldn't be denied any longer.

Knowing they could be seen, including by the kids, he took a step back, swiping his fingertip across her bottom lip. "Damn, I missed you."

Her eyes sparked with heat and something he couldn't decipher. "I missed you, too. Hi."

"Hi, yourself." He reached over to the counter. "I brought you flowers. And I brought your sister flowers, too, for different reasons."

She laughed. "Noted. And thank you."

The back door opened and Hazel walked in. "Oh, hey, Eugene."

Eugene gave Hazel a smile. "Hi, Hazel. Thanks for hosting my family tonight."

"I'm happy to do it."

He picked up the bouquet of wildflowers. "Brought these for you. Along with beer and booze."

"All are appreciated. Thanks for thinking of me. Your brother Warren texted about five minutes ago to tell us they're on the way."

"Okay, thanks."

"Linc's outside if you want to join him."

"I will." He turned to Natalie. "Are the kids outside, too?"

"No, they're with Sean tonight. Sean and his girlfriend, Madison, who I met today, wanted to take the kids to the new kids' movie. He asked if it was okay if he could have them tonight."

"Wow. How very outstandingly parental of him."

"I know, right?" Hazel said. "I'll be outside."

After Hazel left the room, he asked, "So, Sean has a girlfriend. How do you feel about that?"

"I feel fine. Madison is actually very nice. She teaches fifth grade at Cammie's school and she's apparently great with the kids. Cammie can't say enough good things about her, and Christopher said she's fun."

"I guess that's pretty good accolades, coming from the kids."

"Agreed. And I think she's opened Sean's eyes to the concept of spending more time with his children. And if she can do that, how can I possibly have any objections?"

"If you're sure that's all it is."

She frowned. "What do you mean?"

He should probably shut up, but when did he ever do that? "I mean, I hope Sean wants to spend more time with Cammie and Christopher because he wants to. Because they're his kids and he loves them. And not to impress some woman he's dating."

She opened her mouth, and he knew she wanted to object. She had every right to, and this really wasn't any of his business. But she closed her mouth and cocked her head to the side.

"You know what? That thought had never occurred to me."

"Of course not, because you think your kids are awesome and who wouldn't want to hang out with them all the time?"

She reached for his hand. "You mean, like you do?"

"Hey, I like kids. I especially like your kids, which has nothing to do with how I feel about you."

"Oh yeah? And how do you feel about me?"

He leaned into her. "Oh, we don't have the time to get into that right now."

"Really. How come?"

"Because you're wearing too many clothes. But I'm happy to get into it in depth with you later, when we're alone."

"Sounds ideal. Now, what kind of wine did you bring? Hazel has reds and some sweet stuff."

"I got your favorite, a pinot grigio."

"Excellent. Pour me a glass and let's go outside. It's a beautiful night and we might as well enjoy it before the heat and bug season starts."

"Before we do that, and since we're alone . . ." He drew her into his arms and they lost each other in another deeply passionate kiss, making him wish they were actually alone so he could explore every inch of her. But they weren't, so their kiss was woefully short.

He'd fix that later, though. For now, they headed outside to join Hazel and Linc and all the dogs.

"You've been busy," Linc said once Eugene took a seat next to him. "I've hardly seen you."

"No one has seen me." He explained about all the fuckups at work, and what he and his team had to do to fix them.

"Ugh," Linc said. "I hate when something goes awry and it takes forever to fix it. It's like the faulty wiring in this house I'm working on right now. Had to rip it all out and start over from scratch."

Eugene gaped at him. "Dude. You're working on my house."

"Huh. I am, aren't I?"

It took him a few seconds to recognize that look on Linc's face. Eugene rolled his eyes. "Asshole."

Linc laughed. "Yeah, but I had you going for a while didn't I? Anyway, you should come by and see the house. It's nearly done."

"Yeah? I've tried to stay out of the way so you and your crew can do your jobs."

"And we have. Come by."

"I'll do that."

"Bring Natalie, too."

"Will do."

"How's that going, by the way? With Natalie?"

Eugene looked over where Natalie was engaged with Hazel and the dogs. He smiled. "It's good. Really good."

The back door opened, and Warren and Joe walked through. "We were told to let ourselves in."

Eugene was surprised when their mother strolled in with them. Before he could say anything it was instant chaos with a barrage of barking dogs and everyone going over to greet them. Once the dogs had been properly greeted and petted and Hazel had taken them to their section of the property with a treat, Eugene went over and took Natalie's hand.

"Come meet the rest of my family."

She looked up at him with a nervous smile.

"Natalie Parker, this is my mother, Lisa Kennedy. And this is my brother Warren and his husband, Joe."

Natalie shook hands with them one by one. "It's so nice to meet all of you. Hazel has told me wonderful things."

"That's because we're all awesome," Warren said with a wink. "Great to meet you."

They all went inside for drinks and snacks. Natalie pulled up a spot at the kitchen island next to Lisa. Eugene poured them both glasses of wine.

"Nice to see you, Mom," he said, squeezing her shoulder. "It's a good surprise."

She patted his hand. "I'm happy to see you, too."

After Eugene wandered off, Natalie asked, "Wow. Three boys, huh?"

"Yes. And, yes, they were a handful, especially being so close in age. But they were each others' playmates and best friends."

Warren coughed. Eugene choked back a laugh. Linc outright snorted.

"Okay, you three." Lisa shook her head. "So, Natalie, tell me all about yourself."

Natalie realized that Eugene hadn't told his mother anything about her. About them. Which was fair. If her mother didn't live so close, she likely wouldn't know anything about her dating life, either. "I'm an interior designer, I'm divorced, and I have two kids. Camryn is seven and Christopher is five."

Lisa's eyes sparkled with delight. "Oh, you have children. That's wonderful. They must keep you very busy."

"They do."

"She also just got a dog," Hazel hollered from the dining room. "Grizelda is outside wrestling with Freddie."

Lisa craned her neck to see the little fluffball tangled in a fun free-for-all with Hazel's dachshund. "She's cute."

Natalie smiled. "Yeah, she is. The kids love her, and they really like taking care of her."

"That's good." Lisa looked around. "Okay, they've all moved into the living room. Tell me about you and Eugene."

"Oh. Well, we're dating." She had no idea what to tell Eugene's mother about their relationship. And she sure couldn't define it for Lisa when she had trouble doing that for herself.

Except you can define it because you love him and you know it.

Dammit. This was not the time for those thoughts to pop into her head.

"Well, of course you are. I already knew that." Lisa laid her hand over Natalie's. "And I'm pressuring you for information about your relationship. I'm so sorry."

"It's fine, really."

"No, it's not." She leaned in closer, keeping a close watch on the crowd in the living room. "It's just that Eugene very rarely introduces me . . . no, correction. He has never once introduced me to any woman he's dated. That makes you special. Unique. Like a unicorn."

Natalie sputtered out a laugh. "Well. I do feel special now."

"You should, Natalie. He told me you two were together."

"Wait. He did? So this isn't the first time you're hearing about me?"

Lisa laughed. "Of course not. Eugene tells me everything. Well, I mean, not everything, of course. But he talks to me about what's important to him. Which means you are important to him, Natalie. That's one of the main reasons why I'm here. And, of course, to see Linc and Hazel's place."

It took a few moments and regulating her breathing for Natalie to be able to respond. She didn't want to make a big deal about this. Moms often read into things that weren't there when it came to their children and their love lives. This was probably no different. Still, she owed Lisa a graceful and grateful reply.

"I appreciate that, Lisa. It means a lot to me that he talks to you about me. I think very highly of him."

Lisa gave her a knowing smile. "Keeping your cards close to the vest. I can appreciate that, and your relationship with Eugene isn't my business, anyway."

She tilted her head toward the living room and saw Eugene's apologetic smile. She gave him a reassuring one in return before answering Lisa. "I didn't mean to insult you."

"You didn't insult me at all. You don't know me, and I could be one of those overbearing moms for all you know. Which I'm not, by the way, and you'll eventually figure that out. But I'm super happy to meet you and I can appreciate what Eugene sees in you. You don't spill secrets, and I can tell by the way you skirt glances at him and the way he smiles at you that there's something special between the two of you. What that is I have no idea, which is just fine."

Okay, now she felt better. "Thanks, Lisa. I hope I'm just as protective but still open with my own children when they're grown."

"I have a feeling you will be. Are they here?"

"No, they're with their dad tonight. He wanted to take them to the movies."

"Oh. Hopefully I'll get a chance to meet them."

"I hope so, too."

Hazel came over and put her hand on Lisa's shoulder. "Okay, enough monopolizing Lisa's time. And I need the kitchen for dinner."

Lisa grinned at Hazel. "What can I do to help?"

"Me, too," Natalie said.

"Nothing. You can both go into the living room while I finish up dinner. I already preprepped everything and salmon takes no time at all to cook. So get out. Lisa, go visit with your sons."

"Is she always this bossy?" Lisa asked.

"It used to be me being the bossy one," Natalie said as they stood. She gave Hazel a look over her shoulder. "But lately, she's grown into her bossiness. I'm very proud of her."

JACI BURTON

Hazel tossed her a dazzling smile. "Why, thanks, sis."

They made their way into the living room, where a fierce argument amongst the brothers was currently taking place. Lisa seemed nonplussed about the raised voices, so Natalie took her seat and sipped her wine, while the guys voiced very strong opinions about . . . paint color?

"Everybody knows flat is the way to go," Warren said. "It blends easily into the walls and gives an old world look."

"You're totally off base, Warren," Linc said. "Semigloss is easier to clean. It's the only thing I put on my walls."

"You're both wrong," Eugene said. "Eggshell finish is more durable and looks great on the walls."

Linc shook his head. "No, you and Warren are wrong, and I'm the expert, so my vote is the only one that counts."

Natalie looked over at Lisa. "Was it always like this?"

"Unfortunately, yes."

"What about you, Joe?" Natalie asked. "Are you weighing in on this?"

Joe looked up from his phone. "Me? I try never to get involved in their skirmishes. Besides, I'm watching baseball." He lifted his phone to show her the game.

She laughed. "Probably a wise choice."

"You're the designer, Natalie," Eugene said. "You agree with me about eggshell, right?"

"Actually, I think it depends on the area of the house. High traffic areas that get a lot of moisture can get messy, and can benefit from semigloss or satin. Your lesser used rooms would be fine for eggshell. And the only place I'd paint with flat is ceilings."

They all stared at her, and she was sure she'd angered all of them.

Then Warren laughed. "She's smarter than all of us, including you, Linc. You should hire her."

"Hey, she's doing the design on Eugene's house," Linc said. "She's just not painting it."

"Thankfully," Natalie said.

"Speaking of," Linc said. "I told Eugene to come by and look at the house. It's almost finished, so you two should walk through together. I figured you might want to finalize your design ideas."

"Sure. We'll put our calendars together and figure out a date."

"I'd love to see some of your work, Natalie," Lisa said.

"Well, some of it's right here," Hazel said as she entered the living room. "Natalie did the design for our house, and we just love it. In the meantime, dinner is ready, so let's gather in the dining room."

"With Hazel's permission, I guess you can give me a tour after dinner," Lisa said.

Natalie looped her arm in Lisa's. "I'd love to."

CHAPTER THIRTY-FOUR

It had been a good couple of days. Eugene had missed having his family together, and Mom showing up with Warren and Joe had been a huge surprise. The fact that Natalie fit in so well with his family, however, wasn't a surprise at all. She was currently having a girls' day with his mom and Hazel, the threesome apparently having become besties in a matter of two days. Not that that should surprise him. He'd gotten close to Natalie quickly. She was warm and open and easy to talk to, and his mom was the same way. It was logical that the two of them would bond.

Today he was on the golf course with his brothers and Joe, and they were talking—of all things—babies.

"So the baby is due in early November," Joe said, unmistakable excitement in his voice.

"Which means, if it comes early, it could be a Halloween baby," Linc said. "Do they put the newborns in costume in the hospital?"

Warren rolled his eyes. "No, jackass. They're babies."

"Oh, come on," Eugene said. "If it's a Halloween baby you have to bring it home in some kind of costume."

"You're both assholes," Warren said. "And now I'm hoping it's born in November."

"Then you could dress it like an ear of corn." Linc grinned.

Eugene shrugged. "A pumpkin still works."

Joe shook his head, but his smile was evident. "Worst uncles ever." He looked over at Warren. "You know we'll never be able to trust our child with either of these two."

Warren nodded. "Obviously."

"Hey." Eugene frowned. "I'll have you know I'm great with kids."

"Based on what?" Warren asked.

"I hang out with Natalie's kids all the time. They like me."

Linc snorted. "I think he pays them."

"No, I'm just a genius with children."

Warren coughed. Joe snickered a laugh. Linc said, "I think I'll just ask Natalie."

"You do that," Eugene said.

They walked the next couple of holes, and while Linc lined up his next shot, Warren came up beside him. "Taking us teasing you about kids pretty seriously, huh?"

"Hey, I like Natalie's kids. And they like me back."

"I know that. But we're your brothers. We're supposed to give you shit, you know."

"Yeah, yeah."

"So what is it that irritated you?"

He gave Warren a look. "Honestly? I don't know. Maybe it's because I'm the youngest and no one expects me to ever grow up. But I have, with responsibilities that I take seriously. I sometimes think you and Linc still see me as that goofy kid you used to push around and make fun of."

Warren frowned. "No one thinks that about you, Eugene. You've made a tremendous success of your life. And Natalie is amazing. It's obvious she cares about you. I haven't met her kids so I can't judge you on that. Yet." He gave Eugene a wink.

"Well, you will tonight since we're all having dinner at her place."

"True enough. So I'll withhold judgement."

Eugene was about to say something, but Warren gave him a teasing smile, so instead, he rolled his eyes, and they walked on.

Their golf game was fun, though Eugene sucked at it. But his brothers and Joe enjoyed it so it was something he endured in order to hang out with the guys. After, they had lunch at the club-house and talked all about their lives.

"So you're happy building houses with occasional visits to your finance company?" Warren asked Linc.

Linc shrugged and took a sip of his iced tea. "It's working. I have a phenomenal management staff who don't need me there every day watching their every move. And if they do need me I'm only a phone call away. Plus I'm in the office a few days each month for meetings."

"Sounds like a perfect setup to me," Joe said. "With the baby coming, I'm doing the same with the health clubs. I've pro-moted some people to top-level management positions so I can spend less time at the clubs. I want to be home more with the baby."

"That makes good sense," Linc said. "We all know Warren will nod at the baby when it's born and then head straight back to the courtroom."

"Hey." Warren shot Linc a look. "I plan to take a month off."

"I'll believe that when I see it." Linc smirked.

"Believe it, bruh."

"I have a question," Eugene said. "And it might be a sensitive topic, but who's the daddy of this kid?"

"We don't know, actually," Warren said. "We each provided sperm, and then the fertility doc separately fertilized the donor embryos, which were frozen until a surrogate was found. They implanted the ideal one, which meant the one with the best chance for survival. We didn't care about the sex of the child, and we honestly don't know whose sperm got used."

Joe slung his arm around Warren's shoulder. "It's our baby, no matter what."

"Well, you're Black, and Warren's White, so I think it'll be obvious once the kid arrives."

Joe laughed at Eugene. "Yeah, we know. But it still won't matter."

"We're both the child's legal parents," Warren said. "So in case—God forbid—something happens to either of us, or in case of a divorce . . ."

"Which will never happen," Joe said.

Warren nodded. "Right. Anyway, in case of . . . well, dire cases, we both share legal custody equally even though only one of us will actually be the biological parent."

"Helps to have a lawyer in the family, huh?" Linc asked.

Warren nodded. "Yup."

Eugene couldn't help but grin. "You guys are gonna be the best dads."

"Thanks, Eugene," Joe said.

"Yeah, thanks, kid," Warren said.

Eugene shook his head. Sometimes he hated being the youngest. He'd always be the kid to them.

But maybe that was okay.

He smiled and took a drink.

*N*atalie wriggled her toes, admiring the shining pink polish as the woman at the nail salon put the finishing touches on her pedicure. Next to her, Lisa regaled both her and Hazel with hilarious stories of Linc's and Eugene's childhoods.

"And then the three of them decided it would be fun to climb inside a cardboard box at the top of the stairs and ride it all the way down. They crashed into a wall. I thought I'd be running to the ER with at least one or two of them with broken bones. Instead, all of them came tumbling out of the box, laughing hysterically, not a scratch on them."

"Oh my God," Natalie said. "Kids will scare the life out of you, right?"

"At least once a week, if not more than that. I have way too many stories like that."

Natalie shook her head. "Mine have been minor. So far. Maybe mine aren't daredevils like yours were."

"Or maybe they're just lulling you into a false sense of security,"

Hazel said, "only to spring the dramatics on you when you least suspect it."

Natalie gaped at her sister. "Oh, thanks, sis."

Lisa laughed. "Hey, it could be that you just have good, non-destructive kids."

"Ha. I don't think any kid lacks a destructive side. Or at least the inability to keep themselves from harm."

"That's true. Eugene was the worst of them. Too many trips for stitches and broken bones with that one."

Now it was getting interesting. "Do tell."

"Well, being the youngest, he always thought he could keep up with his big brothers. So he'd jump off things he wasn't big enough to jump off of, or climb things he shouldn't be climbing. He did a nosedive off the top of the slides, taking a short cut because Warren and Linc had taken off, and ended up with a broken arm."

Natalie winced. "Ouch."

"And then there were the stitches on his head when they all decided throwing rocks at each other could be a fun game. Eugene, being the youngest, didn't have as strong an arm as his brothers, but that didn't stop him from pitching rocks at them. Unfortunately, Warren hit him just on the temple with a jagged one, and he ended up with six stitches."

"Oh no," Hazel said. "Did Warren get in trouble?"

"They were all in trouble, but then again, Eugene loved every minute of it because his brothers praised him for taking the stitches like a champ."

"I don't think I ever want to have kids," Hazel said. "No offense to either of you."

Lisa laughed. "None taken."

"Christopher had stitches a couple of months ago. It's like my heart stopped. But he was barely bothered by it."

Lisa reached over and patted her hand. "Kids are resilient. They bounce back faster than our worries for them."

Her heart swelled with emotion, with joy, with understanding for this woman who'd raised three incredible men, including the one she lov . . .

Just say it. At least think it.

She loved him. Okay, fine, she'd thought it. But thinking it and doing anything about it were two different things.

She was having a fun day with Lisa and Hazel, and that's all she was going to think about today. Anything else was too much to handle. So she shoved it aside, at least until she got home and started prepping for tonight's dinner. Hazel had followed, and so had Lisa, and then her mother had showed up, so she got to introduce Eugene's mom to her mom.

"I'm so glad you're here, Melinda," Lisa said to Natalie's mother as they sat at the table sipping wine while Natalie and Hazel worked at the kitchen island. "I was hoping we'd get a chance to meet before I left."

"I'm happy that Natalie invited me," her mom said. "I would have been upset to miss meeting you, along with Eugene's other brother. Hazel and Natalie both tell me that your sons are amazing men. You must be very proud."

Lisa smiled. "Thank you, I am. And you as well. Your daughters are remarkable, successful, amazing women."

Natalie shot Hazel a look. Hazel shrugged and grinned.

Okay, fine. So it was going well between the moms. Still, this was a little weird that her mom was meeting Eugene's mom. Then the realization hit her that Lisa was also Linc's mother, so it made sense they should meet each other since Hazel and Linc had been together for a while now. It really had nothing to do with her and Eugene.

Christopher came running in. "Mom, can I have a snack?"

"Not before dinner." She held up a carrot. "Unless you want a veggie?"

Christopher wrinkled his nose. "Ew. No. Can I have a cracker?"

"Nope. But how about I slice an apple, and you can share it with your sister?"

"Okay."

"I've got that," Hazel said. "Christopher, go get Cammie while I get your apple ready."

He disappeared and then came back, Camryn in tow. They took seats at the kitchen table and Hazel put their apple slices on a plate. Both Lisa and her mom engaged the kids in conversation while they ate their snack.

"That's going well," Hazel said, keeping her voice low.

"Which part? The moms or the kids with Lisa?"

"Both."

Natalie looked over to see Lisa having an in-depth conversation with Christopher. As she listened in, she couldn't help but smile as she realized it was about different types of construction trucks. Yeah, Lisa was definitely a mom of boys. And yet, she turned her attention to Cammie and oohed and ahhed over Cammie's pink painted fingernails, then remarked about Cammie's bracelet, which made her daughter so happy.

Lisa was going to be a fantastic grandmother.

The guys showed up, regaling them with tales about their golf game, and then how Eugene had taken them to his office to show them the ride he was creating.

"It's damned impressive," Warren said as they took seats in the living room.

"We will definitely be back once it's done," Joe said.

Natalie got involved in helping Hazel fix their dinner. They were having shrimp tacos with cilantro lime slaw, fresh avocados, rice, and salsa and chips. And chicken with pineapple on skewers for the kids, which they were going to love. Natalie made margaritas for the adults and lemonade for Cammie and Christopher.

School had ended and summer was just beginning. It was such a fun time of year, even though it was already humid and hot. But that meant more outside time in the pool, and the kids always enjoyed that.

They ate inside at the table, and there was plenty of room for all of them, though they did have to squeeze together. Not that Natalie minded being huddled close to Eugene.

"Have a good day?" he asked as he brushed his shoulder against hers.

"I did. You?"

"Yeah. Missed you, though." He leaned over and gently glided his lips across hers, and she realized how natural and usual that had become, even in front of her children, who didn't notice anymore. Then again, her kids were too busy talking Warren and Joe to death about cars and trucks and jewelry and art and anything else that came off the top of their heads.

She supposed it was good practice for when they became dads.

"Warren, Joe, if you need rescuing, let me know," Natalie said.

Warren grinned. "Are you kidding? This is the highlight of our day."

"Seriously the highlight," Joe said, turning his attention back to Camryn, who explained to him that he'd look even better if he'd let her paint his nails tonight.

After dinner, Natalie let the kids hang out for a bit, then sent them to their rooms to get ready for bed. Her mom went in to help them change clothes, and Lisa went with her. The rest of them moved into the living room.

"How's the house coming along, Eugene?" Joe asked.

"It's done," Linc said.

Eugene frowned. "Since when?"

"Since the end of this week. Okay, by the first part of next week I'll be ready for you to do a final walk-through."

Eugene looked over at Natalie. "Ready to walk through it with me?"

"Absolutely." She made a mental note to go through her

301

design notes and make sure everything she'd ordered was ready for delivery. "Linc, you're sure it's finished?"

Linc grinned. "Of course. I wouldn't say so if it wasn't."

She was excited. Getting Eugene in his house was everything. It spelled permanence, even though she knew he wasn't staying here forever.

Was he? No, of course he wasn't.

But had things changed? She hadn't asked him. She couldn't. Wouldn't.

Why not? Tell him how you feel. Then ask him. Ask him to stay. Not just for the duration of his project, but permanently.

No way.

"You have a faraway look on your face. What's on your mind?"

She looked up to see Eugene smiling down at her. "Oh. Just thinking about how much fun it's going to be to decorate your house. Are you excited?"

He grinned. "Yeah. I mean, the rental is fine, but it'll be great to be in the house. Are you looking forward to decorating my place?"

"Of course." She laid her hand on his chest. "I can't wait to make it feel like home for you."

"I can't wait, either."

He slipped his arm around her and leaned in, whispering in her ear. "We'll have to christen the house."

She tilted her head back, gazing into his incredibly sexy eyes. "With champagne?"

His lips lifted. "No. With sex. In every room."

Heat surrounded her, filled her, desire blooming within her. The way he could do that to her so easily made her think . . .

Well. It made her think exactly what he was thinking.

"Yes. We should definitely do that."

He laughed. "I can't wait to move in."

Neither could she.

CHAPTER THIRTY-FIVE

The house was perfect. As Eugene walked through, watching Natalie fluff pillows on the incredible sectional and smooth out the rug in the living room, he stared up at the huge arched ceiling with wood beams and felt more at home than he'd felt in a very long time.

The main bedroom was spacious, bed was huge, bathroom was like a spa, and he could already see Natalie and him enjoying some hot sex in that oversize shower.

Backyard was even better. Full outside kitchen, incredible pool with tons of lounging area, and an awesomely oversize green area with amazing trees that provided shade. He could picture parties here. Kids here.

A family. His family. A family he wanted to create. And that was new. Kinda scary. But exciting, too. For the first time since he'd moved here, he exhaled.

"Yeah, this'll work."

"So you like it."

He turned to face Natalie. "I love it. How about you? Do you love it?"

She grinned. "I decorated it. Of course I love it."

"I mean, would you live here?"

Her smile turned to a confused frown. "I don't understand."

"I mean, if you were buying a house, say for you and the kids. Would this be the kind of house you'd choose."

"Oh. I see. Yes, for resale. Yes, I think a family would love this house. Plenty of space and the backyard is totally family friendly. Who wouldn't love this place?"

Not at all what he'd asked, but he didn't want to push. They hadn't really even talked about feelings yet. He should really do that.

"Natalie, I was wondering . . ."

Her phone rang. "Oh. Hang on, I need to answer this."

She walked away as she took the call, so he wandered off, walked outside, answered a few emails, but realized he was distracted when he read the same email three times and still didn't know what it said.

Because he needed to have a conversation with Natalie. An important one.

He turned to go inside, but Natalie walked out. "Hey, it's a prospective client and kind of important. I'm sorry, I need to go."

"Oh. Sure. Thanks for coming over to look at the place. See you tonight?"

She leaned against the doorway. "I'm sorry, I can't. I have the kids this week. Now that it's summer, Sean and I divide up by whole weeks, and this week is mine. But we'll get together for sure. I'll call you?"

He hated the sound of that. It sounded a lot like she was

avoiding him, which was probably his imagination. "Sure." He walked over to her and brushed his lips across hers, hoping to take it deeper.

But she stepped back. "I've gotta go. Sorry. We'll talk soon."

"Okay." He walked her to the front door, and she headed out to her car and pulled down the driveway, leaving him alone.

He had planned on having some alone time with Natalie today, but instead, she had to leave. So, he grabbed his keys and got in his car, figuring he could get some work done at the office.

He'd make plans with Natalie some other time.

And then they'd have that all-important talk.

CHAPTER THIRTY-SIX

*I*t was a full house, and Natalie couldn't be happier for Eugene.

They had been planning this housewarming party for a couple of weeks. He'd invited his coworkers, some of the new neighbors he'd met, Ned the contractor, and, of course, Linc and Hazel, along with Natalie and the kids. Natalie's mom and stepdad had stopped by for a short visit but had to leave early to go visit a sick friend.

It was nice to finally meet the people who worked with Eugene.

A couple of the neighbors had brought their kids, and fortunately, since Eugene's house was close to hers, Natalie also knew these neighbors. And Cammie and Christopher already knew the kids, which was perfect. So the kids had all run off to have some fun in the pool. And with parents surrounding the pool area and agreeing to keep an eye on her kids, Natalie could take a break and go look for Eugene.

She already knew she'd find him in his media room, his pride and joy. It was totally soundproof and wired up for sound and video like nothing she'd ever experienced before. The room was filled with his coworkers, who were all suitably impressed.

"Dude," Heath said. "This setup is sweet. You never have to come in to the office anymore."

Eugene laughed. "You're just saying that so you can goof off if I'm not there."

"Nah. I like the design we're doing. I want to take it to the finish line."

"Speaking of," one of the women said, "what do you think of the new matrices and vectors we set up? I think it helped speed up the processors and gave the ride a smoother look."

That's when Natalie tapped out, because if they were all entering the matrix or vectored to another world or whatever video or wild ride thing it was that they did, it went way over her head. She made her way back to the pool area and found Hazel and Linc sitting poolside, their gazes focused on Cammie and Christopher.

"Are you monitoring my children?" she asked as she pulled up a chair next to them.

"Watching your kids is enjoyable," Hazel said. "They're so sweet, Nat."

She couldn't help but smile. "They can be. They can also be small terrors."

Linc shrugged. "That's how they learn survival instincts to help prepare them for adulthood."

Natalie laughed. "I suppose you're right."

Her dog, Grizelda, came over for some love, then ran off after some of the kids. The great thing about Grizzie was that she loved the kids, and the neighborhood kids—including her own—also loved her.

Suddenly a blur flew past her and landed with a splash in the pool. The kids screamed and laughed, and Natalie realized it was Eugene. The kids all flung water at him and laughingly smacked him with pool noodles. He grabbed a water cannon and started spraying them.

"He's like a kid," Linc said. Then he stood. "Still, I should probably assist him before the kids take over."

"Yes." Hazel gave him a smile. "He looks like he's in dire need of your help."

Linc pulled off his shirt and made his way into the pool, diving in and finding himself under similar attack from six very adorable children.

"Siblings," Hazel said, rolling her eyes.

"At least yours seems calm and rational. He's just throwing the ball with the kids. Eugene is jumping all over the place giggling and laughing like a child."

Hazel laughed. "Hey, he enjoys playing with them. Not too many men will get down to a kid's level. He's a kid at heart. He's going to make an incredible father someday."

He's going to make an incredible father someday.

That sentence hung in the air, nearly choking her with panic and dread.

She'd been prepared to have a conversation with him later today about her feelings for him. Tell him that she loved him. But with that one sentence, the cold realization hit that if she entered a serious relationship with Eugene, if she pondered a future with him, she'd be denying him the one thing he was so good at. The one thing he might truly want someday.

A family of his own. The opportunity to have children of his own. Because she was done having kids. She'd made that clear, and she knew in her heart she didn't want to start over having babies. Which didn't mean that Eugene wouldn't want to start a family. Of course he'd want to have his own kids. He was so good with her children, dove in right from the start with Cammie and Christopher, and they'd accepted him immediately.

How could they not? He was charming and fun and sweet and she owed him honesty about how she felt.

Oh, she could never tell him now how she truly felt. At least not what was really in her heart, how much she loved him. That would be so unfair to him.

No, she'd have to sit him down and explain the reality of the situation. That their age difference had finally reared its ugly head.

They were in two different places in their lives. His was just getting started. With everything, to be honest. New job. New house. He had a chance to start a new relationship. Find someone to fall in love with, get married, and have a family with.

Whereas she was in a different place, somewhere completely different. Divorced, free, independent, and raising two incredible children. She was moving forward with her life as it was. She wanted . . . well, she didn't know exactly what she wanted yet, but she'd eventually figure it out.

Liar. You do know what you want. You want Eugene. You love him. You want him to be a part of your life, your kids' lives. You want that happily ever after with him.

She stared out over the water, the splashing and laughter and the way her kids clung to Eugene like he was everything to them. Their protector, someone who was important in their lives. Her heart twisted as she thought about the kind of future they could have together.

No. That wasn't her life. Or, it could be, but that would be so incredibly unfair to Eugene. She refused to do that to him.

So, later tonight, they'd talk. She'd be honest with him. He'd understand, and, of course, he'd see the logic in all of this. He'd realize that she was right, and they could go their separate ways without hurting each other.

It was all going to be just fine.

Ugh. I'm so full. I shouldn't have had two burgers." The party had dwindled, leaving just Eugene and Natalie and the kids, along with Hazel and Linc.

Linc looked over at his brother. "You ate two of those monster burgers?"

"Hey. Chasing little kids around the pool worked up an appetite, okay?"

"Uh-huh. You poor thing. I'm sure you were wasting away waiting on the food to be ready. And now you ate too much and you want to die."

Eugene sank farther into the chaise. "Didn't say that. I just said I was full. Satiated. Appreciated a good meal."

Linc snorted. "No, that's not what you said."

Hazel came outside. "Kitchen's clean and we have puppies to tend to. You ready to go?"

"Yup." Linc got up and so did Eugene. He pulled Eugene into a hug. "Great house and awesome party, bruh."

Eugene hugged Linc tightly. "Thanks for everything. Love you."

"Love you, too."

He walked with them into the house. "Where's Natalie?"

"Oh." Hazel turned around to face him. "She said to tell you that Mom and Paul are home now, so she's running the kids over to their house to spend the night, because they're going on some farm tour early tomorrow morning. She'll be right back."

"Okay." He hugged Hazel. "Thanks for all your help."

"You have a great house, Eugene. And my sister did an incredible job decorating, which I've told her about ten times already."

"She did, didn't she?" He walked them to the front door and said goodbye again, then waited while they made their way to their car before he shut the door. He wandered back into the backyard to put chairs away, reorganize the tables, and make sure everything was put away.

After, he went inside, smiling as he realized how clean it all was. He had Natalie and Hazel to thank for that. Grizelda looked up at him with an expectant tilt of her head.

"Wanna go outside?" he asked.

She wagged her tail.

"Okay, girl." He opened the door and she bounded out to the backyard.

The house was so quiet now. He'd always enjoyed the quiet. Being alone had always suited him. But now he'd gotten used to kids and dogs and noise, so he found the silence . . . well, silent. It was weird.

After letting Grizelda inside, he flopped down on the sofa and took out his phone, scrolling through his photos to review the pics he'd taken during the housewarming tonight. He smiled at the one of him and Natalie sitting on the front porch with the kids and the dog.

They all looked so good together. Like a family. Like they were meant to be together. All of them.

He stood, pacing the room, realizing how much he needed to talk to Natalie, to express his feelings to her. To tell her how much he wanted her and the kids to be a part of his life.

Tonight. He'd do it tonight.

And now he was more nervous than ever.

But excited, too.

Natalie pulled up in the driveway, turned off the engine, then just sat there, going over and over in her head how she was going to break up with Eugene.

Just the thought of it tightened her throat. She couldn't fathom hurting him. Losing him would devastate her. She couldn't even imagine how upset the kids would be. They'd grown so attached. How was she even going to explain it to them? And what about Linc and Hazel? How would that go once she and Eugene broke up? They were always together as a foursome—as a family. But after tonight . . .

This was going to hurt a lot of people. She'd bungled this so badly. She knew better than to get involved, yet she'd done it anyway.

She gripped the steering wheel, contemplating backing out

and going home. But that would only delay the inevitable. It was better to be honest, to just get it over with, no matter how much it hurt.

At this point she wasn't certain she was going to get through it without falling apart.

She got out of the car and walked to the door, her finger hovering at the doorbell. She inhaled several head-clearing breaths and pushed the button.

Eugene opened the door, his bright smile making her doubt she'd be able to do what needed to be done.

"You're back."

"I am." Grizelda was there to greet her so she bent over to scratch the pup behind her ears. She walked inside and followed him down the hall toward the living room.

"Get the kids dropped off okay?"

"I did. They're so happy to spend the night with Gramma and Grandpa. And even more excited about going to the farm to see the chickens, cows, and goats tomorrow."

He wrapped his arms around her and tugged her against his chest. "Aww. I'm sure they're going to have a great time. I can't wait for them to tell me all about it."

Dammit. Tears welled in her eyes. She blinked, frantically forcing them back. She was relieved to know he wasn't looking at her.

But then he turned her around. "So, there's something I need to tell you. Something I've wanted to tell you for a while now."

Oh. Maybe *he* was breaking up with *her*. The thought made her stomach plummet, but then she realized how ridiculous that was. Wouldn't it be easier if he dumped her, so she wouldn't have to be the one to crush his heart? Though it was still going to hurt either way.

"Okay. Tell me."

He swept her hair away from her face. His touch gave her goosebumps. Always had. And when he stroked his thumb across her bottom lip, her knees went weak.

How was she going to survive without those butterflies, that feeling of being swept away by his every touch?

"I love you, Natalie. I'm in love with you. I want you in my life. Every day."

Oh no. She hadn't expected this. Those words, the look of utter, truthful love on his face. Before she could utter a rebuttal, he kissed her—a deep, passionate, curl-her-toes kind of kiss with lots of hot, delicious tongue that sent desire swirling through her nerve endings.

She wanted to object, to push him away, put a stop to this. But then he pulled the neck of her top down and pressed searing wet kisses along her throat and collarbone. His hand moved to her ass and squeezed, massaged, drew her against his hard cock, making her dizzy with the need to feel him inside of her. And then all thoughts of having any kind of breakup conversation fled.

With desperate intent she pulled up his shirt, sliding her hands inside to feel the hard planes and angles of his abs. She slid her hand into the waistband of his shorts, grasping his cock and stroking up, then down, focusing her gaze on the burning-hot look in his eyes.

"Naked," he groaned, jerking the waistband of her pants down. "Now."

Clothes were flung everywhere and suddenly they were both naked in the living room. Natalie spread a blanket out on the sofa while Eugene disappeared for a few seconds to grab a condom. He came back and kneeled down in front of her on the sofa, pulling her down so her hips rested on the edge.

"I've been dying to get you alone," he said, pressing his fingers on her thighs. "I need to taste you, make you come."

He put his mouth on her sex and she arched her hips, moaning with sheer delight at the exquisite sensations. Eugene was relentless, never letting up as his mouth and tongue took her right to the edge, then over. She was certain that scream was hers as she shook through the intense waves.

Shaken after that incredible orgasm, it took her a minute to do anything other than lie on the sofa like a limp mop. Meanwhile, Eugene had gone into the kitchen and come back with a glass of water. She took a sip, coating her parched throat. She handed the glass to Eugene, and he took a few sips, then laid the glass on the table.

Then she pushed him to sit on the sofa and straddled him.

"I like where this is going," he said, sliding his hands around her hips.

She reached over where he had put the condom, flipping the package back and forth in her hands. "Since your cock is still hard—which is very impressive, I might add—let's get this on."

"Hey, you're naked and you just screamed so loud when you came I think I'll be hard for the rest of the night."

"Ooh. A challenge. I do like a challenge." She leaned over and cupped his face in her hands, then put her mouth to his, taking in his breath, his lips, his tongue, the way his hands swept over her back and lower. The combination drove her wild with desire.

She ripped open the condom package and applied it to his cock, then rose up and slowly slid down over him. The feel of him entering her, the way he filled her so completely, made her insides quiver with sensation. She took a shuddering breath.

"You okay?" he asked.

"Mmm. More than okay." She leaned over him, lifting, then filling herself with the length and thickness of him. The eye contact between them intensified her pleasure, making her lose herself in the beauty of his face. This face that she was going to let go of, that she was going to allow to leave her forever.

Don't think about it. Not now. Not yet.

"What you do to me, Natalie," he whispered as he grasped her hips and dragged her clit across his pelvis.

She gasped, leaning closer to him, using his shoulders to help her balance as she grew closer to orgasm. "Yes. Like that. Don't stop."

He didn't, just kept going until she came apart, and then he drove deeply into her and shuddered with her. She dropped down on top of him and he wrapped his arms around her, both of them shaking with the force of their orgasms.

And then he just held her like that, for the longest time, smoothing his hands up and down her back. She could have fallen asleep like this, could have let him hold her like this forever so she didn't have to face reality.

At least until her hip started to cramp.

She climbed off and went to use the bathroom, freshened up a bit, then came back to the living room to grab her clothes.

"Whoa, wait a second. What are you doing?"

She turned around to see a deliciously naked Eugene leaning against the wall. "I'm getting dressed."

"No, you're not. We're not finished."

She needed to talk to him. About important things. Though at the moment he was naked and so was she, and she had to admit her brain was a bit sex addled.

Surely that important conversation could wait, couldn't it?

She held out her hand. "Sofa again, or would you like to bend me over your outstanding kitchen island?"

He arched a brow and took her hand. "Lead the way into the kitchen."

CHAPTER THIRTY-SEVEN

*E*ugene woke up to find an arm draped across his chest. He couldn't help but smile at the feel of Natalie's warm body pressed against his.

He slid out of bed to use the bathroom, then came back and climbed into bed and pulled her against him, nuzzling his face in her neck.

Last night he'd told her he loved her. She hadn't said anything in return, which was fine. He had no expectations other than letting her know how he felt.

She wriggled against him and he got hard. Of course he did. He wrapped his arm around her, snaking his fingers down her body and between her legs, massaging her clit with slow, gentle movements until she began to writhe against him and make soft moaning sounds that made his balls quiver.

She came with a whimpered cry and a shudder. He continued to stroke her easily, then waited until she relaxed. He reached over and grabbed a condom, put it on, then slid inside of her, her body still quaking with the aftereffects of her orgasm. He reached up to tease and stroke her nipples while he thrust inside of her, and when she came again, this time he went with her.

After, she got out of bed and went into the bathroom. He went into the guest bathroom, then came back and put on his shorts, let Grizelda outside, then made two cups of coffee, pouring cream into one of the cups for Natalie.

She came down the hall wearing one of his T-shirts—and apparently, nothing else.

He leaned against the counter, coffee cup in hand. "You trying to get me hard again?"

She smiled, then came over and picked up the other cup. "Thanks for making me coffee." She took a sip, then sighed. "That's good."

"Feel like some breakfast?"

She paused as if she were about to say something else, then gave a quick nod. "Sure."

He got out bacon and eggs and bread, along with fruit. Natalie came over and helped, and they fixed breakfast together. He could envision doing this on weekends, with the kids running around and Grizzie chasing them.

Kind of a perfect life, actually.

Once breakfast was finished, Natalie poured orange juice for them, and they sat at the island to eat.

"Party was good last night, wasn't it?" he asked.

"Mm-hmm."

"Have you talked to your mom yet today? See how the kids were doing?"

"No. I'm sure they're fine."

"Okay." Grizelda wanted back in the house, so he let her in and poured out dog food for her that he'd bought to keep at his house. He poured fresh water into her bowl, then slid back into his chair to continue eating.

"I bought the same dog food you have at your place."

"Oh. That's nice. Thanks."

Obviously Natalie wasn't interested in having conversation this morning, so they finished their meal in silence. When they were done, he took everything to the sink and piled it up, then went to take a shower. When he got out and went to the bedroom, he saw that Natalie had gotten dressed. He slipped into boxer briefs and clean shorts, then pulled on a sleeveless shirt.

"I used some of your toothpaste to brush my teeth," she said, using an elastic tie to put her hair in a ponytail. She went downstairs, so he followed her down there.

"Maybe you should start leaving a change of clothes here. And a toothbrush. Some favorite shampoo?"

"Yeah, about that. Can we sit and talk?"

"Sure." He walked with her to the sofa. She sat and he took a spot next to her.

"I had a really good time last night with you, Eugene. These past few months have been amazing."

Uh-oh. He knew what that meant. "Yeah, it's been really great."

"And when you told me you loved me last night—"

"It freaked you out, didn't it?"

She shook her head. "No, it didn't. Because I love you, too."

He grinned. "You do?" He picked up her hand. "That's a good thing, right?"

She inhaled, let it out. "Not for us, Eugene."

"Why not?"

"Because you're almost five years younger than me. And I see you with my kids and my dog. You have this huge capacity for love and family. The thing is, I have a family. I have Camryn and Christopher. And they're everything to me. My life is just the way I want it to be—family-wise. I'm done, Eugene. But you . . . you're just getting started. You're going to want to make your own family someday, have a child of your own. And I can't do that for you."

He sat there for a minute, absorbing everything she'd said before he responded. Emotions swirled around him from hurt to anger and back to hurt again. "You've decided this all on your own, huh? You know what's best for me? For what I want in my future?"

"Eugene . . ."

She squeezed his hand, but he jerked it away and stood.

"I don't get it, Natalie. You and me, we've been on this same trajectory almost since we first met. We clicked in ways I've never clicked with anyone before. You were so snarky and determined not to like me, until you just couldn't help yourself. And I wanted to tease you into liking me, and it finally worked. I thought you and I could have some fun. That's what we both agreed to. No big deal, no commitments, right? But then something happened, because with every passing day I fell harder and harder for you, until that turned into love.

"I had to tell you I loved you, realizing it was a risk, because while I thought you might love me, too, I wasn't a hundred percent sure. And just now, when you told me you loved me?" He raked his fingers through his hair. "Man, it was the greatest. Because while you can't see our future together, Natalie? I can. I see it perfectly. I see you and me and Cammie and Christopher and Grizelda and maybe another dog to keep Grizzie company. I see us getting married and living happily ever after in my house or your house or wherever you want to live. I don't need some genetic marker to make kids my kids. I love your kids, Natalie. I love your kids as much as I love you. I want forever with you. I wish you could see that, could feel as confident about that as I am."

She looked up at him. "You say that now, Eugene, because you're in the throes of new love. But someday you'll change your mind."

"Oh, because you know how I feel? You know how I'll feel in ten years? Twenty years? That's pretty impressive."

She stood. "I just . . . I don't ever want to put you in the position of having regrets, Eugene. I love you too much to tie you down to me, to a family you might regret having someday. It would hurt everyone involved. And I have to look out for my kids. I can't have them get hurt, either."

He took a step forward, coming face-to-face with her. "Do you think that there's any chance that I would do anything to hurt those kids? Because if you do, then you don't know me as well as you think you do, Natalie. And that really hurts."

He saw the tears filling her eyes, but he was so wrapped up in his own pain he couldn't acknowledge them.

She went to the counter and grabbed her keys, calling Grizelda. "Give yourself some time to think about this, Eugene. You'll realize I'm right."

He went with her to the door. "And you give yourself the same amount of time, Natalie. You'll realize how wrong you are."

She walked out without a word, Grizelda following her out the door.

He closed the door and walked down the hall, that familiar emptiness surrounding him. Only this time it felt a lot more permanent.

CHAPTER THIRTY-EIGHT

N atalie. Are you out of your mind?"

Natalie winced as she listened to her mother rail at her on the phone about breaking up with Eugene. Mom had invited her and Eugene to a charity dinner, so she'd had no choice but to tell her. And maybe she'd just needed to unburden herself. It hadn't gone well. Her mother had told her she was wrong about everything. She refused to argue with her mom about it, so she listened and told her mom she'd call her back later.

After hanging up, she picked up around the house and did a few meal prep items to stick in the freezer to take to work.

The doorbell rang and she went to answer it. Her sister stood there giving her that judgmental look, the same one she'd seen whenever she'd looked in the mirror over the past several days.

"Come on in."

They walked inside the house and into the kitchen. Hazel turned to face her.

"You broke up with Eugene?"

"I did."

Hazel threw her arms around her and hugged her tight. "I'm so sorry, Natalie."

That hug felt good. Tears welled up, only this time she didn't try to fight them back. She let them roll down her cheeks. "I feel awful."

"Aww, honey. Talk to me."

"I thought I was doing the right thing. Eugene deserves to build a family of his own."

Hazel went to the cabinet and pulled out two cups, then made tea for both of them. She slid a cup to Natalie. "Maybe you should allow Eugene the opportunity to make his own choice? He knows who you are, Natalie. He knows who your kids are. He loves all of you, right?"

"So he tells me." She wrapped her hand around the warm cup, and even though it was hot and humid out, there was something comforting about that warmth.

"And you don't believe him?"

"I-I don't know. I want to, but what if somewhere down the road he decides he wants something that I can't give him?"

Hazel cocked her head to the side. "You do realize there aren't any guarantees, right? All we can do is love each other fiercely, be honest and open and communicate with each other. And then we hope for the best lives we can live with the ones we love the most."

Those tears continued to fall. "I'm so hopelessly in love with him, Hazel. And I'm so scared."

Hazel slipped off her barstool and pulled Natalie against her, holding her while she cried out her sorrows.

Finally, Natalie lifted her head. "What do I do now?"

"What do you want to do? Go back to your life before Eugene, or the life you started to build with him in it?"

She shuddered in an inhale, then let it out and looked directly at her sister. "I miss him so much I can barely breathe. I need him. We all do."

"Then go do whatever it takes to get your man back."

CHAPTER THIRTY-NINE

*E*ugene was knee-deep in ride modifications, working in his state-of-the-art home office when his phone pinged. Deciding to ignore it, he continued on with the work.

That is, until his phone pinged again. Then again.

"Dammit."

He swiveled to his other desk and picked up his phone to see a text message—or rather several text messages—from Natalie.

I know you're home. Answer the door.

I'm out front and I'm not leaving.

Come on, Eugene. I need to talk to
you.

He thought about ignoring her. Thinking about her still stung. Seeing her would be even worse. But it wasn't his style to ignore a problem, so he went downstairs and opened the door, leaning against the doorjamb with his arms crossed. "'Sup?"

"Can I come in?"

"I don't know, Natalie. Do we have anything left to talk about?"

"I have a few things I'd like to say."

"I think you said more than enough last time we talked."

"This is different." When he didn't say anything, she said, "Please, Eugene."

"Fine." He moved out of the way and she stepped inside. He closed the door and followed her into the living room.

"Something to drink?" he asked.

"Wine, if you have it."

He pulled out a bottle of her favorite wine and opened it, poured a glass, and grabbed a beer for himself. He went into the living room and handed the glass to her.

She looked up at him and smiled. "Thanks."

Her smile was a gut punch. He had to get her out of here as soon as possible. He'd been so broken by her dumping him that his heart felt like it had been squeezed dry, and there was nothing but a dead husk left in his chest. But he'd be damned if he let her see how she'd crushed him.

So he plopped in the chair, opened his beer, and took a couple deep swallows, trying his best to look nonchalant while she casually sipped her wine.

"How's work going?" she asked.

"Fine." He took another swallow of beer.

"Okay. Anyway, mine's going well. I picked up two new clients this week. One wants a total redesign of—"

"Why are you here, Natalie?"

"Oh. We're getting right into it, huh?"

"Don't want to waste anyone's time, do we?"

"I . . . guess not." She nervously tucked her hair behind her ears. "Okay, so, here's the deal. The things I said before. I may have been wrong."

"Excuse me? The things you said? When you said because I was younger than you that I couldn't know what I wanted? That what was in my heart was bullshit? Those things?"

"That's not at all what I said."

"Pretty much the same thing. I told you I loved you. I broke down our future for you, at least how I saw it. And then you came back and said nah, that's not how it is, dude. Because this is what you're really gonna want down the road—you know, when you're older and more mature, as if I'm some kind of kid who couldn't possibly make adult decisions yet, who doesn't know his own heart. You're not gonna want the woman and children you love, you're gonna want some other woman to make some babies with and have your happily ever after with. Am I close, Natalie? Isn't that pretty close to what you said?"

*E*ugene was angry. He had every right to be. Natalie had taken all that love he'd poured out to her, and she'd casually thrown it right back in his face as if he had no idea what love was about.

She had to fix this, to make things right between them. She just didn't know exactly how.

"At the time, I thought I was doing the right thing. I didn't want you . . . down the road, to have any regrets."

He crossed his arms. "I don't even know what to say to that. You think love has an expiration date?"

She shrugged. "I do have first-hand experience with that happening."

"Okay. You make a good point. But do you feel like you and me are the same as you and Sean?"

She frowned. "No. Not at all. But I'm scared, Eugene. I don't want you to get wrapped up in a relationship that you might regret later. There are a lot of people here that could get hurt besides you and me."

He got up and came over to her, knelt in front her, laying his hands on her knees. "If I thought for one minute that this whole thing between you and me had an expiration date, I would have never told you I loved you. I'd die before hurting Cammie and Christopher. Or you. I'm in this, Natalie. For the long run."

And here came the tears again, because she believed him. She slid off the sofa and sat on the floor with him, sliding her hands into the softness of his hair. "I'm in this, too. Forever. I'm sorry I said the things I said. I didn't want you to have any regrets."

His gaze was so filled with love she was overwhelmed. "I could never regret loving you, Natalie."

Her heart felt like exploding. She felt so much she couldn't take a breath, and yet she did. "I love you, Eugene."

She lifted her lips to his, and he met her lips. That kiss, so powerful and passionate, mended the break that had torn them apart. With Eugene's arms around her, his body against hers, she felt whole again. She was right where she belonged.

He pulled away. "You are mine."

She smiled. "And you are mine."

She climbed onto his lap and swept his hair away from his face. "I'm so sorry. I screwed up, and I'm sorry I hurt you."

He ran his hand up and down her arm. "It's okay. You can spend the rest of your life making it up to me." He finished with a grin.

"That sounds like a very good plan." She kissed him again, and before long they were rolling around on the living room rug, and she was so happy to be in his arms again she could explode from pure joy.

But then her phone rang. She was going to ignore it, but she couldn't because of the kids. She got up and grabbed her phone, her stomach dropping when she saw it was Sean on FaceTime. He still had the kids so her first thought was that one of them was sick or hurt.

"Sean," she said after she punched the button.

It wasn't Sean, it was Cammie, who excitedly told her she had lost a tooth this morning at breakfast, so they talked about how she was going to put it under her pillow tonight. Seeing her daughter's sparkling smile gave her so much joy.

"I miss you, sweet pea," she said. "Oh, and Eugene's here. Do you want to say hi?"

"Yes."

"Hey, punkin," Eugene said as he looked over Natalie's shoulder. "Let's see that smile."

Cammie smiled. "I lost a tooth, Eugene."

"I see that. Good job. Before long you'll have a pretty new tooth to take its place."

They talked for a while, and then Cammie said she had to go, so they hung up.

"She was excited," Eugene said, leaning against the kitchen island.

"Yeah. She loves losing those baby teeth." She laid her hand against his chest. "Sorry about the interruption."

"Hey." He wrapped his hands around hers. "Our lives are always going to have these interruptions. We have kids."

Tears sprang fresh at "We have kids." "I love you, Eugene. Let's go build that life together."

He smiled at her, and she saw her forever in that smile. "Yeah, let's."

ACKNOWLEDGEMENTS

A book is never created alone. Sure, my name is on the cover, but I didn't create this cover. The Berkley art department has made magic with every one of my covers, and they've all been spectacular. I cannot thank them enough.

The words inside the book are mine, but they've been made better by my editors over the years—Kate Seaver and Leis Pederson—who've made my words shine like a diamond.

Those words were polished even more by the copy editors who made sure I didn't change a character's name midway through the book. (I'd like to say I've never done this, but . . .)

My fantastic agent, Kimberly Whalen, has been there for me through countless books and crises and meltdowns, and I couldn't do this without her expertise.

A huge thanks to my bestie, Shannon Stacey, who has been by my side from the very beginning to offer advice, laughs, and sometimes a shoulder to cry on. And often has provided the best book titles ever. Thank you, my friend.

And, finally, and most importantly, to my husband, Charlie, who got me started with encouragement and has held my hand through the ups and downs of writing and life. Love you always.

Photo by Claudio Marinesco

Jaci Burton is the *New York Times* and *USA Today* bestselling, award-winning author of more than eighty books, including the Play-by-Play, Hope, and Brotherhood by Fire series. She has been a Romance Writers of America RITA finalist, and she was awarded the RT Book Reviews Career Achievement Award. Jaci lives in Oklahoma with her husband and dogs.

VISIT JACI BURTON ONLINE

JaciBurton.com
f AuthorJaciBurton
𝕏 JaciBurton